River of Hope and Hatred

Lords of the Underworld
Series Book 3

Maggie White

The following text is a work of fiction. All the characters, organizations, businesses, and events portrayed in this novel are products of the author's imagination or used fictitiously.

River of Hope and Hatred by Maggie White
Book 3 of the Lords of the Underworld Series
Story Copyright 2024 Maggie White
Editing by Jenny Raden
Map by B.C. FaJohn Books

The book you're about to read includes the death of a characters on page, moments of violence and danger, mature language and situations. For a full list of possible triggers, please visit www.maggiewhitebooks.com.

Contents

Yes, it's true. Kharon is the only brother who doesn't have wings or horns…but hear me out…he can hold his breath for a really long time.

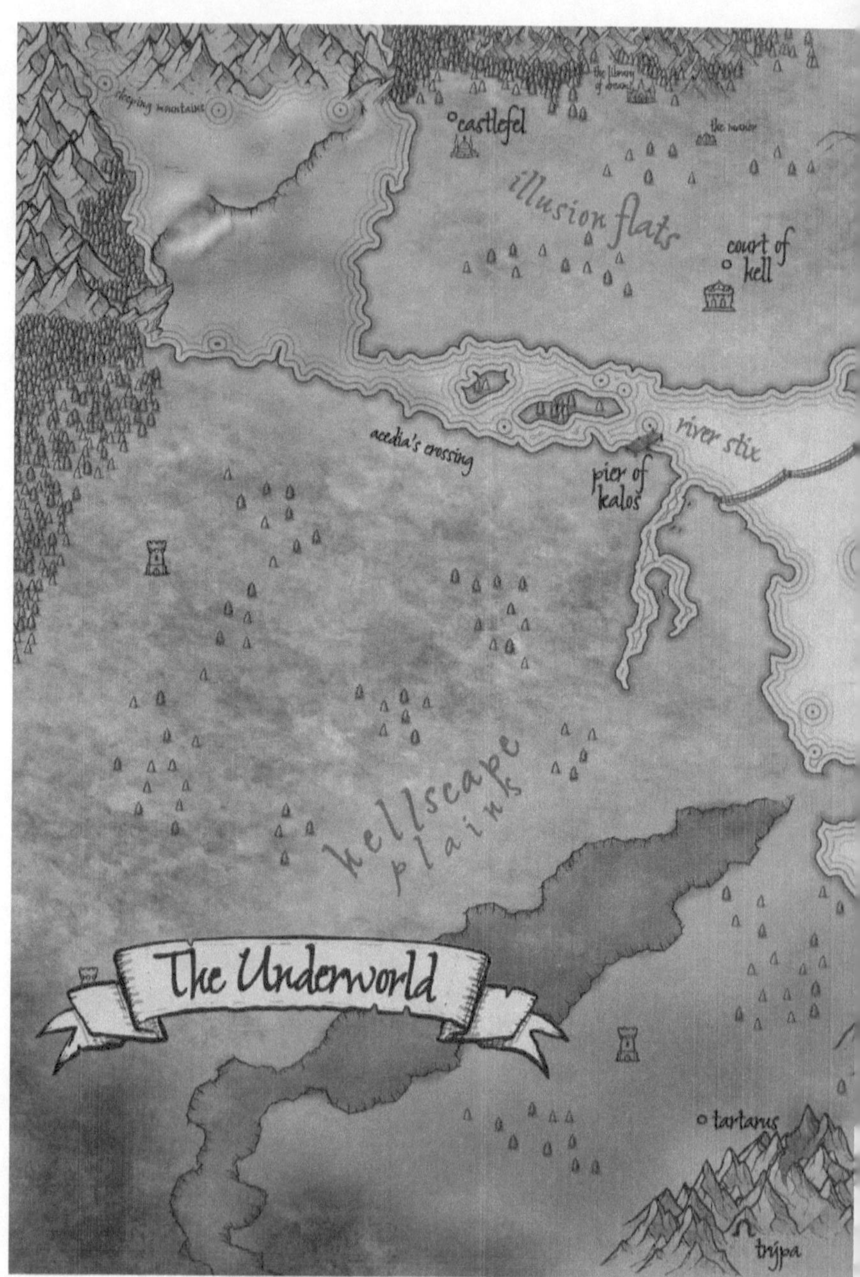

sleeping mountains
castlefel
the library of dream
the manor
illusion flats
court of hell
acedia's crossing
river stix
pier of kalos
hellscape plains
The Underworld
tartarus
trypa

the
courthouse
elysium
elon's
isle
kell's
pointe
Wastelands

1

Frothing gray waves lapped hungrily at the hull, rocking the large commercial fishing boat that I stood upon. I braced my feet wide as I stared wide-eyed over the edge of the bow, fascinated and terrified by the ever-changing water just beyond. My life jacket was tight enough that it could choke me, but I didn't dare take it off before I was told to.

Slowly, my eyes moved across the deck, the wood slats still damp from the early morning mist. From here, I could see around the carefully tied rigging and netting and into the helm, where a trio of men stood. Each of their heads were bowed low, their words snatched away by the sharp sea wind the moment they crossed their lips. I didn't dare cast my magic towards them to try to listen in. Not here. Not when I already had a horrible suspicion of what topic they discussed. I had but one purpose in their minds.

Dry… My lips were so dry it burned to part them. My tongue slipped out to wet them, but another moment later, they were dry once more, a victim to both my nerves and the brine that blew around us in the unseasonably cool, overcast Florida morning.

When I had pictured Florida, I'd been hoping for sunlight and warmth. Palm trees. Maybe the chance to sink my toes into a real beach. This was nothing compared to the stories I read when I wasn't working. I was desperate for it in some ways, for the reminder of what a simple joy life could bring. But now all I had was the blur of dark clouds and the ominous sound of the waves against brightly painted carbon fiber. Nausea rose in my throat, bubbling up as a larger wave tossed us to one side then the other, causing me to stumble once more.

This must be the storm they'd whispered about on the plane, the one they claimed was necessary for my task to be completed. Anxiety bloomed fresh in my chest, and I found myself suddenly wishing wholeheartedly I was back with the Drude. He would've understood that I didn't need water or a natural resource to use my magic. But in all my years of training alongside him, one thing my master knows is that fear does bring out the best in me. Or rather, the worst.

He'd said he couldn't be there. That it would be too hard for him to witness my fear and not intervene. Instead, he promised that his best soldiers would accompany me. That they would keep me safe from the monsters we wished to destroy. He had promised.

I swallowed back the whimper that rose in my throat as another wave buffeted the fishing boat that we'd chartered upon arrival in St. Petersburg. Only a muffled noise slipped out as I braced myself harder against the slick rail.

One of the men turned, meeting my eyes for a long moment before a slow smile curled his lips.

A Corrupted.

My master's chosen soldiers. They were my allies. My roommates. They were human bodies my master had stolen and implanted into them souls loyal to him that he'd brought straight from Hell. The magic binding them to this dark second chance at life bound them to the Drude. There would be no betrayal. No fear of uprising. They were loyal and would remain as such until the day my master ran out of tasks for them.

Then they would be gone.

No soul. No body. No trace of the being that had served our quest to return the Underworld to its proper glory. The Drude had pulled me aside when he had first begun to create them. He'd shown me the magic, the binding, the all-encompassing control over them. He had wanted me to understand two things, I thought.

One, that they served only him.

And two, that there was always something worse than the sheltered, hidden life that I kept to. The message was just as clear as the darkness of their soul. I could be like them. He could *make* me like them.

He didn't need to worry though. He had all the power over me he would ever need. Instead, I had merely nodded and continued on in my training. First there was one team, then two. Slowly, as the Drude grew in power, he grew his numbers. And now, they were a part of my everyday life. I had to trust them, especially now that it was just us on this task.

I forced a smile to my lips, ignoring the fear that continued to pull at me. This Corrupted was a new recruit. He still looked uncomfortable in his new body, like a child wearing their father's too-large shoes. He swaggered towards me, and unlike my lightweight slip-ons, his heavy boots echoed across the empty ocean.

I did not like the way he was looking at me. Away from headquarters, so many of these souls were like wild animals when the Master granted them their new life. They were forbidden from hurting me, that I knew. But there were other things that they liked to try, to see how far they could go and get away with.

The day that one had chopped my curls off at dinner, I had sobbed to the Drude. He had tsked, petting my bobbed curls, and told me that it wasn't up to him to establish my own boundaries. "Freedom within reason," Master had said. "That's what I offer."

I think he'd wanted me to lash out at them. Impress someone with my magic. But I hadn't. My magic had only brought pain and embarrassment. Unless I was ordered to do so, I preferred to keep it to myself. Something no one else could touch.

Now, as I watched the Corrupted approach, deep in my chest, my magic swirled to life, ready to defend. In most cases, the new recruits feared the Drude's wrath so much they didn't give me two looks. But here, so far from Master, things felt different.

And just as my magic began to warm my palms, another man stepped in between us, throwing his arm up in front of the recruit. "Back off, Lang. We still need her." The two shared a heavy look before the second man, this one named Paul, released his comrade. Paul Groves was their leader and the only Corrupted who had made the journey from our midwestern home base to Florida with me.

The other two, both newer recruits, had been waiting for us here when we'd landed in the private airstrip outside of town. They had puffed up around us, but I knew better. Every time I looked at them, there was a tendril of fear in their eyes. Not fear *for* me. Fear *of* me. And I hated it. I curled my chin to my chest as Paul halted in front of me. He clucked his tongue, cold gray eyes appraising me sharply.

"Are you afraid of the water, witch?" Paul asked, already knowing the answer.

"No," I lied, tucking my hands behind my back. The dress I'd been so comfortable in earlier suddenly felt like not enough armor against his surveillance.

"Sure, whatever you say. You can lose the jacket," Paul said, the order making me flinch, even as he continued on. "You won't need it much longer." His gaze strayed to the side, glancing to the west as the third in their group pressed the vessel into a higher gear. The engine rumbled to life and took us slightly closer to the boardwalk.

From here I could hear the crowd noise, the music of the festive atmosphere that seemed to be a constant in this part of Florida. My heart swelled in my chest at the sounds. Human nature at its best were the bright, happy sounds that filled my ears. How funny that I could be this close and feel so very far away.

A lifetime away.

My eyes shuttered for a long moment as I spoke out one final, silent prayer. Then, with numb fingers, I began unfastening my life jacket, the glowing orange color, once meant to highlight my body in the water, now seemed too dull as I dropped it to the deck of the ship. It was unnecessary from this point forward.

I stepped away, my soles squeaking a little against the deck, and moved quietly to the edge of the boat. My fingers wrapped around the edge, heart rate spiking as I stared down into the frothing water.

Dark, blue, deep.

I breathed raggedly through my nose. My magic, and that nameless second thing, the one that twisted and turned even deeper inside, vibrated. A warning. "Too late," I whispered aloud. I had made my bed. Now I had to lie in it.

"Are you ready, witch?" The second recruit was leering at me. Just how deep in hell had they found his soul? He appeared more alive than ever as he thought about what he was going to do today.

I tried one more time in vain to wet my lips. "Yes, Corrupted. I'm ready." To my credit, my voice did not shake. Did not give me away.

Paul urged me closer, his hands falling to my shoulders as he held me in place. The other two were moving now, the clanging of metal and the soft chanting of spell work behind me making my chest ache.

Regret filled my mouth, making it taste like metal, as he turned me, guiding me towards the back of the boat where a small ladder had already been lowered into the water. I paused there, frozen as another wave of fear crawled across my skin, making me shiver. In the distance, I could see the crowds once more. I could nearly see the smiling faces of the families vacationing on the beach.

"Are you sure this is the right spot?" Paul shouted over his shoulder.

His cronies answered immediately. "Yes, sir. This is it."

Paul leaned over me, forcing me to slump, even at my tiny size, as he pressed his mouth against my hair. "You hear that? This is it."

A single tear slipped out, running down my face, hot in comparison to the splashes of seawater that flew up to touch my face. "And you're sure…about me?"

The gentle crash of waves was the only sound for a long moment, and then Paul chuckled darkly. He was no longer

Paul. Not really. Instead, the Drude spoke through him, a supernatural microphone that was installed as each pledged themselves to the cause. "Oh, sweet girl." Paul, or rather the Drude, stroked my hair. "I have always been sure about you."

I swallowed, trying to focus on that reassurance and the Master, who I had always trusted. "Now what?"

He sighed, his breath hot down my neck. "You were born for this, Faye Sullivan. Born to change the world."

I quaked against Paul's hold, the thick hands that swept down my shoulders to grip my lower back as his body leaned on me. "All you have to do…is die."

And then, without a moment of hesitation, Paul shoved me into the Atlantic Ocean.

***

Kharon

There was very little that happened in the Underworld without me knowing. Perhaps it was to my brother's chagrin, but I was easily the most informed of all of Lucifer's sons. But perhaps that was also because I spent my days surrounded by the most educated and most outspoken guests of the underworld.

And by that, I meant the dead.

No matter how my powers dimmed in these past decades, I still had lost no control over the information that was coming into the Underworld, and that made me unique.

Who needed spies when you had humans? They could no better keep their secrets to themselves than to stay alive forever. Which obviously meant the dead had a lot to say. Good thing I had nothing better than to listen to them chatter on as we ushered them downstream. Hell hospitality. It was a new trend I was trying out.

Humans. Delightfully flawed and full of all kinds of tasty tidbits that my father only wished his people knew.

My bare foot stepped onto my ferry, and I rolled my shoulders back, listening to it crackle and shift, preparing for the first of several journeys down the river today.

"Another day, another ferry full of dead people waiting to pay me." I sighed, leaning my head back until I was staring up at the endless spread of my father's homemade version of the sky. "It's going to be a good one. That one over there, the really floaty one, he died in an actress's bed, and not the one he was married to. I can't wait to hear his side of the story. Poor Nephesh is sending him to Tartarus for sure, but I can get all the tea first."

"What a life you lead, sire." Sarcasm dripped from decrepit vocal cords.

My eyes snapped open, and I groaned as I turned to stare down at the soul lounging beside me. "Would it be so difficult for you to keep the sarcasm to a minimum, Chris? I'm trying to set the tone here."

"Sorry, sire. I thought I was doing a better job." The soul floated closer; the glowing outline of their form visible in the clear Underworld light. "But in my defense, you say that every day."

"Well, every day I'm convinced the day will be good. Temporary insanity. Or is it glaring delusional madness?"

Chris gave me a long, slow look. "I didn't realize you were adding delusion to your list of specialties. I will immediately amend my perspective."

The soft rocking of the boat was more familiar than my own two feet. "Wonderful," I said. "Thank you for your efforts. Shall we go? The dead cannot wait forever. Or, honestly, they can, but where's the fun in that?"

Chris raised a heavy chin, covered with a shadow of stubble from a lifetime ago. I rolled my eyes at the way his head tilted back, as if he could still smell the scent of rock and cold flowing water.

What a crock this one was. I wasn't sure where I'd acquired him, or even when, it seemed he'd been here since the early 1900s when I'd picked him up in a ferry ride, and instead of falling in line, the soul had simply demanded to stay.

For several years, my brothers had harassed me about the somewhat pompous sailor's soul who had decided that my neck of the Underworld was his ideal afterlife.

But you know what? Fuck them. They all had their Brotherhood warriors, or whatever the hell work wife Maeve was to Elon. And my father kept an entire army at Court. I was keeping Chris. At least he couldn't actually put a foot out of line, I was busy enough between the demanding souls and the hungry reapers. I didn't have the time, nor the interest in retraining a new crop of Brotherhood warriors. This suited me just fine.

"Fare thee well, then," I said, pushing the ferry off the dock and allowing the heavy weight of the pulley to fall into place. When I threw the lever down, the ferry began its storied journey back up the River Styx.

As much as I pretended to detest the rogue souls that I'd somehow acquired here at the Pier alongside the river, it was all a farce. I was lonely. I'd been lonely most of my existence, which was saying something because I was very close to a thousand years old at this point, the providential middle child in my father and mother's bond.

Perhaps if I was being honest, I didn't mind the souls most days. Many were desperate for a final wish, or to plead their case to end up in what they assumed was Heaven. They never understood that I couldn't undo that part of the process. As above, so below, the souls were moving constantly. They lived, they died, they learned or opted not to, and then the best of them were sent back to start over again.

In all honesty, I was only a small piece of their story. But I remembered them now. The same glowing souls, the ones that did good while they were up top. I knew them now. What did that say about my life? That I could count the generations of souls that came through my waters.

Chris sneezed, a strange mockery of human nature trapped in death, and it distracted me. "Did you just sneeze? I didn't even know you could do that."

"I think I died of influenza or something," Chris answered, his voice matter of fact.

I stared at him. He and I went over this on a weekly basis. "You died when your ship went down hauling ass from some pirates, Chris. You showed up in the Styx still holding tight to a barrel."

Chris scratched his chin. "I would never die like that. The indignity." I could see his eyes slipping over to confirm with me though.

Subtly, I nodded. I was telling the truth.

Chris cleared his throat, sniffling loudly. "I must've gotten a cold from your ice-cold fucking river, then. Happens to the best of us with your shoddy hosting skills."

I rolled my eyes, turning away from him once more. "Leave me a note on Yelp."

"What's a Yelp?"

I ignored him, and for a long time, there was nothing but the sound of water around us.

Then, Chris spoke up again, this time his voice surprised. "Captain, is that your brother?"

"Don't call me captain. And which one?" I asked before moving my head to look where Chris pointed. Groaning, I saw that I must've misjudged the day because that was certainly my brother. And not the one I was dying to talk to.

It was also not easy to avoid this one either. I groaned loudly and moved over to one side of the ferry, clearing him a path.

Kadmiel, the second youngest of our brood, born directly after me, landed on the ferry with a flurry of wings and shining armor.

I hummed, fluttering my hands at the feathers he rustled up. The ferry was feeling much, much more crowded suddenly. I blamed his wings. "Could you not?"

Kadmiel blinked at me, slow, calm. "Not what? I needed to talk to you."

I pointed at the shore of the Styx that we quickly approached, thanks to Chris steering us ashore. "And you couldn't wait that long?"

Kadmiel almost seemed to consider it. Then he said a definitive, "No."

Sighing, I brushed a feather off my shirt then crossed my arms. "Lovely. I'm glad someone has inherited Father's audacity. Oh wait." I flourished at the solid ground dramatically as the ferry gently bumped against the landing. "You all did."

Kadmiel grunted, tucking his wings in close and marching straight through Chris on his way to the dock.

The sailor threw up a middle finger at the passing demon, which nearly made me smile. But Kadmiel was still speaking.

"At least one of us is interested in our mother's penchant for the dramatic."

"I am not—" I paused, taking a slow breath and stepping onto the decking "—dramatic."

Kadmiel looked down and then back up, taking in my long black cloak, the hood of which still covered part of my smooth blue head. Then he looked past me to the ferry still covered in deep-brown feathers. "Uh-huh. Sure, Kharon, whatever you need to say."

Chris cruised by me, still muttering curses out at Kadmiel as he passed, and then vanished into the walls surrounding my home. Built straight into the docks of the Styx, it was designed to meet my every need. Pillars drilled through the Styx kept me from washing downstream, and I had access points to the water at all times.

Arafel had called me crazy when I told him just how many trap doors through the floor to water I wanted in my house, but I'd ignored him. After all, they might have their wings, but I had the water. I was built to swim through it, my power boosted by its very presence. It was my one nonnegotiable when I took over this home.

Ignoring Kadmiel, I walked through the front door, letting my brother follow in my wake. When he stepped through the entryway, he froze immediately, his power, or what was left of it, spiking in warning. I rolled my eyes.

"A human has been here." He actually spun around a little, looking more like a harried rooster than the leader of my family's soul guardians. The charms that he wore across the small white horns that curled tight against his hair made happy little noises as they clinked together. The sound was completely at odds with the golden glow of my brother's eyes.

I shrugged, moving towards my favorite chair and plopping down with a high-pitched sigh. My hood slipped back, and I ran a hand over my smooth head.

"Calm yourself. It was only Lucia. And that was, I don't know, weeks ago, maybe?" I hummed a little, thinking about the night Nephesh, the heir to our father's throne, brought my other brother's human and very much still alive mate to my doors. Insisting I take her back to the living world. If I hadn't enjoyed the spunky little human's company so much, I would've thrown Nephesh straight back out on his pompous ass.

"Arafel's mate?" Kadmiel was clearly interested. "Why was she here?"

"I'm planning on stealing her away from him with my superior wit and ability to hold my breath for hours." I waggled my dark brows, the only hair on my face, suggestively.

Kadmiel blinked slowly.

I sighed, disappointed my little brother wouldn't rise to the bait. "How am I the only one who ended up with a sense of humor? She was here, Guardian, because Nephesh thought it was a good idea to bring her here." I paused, shifting in my chair until my cloak lay nicely across my legs. "Well, in all honesty, it was a good idea to get her here. I was able to get her back to the living world when the Drude's Corrupted attacked Castle Fel. Arafel needed to know she was safe. Nephesh could get her here. I could get her there." I slapped my hands together. "Dream team engaged."

"That was some time ago. Lucia has been back in the Underworld for weeks." Kadmiel raised his nose, suspicion still thick in his words. "And yet it is still so strong."

I swung my hands out wide. "You're welcome to look, brother, but there's no one else here." I met Chris's gray gaze. "No one alive at least," I amended with a nod to the dead sailor.

Chris bowed his head, acknowledging my change in answer, and then continued leaning over the stack of music that was sprawled across my desk in one corner.

Kadmiel's booted feet moved, and for a second, I thought he might take me on my search, but something changed in his face. His expression dulled; his shoulders sagged. The golden flare of magic in his eyes dimmed, leaving them a sparkling hazel. "Of course. I'm sorry, Kharon. I shouldn't have asked like that."

What the fuck was wrong with him? I peered closely at my brother. He really did appear apologetic. I shifted in my seat, uncomfortable with the emotion in his voice. "It's fine. Now, tell me why you're here, because I know you didn't just drop in to chat. Not these days, and not dressed like that."

We were too busy for that. Too much power and need stretched across the Underworld as the creatures and souls that claimed the Underworld as home struggled to survive. The power was shifting constantly. Souls fed my family's abilities, but when we were not strong enough to process them, then we lost the abilities that we had used to govern this world for so many generations.

Every soul that came into the Underworld paid a price. Every soul that was rehabilitated in Tartarus or who toiled in Elysium building our world, they were the ones who kept this world going. Until the Drude had come. This creature, whoever he was, he was disrupting the channels of power. He was stealing souls and their power alike.

And we…well, we were struggling. Without the missing half of our souls, we would never have a chance to defeat him. But our parents had believed that splitting our souls would make us more difficult to kill. Turned out it made it just as difficult to live.

To live half a life was not enough anymore. Luckily, Arafel, my brother the Dream King, had managed after searching for hundreds of years to find the human woman carrying his soul. A brilliant student, Lucia, had carried it for him and had defied the odds and pledged her own soul to Arafel. Now she was bound to him in more ways than one.

She was a Queen of Dreams, Princess of Hell. And a delight to talk with. But then, Arafel had always been the best among us. He deserved her.

Again, Kadmiel hesitated. I blinked at him, patting my fingers against the edge of my chair, a reminder about the real matter at hand.

He must've gotten the hint because he blurted out, "Did you…have you…done the thing?"

Biting back a laugh, I scratched at my cheek, hiding the smile that burned in my cheeks. "Your clarification, dearest brother, delights me."

Kadmiel blew through his nose, hard. "You know what I'm talking about. Did you… Did you talk to the souls? The corrupted ones that came through?"

Each of my brothers handled a different part of the Underworld, with my father ruling and king, lord, dictator, and head asshole from the Court of Hell. When he and my mother, a mortal-born witch conceived and raised us, their magic designed us in a way that guided us inevitably into the realm of the Underworld we seemed destined to be lord of.

The Judge.

The Dream Lord.

The Ferryman.

The Punisher.

The Guardian.

But what only a few knew, what Kadmiel wanted to ask me about right now, was because I had a unique ability that was not often spoken about at Court or otherwise.

The souls could not lie to me once they were in the Styx.

You would think that Nephesh would've appreciated that skillset as the Judge of Souls, but nope, that was left to me. In recent years, during the Drude's rise to power, my father and Kadmiel had come to me, asking me if I could "read" the souls that came through the Styx on their way to judgment.

I didn't do it often. I didn't like the way it felt, the way the soul faded after my magic left them. Not to mention the vast amount of energy I had to exert to make it happen in the first place.

But things were not going well. Without Arafel securing his bond with his human mate, Lucia, I doubt the Underworld would be functioning at all. And the dream realm only extended so far. We needed to advance.

We needed to win.

I looked down at my hands. "I spoke with only a few." The lie tasted sour on my tongue, but I didn't need my brother to know I had only been strong enough to read two of them. "They spoke only of humans who came to them on their deathbeds, promising another chance at life if they were to follow the Drude's instructions. When they agreed, the Drude poofed into their rooms, they saw nothing, and then they woke up here, entering the river. Once passing through, they waited for a distraction and raced from the river to gather near the southern Wastelands."

"Exactly like the others," Kadmiel said softly.

"Points to Drude for consistency."

Kadmiel made a face. "Don't talk about him like that. He's not some neighbor we are bickering with. He is a monster, and in case you haven't noticed, he's winning this war."

I waggled a finger at him. "You cope with apocalyptic villains the way you want to and allow me the same courtesy. Hm?"

Was that a smile or a growl, I wondered to myself as Kadmiel bared his teeth at me. "My, my… Things must be worse than I thought." Kadmiel was one of the most even-tempered of all of us. In my opinion, it seemed that as each of the brothers were born, they were a little less demonic and a little more human-like. Which was why, in my eyes, Nephesh had all the reason in the world to want to raze this world to the ground. That much demon blood did that to you. Even our father didn't have that much demon in him, and he was fucking Lucifer.

"It's bad," Kadmiel admitted, crossing the floor and staring out at the Pier of Kalos in the distance. "Lucia's soul bought us time, sure. But there's no way we can keep going like this. Souls are disappearing, and they can only be going one place. Father is demanding an answer."

I snorted. "Father hasn't bothered to tell me of this, nor does he extend any of beloved Brotherhood warriors to my aid. I only have my reapers"—I spotted the soul lingering across the room—"and fucking Chris, so back off. I'm doing the best I can."

"It's not enough."

I was out of the chair too fast for him to move, catching my brother up in a choke hold that rattled the wall. I plastered my body against him, letting him feel just how easy it would be to snap his pretty neck. It wouldn't kill him permanently, but necks always hurt when they snapped back in place. "Tsk, tsk, little brother," I growled up at him, staring at the blue tone of my skin against the smooth pale flesh of his throat. "I can smell your fear."

Kadmiel glared at me, his hands on my wrist as he attempted to brace himself against my hold. After a long moment, I backed down, releasing him with a huff.

Somewhere in the back of my mind, my body ached for him to attack. I hadn't had a good fight with any of my brothers, the only creatures around here that would provide a real competitor, in decades. We'd figured out quickly that fighting amongst ourselves drained our power even faster than fighting the Drude. Probably some kind of sick sibling-protection spell that our mother thought was a good idea at the time.

Sadly, Kadmiel backed away, shaking his head, one hand at his throat. "Have your reapers at the ready." He walked to the door, his wings spreading and flexing. "They're coming, whether we are ready or not."

The door rattled on the hinges as he slammed his way out. Crossing my arms, I moved back to the window to watch him become a speck on the horizon. "And they call me the dramatic one."

"An exaggeration to be sure," Chris echoed from his perch by the desk.

"Why the fuck are you still here? Don't you have someone or somewhere to haunt?"

Chris shrugged. "Only you."

I sighed "Lucky me." I eyed him. "Well, if you're going to be here, let's go ahead and put them to bed, eh?"

Moving around Chris's form, as was common courtesy, I made my way over to the piano that took over nearly half of my personal bedchamber. Sitting on the bench, I cracked one knuckle before picking up the sheet music I'd thrown aside after last night's campaign.

"Let's see what this edition does, hm?" Taking a deep breath in, I pressed into the keys, letting my fingers follow the dark-inked notes on the page. Of all the languages I spoke, this one, music, was the only one that lingered. On quiet nights, on wild mornings, there was always music in my mind.

It hadn't taken my mother long to figure out that the way to transfer my magic into the Underworld was through the music I loved so much. And after my powers became clearer, the magic helped me funnel it into something good.

Something that helped my realm.

The strokes of the ivory keys soothed my soul, washing away the remnants of frustration brought about by Kadmiel's visit. Under my feet, I could feel them gathering, the souls in the river water drawn to the sound.

My head lolled back, and I was swept up in the music, a slow, sorrowful piece that always lured them closer. It was getting late, and I knew that while people were dying all across the world, their souls were flowing by. The few that lingered, the few that needed this moment, they were receiving it. This was what I was made for.

The music poured out of me, carrying what little magic I had left into water below, flowing through the Styx until I could feel them all, every soul, every thought, every pain and pleasure. All of it hit me at once, their souls looking to me for that last taste of assurance.

Through the music, I tried to reach them. Even now, I could feel that my reach was so much smaller than ever before.

Without the other half of my soul, soon I would have *no* reach. My fingers paused after a chord, my head tilted. When the magic disappeared, would that mean I would too?

The river's surface grew choppy again as the souls stirred, restless and waiting. I pushed onwards, the chords resuming.

Minutes, maybe hours later, my fingers grew still. My skin was clammy and tight across my frame. More proof of just how difficult using my magic was currently. I was tempted to take a dip in the river to cool down, but I feared waking the souls I'd just quieted. They were always energized by my presence. Chris had gone, and my home was empty once more.

I rose, peeling my cloak and simple black clothing from my frame. The mirror distracted me briefly, and I stared at my reflection. Unlike my brothers, I had very little hair and no feathers. I was sleek, smooth, save the arch of my brows and the dark lashes that framed my overbright blue eyes.

Lucia, my brother Arafel's bold little human mate, once asked if I would be happier in the magicked camouflage that my mother designed for me. A human form, one I could flicker into with only the smallest use of my magic.

And it had taken me a bit to respond. In the living world, I always maintained my human form. Unlike Kadmiel, who looked nearly human most days, save the glowy eyes and annoyingly square cheekbones, my true form would send living people running.

I ran my hands up my face and over my smooth scalp then down, briefly catching against the soft frill of my gills at the sides of my throat. They were sealed now and tingled at my touch.

In the end, I'd told Lucia no, because regardless of how others might react, this was who I was. I was a son of Lucifer, a Prince of Hell, and I had a role to play.

Each of us did. At least until this world ended.

Striding to my bed, I let my body flop over onto the softness of the mattress. And without my brothers and me finding our missing souls, that ending was looming closer and closer. My belly tightened, and I frowned, pressing a hand against it. Demons like me didn't get stomachaches.

I waited, surprised by the depth of the feeling.

It faded for a moment then came roaring back. I lurched up to a sitting position, my mind a whirl as the pain took over my whole torso, centering on my ribcage. Every move I made intensified it, making my breathing come short in my lungs.

"What is happening?" I grunted as I curled to a sitting position. Stars danced in my vision as I looked around the room. This had never happened before. Had I overextended my magic? I hadn't thought so.

"Lord Kharon?"

I looked up to find Chris in the doorway again, his soul shimmering in the light. I pressed a hand against my chest. "Something is wrong."

The pain in my chest grew sharp again, and I gasped, leaning over. "Find my brother."

"Which one?"

Darkness tugged at the back of my vision. I blinked, trying desperately to focus on Chris's face. "Any of them."

My mind suddenly cleared, the pain in my chest a distant echo as I recognized what might be happening. I'd seen it only once.

In Nephesh. The day his soul bound died.

"Oh fuck," I rasped. It wasn't me in jeopardy. It was my soul bound. And they were hurt. Fatally perhaps.

"I have to go," I told Chris, unsure whether he was even listening now. "I have to go now. Tell my brother that I had to find them. That they were in danger."

"Who?"

I reached down, gasping at the pain in my chest. "My soul bound." And with that, I yanked the trap down on the floor of my bedroom and stared down at the water below.

"Don't worry," I whispered. "I'm coming."

2

Faye

The water was warm. And for the first few moments, I was still, feeling the soft waves push me to and fro in the ocean current. Then that ache in my chest built.

Air.

Oh God, I needed air.

I struck out, my arms pinwheeling in the water as I struggled back to the surface.

Paul leaned over the edge of the ladder, a disgusting smile on his face. "You just work your magic, girl, and we will be waiting."

I clawed at the water, cursing both my fear of water and the insane men who now stared down at me as they slowly pulled up the ladder. My head ducked under, my legs kicking desperately as I struggled back to the surface.

This time I only made it into the air for a moment before the current tugged me farther from the boat. My waterlogged eyes saw no one now, my entire mind consumed with the insanity of this plan. And as dark spots filled my vision, I knew once and for all that while the Drude may have been aware of my witch-filled bloodlines, he was not right about the thing he loved the most about me.

I was not bound to any of Lucifer's sons. Because if I had been, they would've come for me. As water stole its way up my nose, I nearly laughed at the improbability of it all. My entire life planning and training for this one moment.

All to be completely incorrect.

I could go to hell laughing. Maybe my "not" soul mate would laugh too.

We could enjoy this moment together.

My chest burned again, my body tightening with desperate need just as I made one final push to the surface. Only my fingertips broke the surface.

But just before I sank lower into the dark, deadly water, large hands, rough and strong, settled under my armpits. One moment I was flailing. The next my head was breaking the surface, my curls clinging to my face and neck. Those hands held, a solid, warm form bumping into me as my legs kicked out like a child's.

"Please," I whispered. "Please don't let me go."

"Don't worry," a smooth voice said. "I won't."

I shivered, his voice settling over my mind like a balm. He spoke English, but the accent was a little off. Swiping at my face, I pushed hair and seawater out of my eyes. I could feel it was tugging us somewhere, and I prayed to everyone listening that it was the boat. Forget the plan. I wasn't getting back into this water ever again.

"Are you alright?" my rescuer asked, and this time my eyes focused on the man hauling me along behind him. My heart leaped in my throat. It was… It was just a man. A beautiful one, maybe, but the Drude wasn't looking for a man.

I hadn't just been thrown into the ocean for a *man*.

Pushing back, I stared down at him, willing him to have something different on his body. Something that I could confirm made him a demon. Why didn't he have horns like Nephesh? And his eyes, while beautifully blue, didn't even glow as he towed me along. He looked positively normal.

I gulped, suddenly wishing he'd left me in the water. Where had he even come from? One minute there'd been only water, and then…him.

"I'm fine. I'm fine! Where did you come from?" My voice was raspy, rough from the water I'd swallowed.

The man was staring at me as he swam, his strokes confident and comfortable, even as a large wave pushed against us. "I, uh… Let's get you back in your boat. What are you doing out here with no life jacket? These currents are dangerous."

Unbidden tears filled my eyes. All of that work, all of that training, and it was all for nothing. The Drude was going to kill me, unless Paul did it first. My heart hammered in my ears as the stranger towed me closer to the boat, and then, holding one arm around me, he somehow reared up to yank the ladder back down into the water.

He pushed my legs to the rungs, steadying me with hands on my hips as I climbed shakily up the ladder. I stumbled on board, gasping again as water dripped off me, pooling against the polished wooden boards.

I had failed.

Paul would be out here any moment.

A palm pressed against my back, warmth radiating into my body, making my burning lungs relax. Quiet stole its way through my body, even as my mind raced. I dared to look at him one more time to make sure I hadn't just missed something. Our eyes met and held, his gaze wild and eager as it raced over me.

"Can I get you something? Were you out here all alone?"

I shook my head, past the point of lying. Weakly, I turned, pushing at the bulk of him as he kneeled beside me. He had to leave. Now. There was no other opportunity. As soon as they came out and saw this, it would be over.

"No, but you have to go." *Poor, random guy in the ocean. You have no idea what you're stumbling into.*

His dark brows lowered, and he didn't move an inch. "I want to be sure you're safe."

I couldn't stop the hysterical laughter. "It's been a long time since that one was true." Settling back on my legs, I stared into his eyes as he remained kneeling in front of me. They, like the rest of him, were stunning. A bright blue, nearly the same tone as the ocean around us.

Slowly, he reached out, intending to brush more of my curls out of my eyes. I froze, my chest rising and falling with more than adrenaline from my near-death experience. There was something humming, deep inside me, under my skin, warm and radiant and powerful. The moment his fingers brushed my skin, his fingertips changed. No longer the smooth tanned skin of the human man before me, but rather a blue, tipped with dangerous-looking black nails.

He jerked away, faster than I believed possible, but it didn't change what I knew. What I had seen.

I stumbled to my feet, my mind and eyes on the door to the below-deck area of the ship.

"Wait, hold on!" the male, the decidedly not human one spoke. "Please, I'm not going to hurt you."

"No, you're not," I whispered as I darted towards the door.

"Fu— Please wait." His voice struck out after me, and I heard his footsteps against the ship's deck as I finally made it to the door on the other side. Memory returned, my mind clearing as I realized what I'd just done. What I was setting into motion.

I held up a hand, my power flickering as fear ruled my mind. "Stop there," I said, the warmth that raced through my blood still present. "I said stop."

But he didn't. To his credit, he did slow. Back in his glamor, he appeared every inch the human man, defenseless, powerless against someone like me. But I knew he was different.

The Drude had taught me differently.

"Don't come any closer," I said, my heart thumping in my ears.

But just as before—as we predicted—he took another step. Then one more.

And that was all it took. Throwing my hands out, I murmured the command that would change the world. His and mine.

"Stay."

Blue light, so bright it made my eyes burn, flared up from the deck at his feet, highlighting the circle that I'd designed and built for this very purpose. I could see the human hands swiping at the light as it engulfed him, during which I felt, rather than saw, Paul and his team emerge from below deck.

"Holy shit, Faye," one of them whispered, fear in every syllable.

My heartbeat slowed as the magic solidified and took hold, no longer needing me to trigger it, but merely to settle and maintain the magical cage that encircled the demon prince within. The light faded, revealing a very different creature.

Gone was the human man with smiling teeth and pretty features. Instead, there was a demon. Blue in color, his skin was covered with casual black clothing, bare feet, and several necklaces that hung around his neck. As he turned his head, sharp white teeth bared in a snarl, I saw a flash of jewelry in one slightly pointed ear. Claws tipped his fingers, and gills lined his throat. Muscle reinforced every visible part of him.

This was Kharon, the Ferryman.

Something twisted in my belly.

Had he come for me? That would mean that I was meant to be his in some insane cosmic joke of fate. Or perhaps had one of his brothers sent him? The Drude believed that Kharon was one of the few princes of Hell still capable of leaving the Underworld without dire consequences. So, while my mind told me that he might not be bound to me, my body blatantly refused that idea.

Because of course it was him.

Every part of me, every molecule and iota of power I possessed, screamed to me to free him.

"What have I done?" I didn't realize I'd said the words out loud until Paul's heavy hand landed on my shoulder.

"Exactly what you were supposed to," he said loudly, walking towards the demon. Kharon was looking to his feet, to the glowing blue ring that was keeping him in place. "Demon, state your name."

That barely got his attention. Instead, he continued to observe the magic flowing around him. "Go to hell."

Paul chuckled, putting his fists on his hips. "A little on the nose for you, isn't it?"

Kharon tilted his head, lifting it slowly to observe the male in front of him. It was a predatory move, an alpha observing their prey. Then instantly, his eyes glowed, and I felt something in my belly contract. It was his power. He was testing the boundaries of my spell. Gulping, I stepped forward, ready to defend the magic if he tried to flee.

I couldn't let him go, even if I wanted to. It was no longer an option. Not with the Drude. If he heard that we'd let Kharon escape, there would be such severe consequences that even I would not be able to survive. There was too much riding on this capture. The Drude needed access to the Underworld. At minimum, Kharon could provide that. At maximum, absorbing the soul of a Prince of Hell would bring the Drude more power than even he could need.

"It's you… You are doing this," Kharon said, a shocking smile tugging at his lips.

I blinked, stepping forward and raising my hands. Magic, my own, flickered to life in my palms.

"I am, and this spell was designed specifically for you, Ferryman. You're not going anywhere."

Somehow, I was right in front of the magical barrier now, close enough I could see the droplets of water on his blue skin. He ducked his chin, bringing his eyes closer to my much smaller height.

"I'm flattered…" His gaze took me in, making my skin tingle. "Witch."

Then, just as fast as before, he stepped back, his shoulder relaxing. Turning away from me, he did a small circle around his enclosed space. I watched him closely, and I was sure the men behind me were too. He did another slow circle around the outside edge, and then with a dramatic sigh, the demon folded his legs under himself and calmly sat down on the deck.

I backed up as Paul moved forward.

One of the recruits coughed then leaned into his friend. "What's he doing?"

Paul was silent as the other recruit shrugged. "Um, not sure, man. Probably some kind of trick."

"*He* can hear you," Kharon said, flashing another smile at us, this one full of fang. "And since you neglected to provide me with a seating arrangement, I've made one of my own." He gestured around himself. "I'm guessing this little spell your witch set up will allow things to enter the field with me, but nothing to leave?"

He was right. My chest constricted, doubt crowding into my thoughts. Had I missed something in the spell? It shouldn't be so…so obvious. Right?

Kharon continued, "So, if you'd like to be polite, you can scoot one of those deck chairs through my way."

No one moved. No one even breathed. He was… Was he joking? I looked quickly at Paul, whose face was grim and strained.

The recruits shifted a little then. "Sir, should I get him—"

"Fuck no, don't get him a chair." Paul stepped forward towards the demon. "I don't know what you're up to, demon, but it doesn't matter. You just sit there, shut the fuck up. The Drude will deal with you when he gets here."

Kharon didn't seem to be listening. He was focused on my magic again, holding his finger a few inches from the barrier, a light-blue line jumping from his skin to the glowing circle.

Without thinking twice, I reinforced my spell. Kharon's lips curled, but he didn't look my way again.

Paul's hands were on my shoulders now, pushing me ahead of him and the rest of the crew as we clambered down the few steps into the galley. The floors rocking under my feet did nothing to stem the ill ease that filled the air around us.

"Will that hold him? Your spell." Paul's voice was quiet, gritted, as he alternated between looking at me and the direction of the captured demon.

I took a mental analysis of my powers, the gentle hum of the spell above deck, holding our prisoner in place. The cords tying me to the spell were strong, glowing with the strength of my power. "I'm fine, in case you were wondering." I crossed my arms. "And yes, it will hold."

Paul swiped a hand across his pale, sweating features. I followed the gesture with interest. The Corrupted were brought back to life with very little survival instincts. Only the ones who managed to survive longer picked up those more human traits once more. Master always claimed that was why he needed new souls all the time. Because the older Corrupted were too human, too emotional, prone to fits of fear or worry.

I hadn't seen Paul like this, looking more human than ever before. Cocking my head sideways, I watched his throat bob in a series of swallows.

He would be gone soon. I could tell already. Maybe even before we were back at Headquarters. You never could tell what Master had in mind, but he would hate to see this unraveling of his warriors. The urge to distance myself from what was definitely going to be one of Master's next kills made me queasy. I stepped back, bumping into the cabinets there, all latched shut tight against the waves.

"Okay, okay. That's good," Paul said, his voice a rasp. "Fuck, though, did you see him? Do you think you can do three days?"

I nodded.

Paul immediately looked to the captain, a civilian man who the Drude had been utilizing for months. He was more shell than man now, seeing nothing, knowing nothing, remembering nothing but the task given to him by the Drude. I didn't even know his name. I wondered briefly if he did. Possession was the ugliest of all Master's abilities. The slow, ebbing destruction of someone's self.

I looked at him standing there, his hands limp at his sides, vacant eyes on Paul as the men spoke quickly. Would I look like him someday? When my worthiness wore thin?

"We're taking the dinghy and going back to the land. Stay the course. We will return soon with your Master. Do you understand me? Stay close. Do not touch the witch or the demon on the deck."

The captain nodded, his hands and eyes never moving as he rigidly moved back toward the navigation panel. Paul didn't wait for his agreement; he didn't need it. Together, the other Corrupted moved to the bunks, grabbing their already packed bags and other personal items off the threadbare blankets.

Reassembling in front of me, they formed a wall. I tried to push back the bulk of male that blocked me from my own items.

I cleared my throat, resisting the urge to stand on my tiptoes in case they didn't see me. "I'll just be a moment."

"Not you, cupcake," Paul sneered at me. "You stay with the prize."

"What? Me stay here?" Dread was a living thing, shrinking me to the floor. I couldn't stay here. The water, the demon, it was all too much. I'd done what I was told to do. Now I was supposed to be taken home again. Or to wherever the Drude needed me next.

The Corrupted leader sighed, as if I was taxing his patience. And I was sure I was. "Master wants to make sure that his new toy doesn't get lost and isn't sure your abilities can stretch all the way to land. We can't risk him getting to somewhere he can call for help."

My skin chilled instantly, my mind scrambling to explain. I could not stay here. Not a single moment longer. "We've trained for this situation. We've tested my reach. It will be nothing."

Paul's shoulder lifted, unaffected by the way my voice shook. "We will be back soon, witch. Don't worry so much. You'll be safe here with the captain."

Stupid, frustrated tears blurred my vision. I blinked them away, desperate to stay focused, to stay grounded. If my emotion got away from me here, I wasn't sure what would happen. "I don't want to stay here; you know how I feel about…"

Paul lowered his face until we were staring eye-to-eye. "Listen up. You may think you're better than us, but in the end, you will live or die by the orders you're given. And the Drude says stay." He rubbed his jaw. "I wouldn't test him, Faye. It's been a rough few weeks since that last one got free on your watch."

My throat tightened, tears now burning the backs of my eyes. He was referring, of course, to me losing a battle against the heir to Hell. One I hadn't even been prepared to fight. I had only been brought to Omaha to babysit the other witch they'd found. Too bad that the demon prince and his human mate had turned out to be something else altogether. And by that, I meant the male had turned into an enormous human-squashing monster the moment his mate was threatened.

I had fought him, sure, but only because I'd been told to. All things aside, the human woman, Justine, she'd been so much like me. I had related to her more than anyone else in the entire compound, and subconsciously I thought I'd wanted them to escape.

I'd never reveal that last part. Not that anyone would ask. They assumed that everything in me was completely devoted to the Drude. I gave them no reason to doubt otherwise. A loyal servant did what she was told.

Just freaking great.

My eyes stared into Paul's. Did he suspect something? More than likely he was just trying to scare me into staying put without a fight. He hadn't been there during the battle with Nephesh, where the Drude had lost so many. But rumors were stronger than steel, and I knew there had been plenty of whispers afterwards.

All the more reason to not screw this up.

Soul mates didn't matter.

Survival did.

Family did.

And as I stared over the railing, watching Paul and his team disappear into the midday sun, I could only hope that I hadn't just ruined my chances of getting out of this alive.

***

Kharon

She was scared of me, this little witch. But not like I had feared at first. After those Corrupted had left, she milled aimlessly around the deck. Her obvious anxiety about the situation practically leaked into the air around us. It polluted the salt air, unsettling my stomach, as if her fear actually made me ill. Or maybe it was that I couldn't do anything about her being so upset. Either way, this was torture.

When she'd leaned in, so close earlier, I'd seen that spark of interest and curiosity. Just before the idiots who had sped off a short time ago pulled her back into their throng. I rolled my eyes. Different goons, same creature giving them an excuse for violence.

It was clear that the Drude was behind this. I'd heard that he was amassing a human army, one with the living souls here in this world as well as the corrupted souls from my own.

But knowing about it and being captured by them were two very different things. And for as much as the Drude appeared to hate us, I'd been surprised by the witch's presence. My family had assumed, incorrectly it seemed, that the Drude was attempting to end all aspects of the Underworld. That would, of course, include the very small amount of witch blood that still ran on both sides of the realm. But here she was, a fully grown witch doing his dirty work with nothing but painful determination.

Faye—I'd learned her name when she and the Corrupted went below deck—paced back by for the forty-third time.

A very pretty witch.

She was freshly dressed in a soft yellow sundress, her dark curls hanging wild around a delicate, feminine face. Her hands clenched and unclenched, occasionally swirling through the air as she marched around the space. Her nails were painted pink, and I could see round pearl earrings dotting the lobes of her ears.

I remained seated, toying with the edges of her spell, trying to learn more about her magic as I watched her. She was quite small, really. If we were to stand toe-to-toe once again, I imagined that her head would likely only reach mid-chest. Not that size was any correlation to power. My own mother, Nicola, famously noted as the first witch, was only a little bit taller than Faye, and she had basically torn the fabric of life and death with my father.

"Would you like to sit down? You have to be tired by now," I asked her as she passed by on lap forty-five.

She blinked at me, dark lashes fluttering over wide eyes. "What?"

"Your pacing… It must be exhausting."

Smooth arched brows rose, and Faye's lips pursed, making my cock twitch. She had a lovely mouth with soft-looking plump lips. I patted the deck, sensing her dilemma. "Sit with me."

"No, thank you." She immediately struck back off for lap forty-six. But her steps were slowed, less frantic.

I tried again, curious if my observation skills were serving me well today. "Are you afraid of the water? Or does being alone with me really provide that much stress to you?"

Faye slowed even more. "I'm not afraid of you."

I shrugged, leaning back onto my palms. "So, you're afraid of water. What did they do? Throw you overboard earlier? I very much doubt you jumped."

She stopped entirely, the magic around me tightening like a fist. I hummed, a shock of pride burning through me at her simple showing of power. I wanted to see more from this witch, the one in which my soul resided. Running my tongue over my teeth, I watched the expressions fly across her features. "Ah, yes. They did, then. Seems odd, considering you could probably turn them all to dust with half a thought."

Faye's sharp little chin jutted out, her head turning in a mockery of ignoring me. "I don't have that kind of power."

She was lying, but not to me. To herself.

I watched the hem of her yellow dress float around her knees in the wind. It was there, a tightness that pulled—no, yanked—at my heart. I knew she felt it too. And after a long breath, I saw her shoulders drop. Step by step, Faye walked towards me, every inch closer she got making that pulling in my chest ache more.

I waited until I could see the soft white of her eyes before I spoke again. "Don't you?"

Her voice was a whisper. "Please stop talking to me. If they find out, Paul will... There will be consequences."

"Would he throw you back overboard?" My shoulders twitched with a need to act. The muscles there suddenly begged to discuss this with the Corrupted when he returned. No one put hands on a female in front of me, and the very idea of anyone hurting this female in particular... The demon blood pumping in my body begged for revenge for her fear.

He had touched what was mine. He had scared her. My fangs burned as they pressed into my gums. I swallowed it back, trying to calm my instincts. This was not the place to go full demon on her.

"No—at least, I don't think so. He needs me to…." Faye fiddled with her fingers again.

"Ah." I tapped the side of my head. "I see now. They need you to keep me under control." When she didn't answer, I continued, "That's very strategic of you. I salute you for the smart planning."

Her head jerked up, obviously offended. "I serve my master loyally. I serve him entirely. There is nothing planned."

"Sure," I said, nodding along. "Does he forbid you from sitting?"

"What? No." She scoffed at me, missing the point of my question.

I smiled at her in a way that I hoped was disarming. "Then sit, witchling, and tell me why the water scares you."

Her eyes flickered over me, a soft flare of her magic making me grin a little internally. Such a clever little thing, checking that I wasn't doing something naughty. Clever witch. She didn't trust me.

Good. She shouldn't.

Just when I thought she was going to resume her pacing, her legs folded, and she lowered herself to the deck a few feet from the edge of her circle. As she did, she swept an arm around her knees, settling the dress across her legs like she was sitting down to tea versus on board a stinking fish boat. It fascinated me, the way her hands moved, smoothing and shifting across the skirt and those smooth, curved calves. My fingers twitched, curious if she was as soft as she appeared.

Settled, she raised her chin in my direction, as if awaiting confirmation.

"Look at you, brave girl," I praised her, clapping softly.

Her face immediately tightened. "The Drude is going to kill you anyway, so it doesn't matter what you say to me."

I nodded, as if agreeing with her. But I shifted my form closer to the spelled barrier. "You know, I'm quite hard to kill. Does he have a plan? Maybe a few. I could help you brainstorm."

Her nostrils flared, and I laughed. "All I'm saying is in my lifetime, enough others have already tried nearly every method. So, he must have at least one plan in motion."

"Of course he does." Her chin was quivering now, the flickers of her temper making the spell around me darken.

Interestingly, that tugging in my chest only intensified. "Oh good. In that case, since it doesn't matter, before I die, tell me why the water frightens you."

Faye played with the edge of her dress, making the hemline dance up the line of her legs. I wondered what the skin there felt like, my entire being suddenly hyper-fixated on that slide of cotton against flesh.

"I never learned to swim. I've been with the Drude since I was a child. It wasn't a priority to learn."

I jerked my gaze back to her, hoping she didn't notice I had been staring at her legs. But her eyes were glued to her lap, where her hands were folding and unfolding.

"Hmm…that's easy enough to fix. I could teach you. Once your master fails to kill me."

Faye huffed a soft laugh, one hand moving to her mouth to cover the sound as her shame-ridden eyes met mine. But it was too late. I'd heard that sound. The softness, the sweetness of that laugh burrowing deep in my brain, forming a memory there, encased in pure steel. Only for me.

"I don't think that will be possible," she said after a moment.

I shrugged, trying to make sure my face remained neutrally smiling. "Fair. Tell me something else." I looked around us as she mimicked the movement. "Where are we? Near Florida?"

Her brows drew together—in surprise, maybe—but she nodded.

"Why Florida? While I can appreciate that it seems like most of the aged souls that end up in the river are coming from here, I see no reason for the Drude to come here."

Faye shrugged. "He doesn't tell me much. I feel like you are overestimating my importance."

"And I feel like you are purposefully downplaying your part in this whole enterprise. After all, how else would a witch come to be in the employment of the Drude?"

"You're assuming I work for him?" Faye huffed then looked nervously over her shoulder. "I have been with the Drude since I was a child. And before you start on the Stockholm syndrome symptoms, I'm not affected in that way."

She swallowed. "I am doing what I need to, to survive. We have a deal."

I scratched my nail against the polished deck, not looking at her, "A worthy cause. I can understand that. The need for survival rises above all else in situations like yours. I imagine any in your shoes would've chosen the same path."

"You wouldn't judge me?" Her voice was soft now, nearly hidden by the sound of waves.

"For finding a way to live?" I shrugged. "No one would judge you for that. I will say that if the Drude really does show up here and sends me back to Hell the painful way, then it might put a bit of a damper on our friendship. But we can work past that."

Her eyes widened, and I could see her consider retreating. But she held her ground, her calves tightening as if prepared to leap away from me. "I don't understand you."

She was an utter delight. I grinned at her. "Most don't."

Faye looked away, back to the water, but not before a soft flash of pink darkened olive-toned cheeks. "You would forgive me…but only because I'm your soul bound. Right?"

I whistled, settling my hands on my laps and giving her a long look. "Now see here, who taught you those words?" I forced a tight smile at her as my heart raced in my chest. "I am sure they aren't on the spelling test for Drude University."

Her lips curled, and a light wind pushed her curls back from her face. "They weren't. But I met someone last week. She was like me, in some ways, and she was…bound to your brother."

My brother, I thought to myself. Fucking hell, which brother? If the Drude had one of my brothers, I needed to act now. Panic threatening, I attempted to keep my voice light. "Which brother?"

I obviously failed at playing it cool. Faye's head tilted as her eyes flickered over me once again. She was clearly assessing me. Trying to decide what to tell me. "I don't want to mess up his name. But he was the angry one…"

"Nephesh," I answered for her. I'd known my brother had vanished, but I wasn't sure if it was just another one of his brooding fests or something else entirely. The fact that this witch had seen him raised every alarm. Without Nephesh, the souls would be trapped, unjudged. Not to mention the considerable amount of power my eldest brother brought to the table simply be existing in our world.

If anything happened to him, hellfire would literally rain on the Drude. There would be nothing left. Nothing even worth saving. I cleared my throat. "Is he… What happened to him?"

"She helped him escape. She…" Faye swallowed hard. "She chose him and defied my master."

"His soul bound?" There was yawning feeling erupting in my chest, replacing the fear for my family with something else. Something darker, twisting and growing as I watched Faye.

Jealousy. Gods, and it was ugly. Nephesh had found not one, but two soul bounds in his lifetime. And I'd had only minutes with mine.

And of course, she was planning on surrendering me to our greatest enemy.

Fucking Nephesh and his luck.

Faye's voice, soft and a little rushed, dragged me out of my tumble of thoughts. "Yes, but it wasn't like that anymore. They were different. She was. She was his mate, she said." She whispered that last part as if scandalized.

I slumped a little in my designated ring. Even Nephesh, the biggest and most accomplished asshole of us all, had managed to find someone to accept him. *Twice.* And it sounded like they could be on their way back to the Underworld even now.

"Lucky ass," I said quietly. I felt like maybe Faye heard me too, because she shifted a little farther from me. I could see her eyes trailing off to the side. She was going to get up. Suddenly, I needed to find a way to keep her here, close to me.

"Where did you learn your magic?"

Her eyes narrowed, but her legs stopped shifting. "Master found me a teacher." She said it as if it were the most obvious thing in the world. And honestly, it was. I huffed a short laugh at my shitty conversation kills.

"Did your parents not have any interest in teaching themselves? In my experience, witch families are quite close."

Her eyes lowered, dark lashes sweeping low. "They were overwhelmed by me. Especially once things got more intense. In school, I…"

She paused, looking over her shoulder again towards the unmoving captain.

"You can tell me. I mean…" I gestured at the circle once again. "Who am I going to tell? Your master is going to skewer me the first chance he gets."

"Someone pushed me during recess, just normal kid stuff. But instead of just brushing it off…" Her hands picked at the edge of her dress. I wish I could capture that hand, hold it in mine, measure how slight and soft it would feel against my palm. "My magic went wild. I froze half of the playground; the other half of the class was drenched in water."

I could feel my brows rise, "Impressive."

"My school principal didn't think so. He was convinced I'd played some kind of trick on them, sprayed the equipment with chemicals or something. My parents' abilities were always less visual, little things. Easy to manage and hide. But mine…"

I answered for her again. "Were not."

She nodded, her eyes still not meeting mine. "The Drude showed up at our door days later, sweeping me away, getting me the best teachers, providing me with everything."

"Except for your freedom."

Oh, shit. I could see the moment she registered what I had said. Her slender shoulders went tight, and just the edge of her fingertips turned pale. No, not pale. Frosted. Something inside me warmed at her easy show of magic, even while holding me in place.

This witch was powerful. No wonder the Drude wanted her.

No wonder *I* wanted her.

I could nearly feel those cold fingers slipping over my body. I would warm her right up.

"The Drude keeps me safe. And for that, I will gladly hold whatever arrogant demon that he asks me to." She paused to push up to a standing position, leaning towards me. "And it'll be my pleasure."

She turned and marched back towards the captain's quarters. My teeth bit down on to my lips, attempting to disguise my smile as she threw her curls back in the sea breeze.

"Oh no, witchling, I think it will be mine."

3

Faye

My knee was bouncing, the rhythm choppy and uneven as the ship rocked gently back and forth. The sky outside was nearly black now, the sharp edge of nighttime biting into my skin as I stared out towards the shore.

Or at least, the direction I thought it was. "When were they going to be back?"

The captain, who was obviously in deep with the Drude's magic, turned glossy eyes to me. "Stay the projected course. Keep the witch alive. Keep the demon on board."

Okay, so not helpful.

I tried another angle. Sometimes that worked. "Did they say when they'd be back though?"

The captain turned the wheel slightly, one pale hand moving to flip over some switches against the dashboard. "Stay the projected course. Keep the witch alive. Keep the demon on board."

I groaned; I knew that I should go down below to the tiny room that I'd been sleeping in before we'd picked up the demon. But I couldn't rest, not yet. I was stuck here, my magic tied so tightly to the demon outside that I felt like I could actually sense his every thought and breath. It was utterly distracting. I was torn at wishing it would stop all together and hoping that whatever he was doing would grow stronger. Because honestly, I could use some distraction, Especially now that soft rolling thunder I'd heard a few minutes ago was coming our way before Paul arrived to take me back home.

Well, to wherever the Drude currently called home, I supposed. I was sure he'd been setting up a new headquarters somewhere, and I wasn't allowed to see if until after we secured one of the sons. That was the price he had given me for safety, and I was more than willing to pay it. Especially after seeing the ferocity that Justine's mate, the demon Nephesh, had fought with.

We needed leverage, and I had gotten it for him. I would be rewarded.

The ship lulled again, reminding me that we were indeed sitting in the middle of the water, surrounded on all sides by something that had always terrified me. Ironic, even my father had said so, since my magic's natural form was ice. Ice, water… You would've thought that somehow, I would've been drawn into it or something. But no. Terrified.

And now I was here.

Closing my eyes, I pushed out of the wheelhouse and back onto the deck, nearly forgetting the demon prince, who was sitting, legs crossed, in the circle I'd spelled him into.

"Are you alright?" he asked, that silky voice slipping over my mind like a caress. Something in my chest hummed as I stumbled to a stop before him.

"You're asking me if I'm alright?" I tried to scoff at him, but I wasn't sure I'd succeeded. "You're the prisoner, not me."

Kharon leaned back a little, rocking on his butt before leaning forward to put his elbows on his knees. "Do you want to talk about it? I'm a good listener." The smile he sent me was blindingly bright.

I sputtered out a laugh before I could stop it. "You're a monster. Don't talk to me."

He shrugged, completely unbothered by my comment. "I won't talk, then. Like I said, I can listen."

"I don't understand. Why are you being so nice to me?"

"Because, Faye, you may hate me on principle, and I accept that, but you and I are both creatures of circumstance. You serve a dark power. I serve a dark power. We are not so different."

I stared at him, at the enormous size of him, at the pale-blue skin and flash of white fangs I could see even now. "We are nothing alike."

Kharon nodded slowly. "If that is what you need to tell yourself, I understand. Lie to yourself—to me—all you want, but I know you. Just like I know that since the moment I hauled you up that ladder, you've been drawn to me."

My chest was heaving. Lurching back to a standing position, I backed away a step too quickly and nearly tripped over a coil of spare rope. And still, Kharon spoke, his eyes glowing teal blue. "No matter what they tell you or what they do to me, nothing can change the fact that we are linked."

"No." That nameless tie in my chest grew even tighter.

Kharon's mouth lifted. "Yes, witchling. But like I said, feel free to continue lying to yourself all you need. I have never been anyone's first choice."

I barely heard his words, still backing away. "I don't need to lie, because I know. I know that ties like this are nothing but a fluke of fate. Being tied to my master. Being tied to you. I have never once known what it is like to choose for myself what my future is. Do you know what that feels like?"

Kharon's face softened. "I know exactly how that feels."

"That is why I know our tie means nothing. Because at the end of all of this, you will be just another line in my resume. A bigger, better way to showcase his power."

When had my words lost their conviction? I pressed a hand against my chest as the glow in his eyes intensified, my words stilling in the air between us.

"Don't hurt yourself with those lies," Kharon said. "It's a waste to use on me, and you'll need more of them when your master gets here."

When your master gets here.

Oh God. My heartbeat was pounding in my ears. What had I been thinking? I internally screeched at my own mistakes. I'd admitted it. I'd admitted that I was tied to him. That I was the one he was looking for. Master had warned me that he'd want to use that connection. That it would cloud my perspective. I'd thought it impossible, even after meeting the other demon and his soul bound, Justine. Yet, I'd only been in his presence for a short time, and my secrets were tumbling free.

"Oh no," I whispered to myself, turning and refusing to look back at the demon, I hurled myself down below deck. I needed a moment, or honestly a few hundred moments, to regroup. And far away from those curious, laughing eyes. Because by "not talking to him," I had somehow still exposed something very important about myself. And him.

I couldn't let myself be caught up in him again. He was already showing himself to be incredibly dangerous.

Still dressed, I crawled onto one of the bunks built into the wall and dragged a blanket over my legs. I should sleep, I needed my rest in order to maintain control of the spell holding Kharon in place. I would not fail my master.

I would be his weapon.

I would be their downfall.

Not because I wanted to, but because I had no choice. And now, now he knew that.

I closed my eyes and surrendered myself to my dreams.

***

I knew in an instant that I wasn't alone in my dreams tonight. She was there. This time we were sitting at a school playground, the one that I had once lost control in, turning the brightly colored plastic into a veritable ice skating rink with a single thought. Not today though, not in this moment. Today the sun shone brightly overhead, warming my shoulders and back. In the distance, I could smell the scent of freshly cut soccer fields, and if I squinted into the horizon, I could make out blurred figures in the distance. My parents, supposedly. My subconscious somehow placed them just far enough away that I couldn't see them, but close enough I knew they were there.

Too close, but also too far.

The breeze swept over me. Habitually, I frowned into it, knowing my curls would never agree with this or any weather. Pushing my hair back with a groan, I turned in a small circle. The mulch under my sneakers was silent.

"You look lovely tonight."

Nicola's elegant form slowly took shape, walking down the chalk-covered sidewalk towards me. How odd that she looked exactly how she did that first day that I met her. I had been nothing but a scared child, dressed in too-big clothes I'd grabbed off a shelf in my master's newly built barracks. The shame and self-consciousness I had felt in that first introduction. She'd been wearing a soft, gossamer gown, the hemline sweeping across the floorboards. Ruby red lips had curled into a smile as I shook her hand in mine. And tentatively, I had smiled back.

Years later, she confessed that I was the reason she was able to stay as long as she did. But it was never meant to last.

She had been there to teach me.

And then Master would send her elsewhere. We had both known it, as surely as we knew that the instant bond between us was born of more than a shared magic. It was a desperate bond between two people torn from their families. Her feet slowed, dress swishing around her ankles as she stopped, so completely at odds with the colorful modern surroundings.

A part of me wanted to reach out, to see if she felt as real as the rest of this did. Her laughter was musical, golden skin glowing. She looked so healthy, so real. "You look exactly the same to me too, little witch."

I blinked, not realizing I had spoken out loud. My cheeks felt warm. "Is this… Are you a memory, then?"

"No, not a memory." She cocked her head, brilliant white gold hair shimmering in the sunlight. "A moment I had stored away in the recesses of that beautiful, wild mind of yours. Tucked away before I was moved. I wanted you to be ready, Faye. I wanted to be the one to make sure you were ready for what all of this would mean. But the fates do not always play kindly, and I'm afraid this is all I can offer you."

I waited, my entire being trembling as her power washed over me. Still powerful, even in this dreamscape, but so unlike the Drude's. Hers was soft, enchanting, sinking into your skin as you absorbed her presence.

Nicola reached out her hand, long cool fingers coiling around my wrist. Her thumb brushed over the veins there, making the power in them pulse. "Sweet girl. Your future is so deeply entangled with my son's. Any way I've looked at it, there is only one answer for it. You two need each other."

She thought we need each other. The demon and me? My mind was slower here, the words on my tongue sticky and unmoving.

Nicola sighed, leaning away, swaying slightly as she began to walk through the playground, her fingers trailing up the edge of a set of monkey bars. I hurried to keep pace with her. Even though we were similar in size, she had always moved with such purpose. I grabbed for her arm but missed, leaving me to lurch into thin air. I straightened, huffing at her nonchalant gaze on me. Patient. Waiting.

For me to ask the right question. "Your son, the one you're talking about—you mean Kharon?"

She turned to the side, showing her profile. I nearly stumbled. Instead of the beautiful face I was used to, there were large open wounds upon it, slicing into her pale skin.

I gasped, "Oh, Teacher…"

She only nodded, the wounds on her face flickering as if this part of my dream was glitching, the power source struggling to maintain her appearance. "It took nearly all I had left to make this. And Gods know, I never wanted you to see me like this, but there is so much you still need to know. The spell I cast on my children, on my boys, was meant to protect them. I would've never guessed that someone would come along, use my magic, my protection against my family. But now, the

69

ramifications are shaking the foundation of my world. Of your world, Faye. You cannot let that happen."

She looked out over the dreamscape playground, down to my feet. My gaze followed hers, my heart pounding as I watched the frost grow and spread, ice growing from where my soles touched the earth. It spread and spread as we watched, slipping over equipment as it slowly encompassed the playground. Nicola didn't move, didn't even flinch as the ice made a ring around her, as if unable to get any closer to her warmth. "Balance must be maintained. As above, so below."

She shook her head, hiding those ghastly wounds behind the curtain of her hair. "And now, everything is hinged on the one thing I cannot control."

"What?" It was so cold now. I was so cold, my magic a living, breathing monster in my center, making my fingers shake as I looked desperately at the woman, I trusted more than any other.

"Your heart."

The scene around us vibrated, and for a moment I felt the earth under my feet shift. My arms flew wide, balancing myself against the slick ice. Nicola moved too, her face swinging back to face me, to push her hands to my shoulders and drag me closer. "Don't let him have it, Faye. You can't."

It was harder to focus on her now. Her face was blurring. "Who? Kharon?"

Tears slipped down her face, and Nicola suddenly reared back, heat burning over my body as the place where her hands held me went white hot. I screamed, desperate to both hold her and push her from me at the same time. In the end, it was she who moved, her head falling back, her eyes filled with a glowing white light so brilliant I was forced to close my eyes. Tripping, I went to my knees, wrapping my arms around my middle, trying to breathe despite the still-horrific pain that coursed through my veins from where she had touched me.

"Nicola!"

I lurched to a sitting position, Nicola's name still on my lips as I looked around the small crew quarters, at the ice that covered every hard surface. Something was wrong. There was more rocking on board the ship. Things were slipping to the edge of the desk now, the pen I'd toyed with earlier falling to the floor and beginning to roll back and forth against the floorboards.

There was a quiet groan, the sound of mechanics and metal straining, followed quickly by another large roll of the ship.

I gulped, panic gripping my chest as I nearly fell into the wall by the door. Deep inside my chest, that humming bond, centered around the core of my magic, flared back to life. But this time louder. More insistent.

"Kharon..." I whispered into the wildness of the moment as the ship creaked again, this time rocking hard enough that I had to slap a hand against the wall to risk slamming back into it.

I threw myself over the edge of the bunk, my feet slapping the cold floor as I dashed out onto the main deck. Violent rain lashed at my face, making it nearly impossible to see. I raised an arm, trying to see the demon I'd left out here just hours ago. If he was gone, everything I'd worked so hard for…

Fear drove me higher, making my feet race across the deck to where I knew he waited. The lights of the deck were useless against the sheets of rain, and I stumbled more than once, relying on memory and the tugging of my magic to find my way to him.

"Kharon?" I shouted over the din of the storm.

"Faye," came the booming response.

I turned my face towards the sound of his voice, the rainwater leaking into my eyes as I frantically pushed my hair out of my way. A thick lightning bolt speared its way across the sky, illuminating everything on board, if even just for a moment.

Kharon stood, tall and strong, his head tilted towards me as he held his hands up against the walls of my enclosure. He looked impossibly unbothered by the rocking of the boat, even as I scrambled over the deck, now strewn with loose netting, to get close to him.

I stood in front of him, fear making my blood pound as our eyes met and held.

"You have to let me go," Kharon said, with no trace of the humor from last night. No hint of sarcasm. Just a deep, commanding request.

My heart raced; my body shook under the rain. "What? No, I can't let you go." The Drude would never forgive me if I let a Prince of Hell slip through my fingers like that. Never.

Kharon's hands curled into fists against the magical enclosure, and it glowed bright in response. "Faye, listen to me. This storm isn't natural. It's isolated to us. You have to let me free; I can help."

"No." I shook my head, my curls waterlogged and slapping against my neck as even more rain poured over us. Kharon's eyes began to glow.

"Faye. You free me, or you die out here."

My throat worked, my mind racing. You, he'd said. Not me. Because of course a little water wouldn't hurt the Ferryman. As for me, I would be a lost cause.

Kharon leaned down. "I won't hurt you. I know you don't believe me, but you can trust me." He stepped as close as the spell would let him, the magic flaring like sparks where he touched it. "If you believed anything about what the Drude told you, you know that I could never hurt you. You carry my soul. My entire being is focused only on protecting you."

I whined in my throat, more confused than I'd ever been in my life. I looked around us, at the dark swirling rain, at the blinking lights above. The boat below us rocked violently, pitching me back and then forward again.

"What about the captain?"

Kharon shook his head, "This isn't about him. It's about us. And as soon as we're gone, I'm sure the water will settle."

My chest actually hurt from the break in my heart, the realization of what I needed to do.

"I... I... Oh God, I can't. I can't. You don't understand."

But before I could explain, there was another massive creak, and it felt like the entire ship shook under my feet. Gasping, I took several stumbling steps backwards then to the side. I couldn't find my balance, and the edge of the deck loomed close as the ship began its violent rocking once more. I leaned forward, my magic blooming in a fearful panic. I was going to fall overboard.

I was going to die here, unable to save myself. Unable to save anyone who mattered to me.

I was useless.

Helpless.

"Kharon," I whispered, just before a roar split the air between us.

I looked up in time to see Kharon's glowing eyes widen, and then, with all the grace and ease of the predator he was, he stepped through the magical enclosure I'd made for him and out into the pouring rain. The glow in his eyes spread to illuminate and outline his entire massive form. In two steps, he reached me, his arms going around my middle as the ship bucked under us.

We slammed back into the railing, his body a cushion against the impact, but only for a moment.

"Trust me," he whispered, just before he slipped a hand up my body to wrap around my throat, tilting my head back to his.

And then he pushed us over the railing and back into the sea.

4

Kharon

The water crashed over us, and the current coupled with my momentum from earlier took us deeper. Letting my magic flare at my fingertips, I shared my magic with Faye, letting her breathe in just as easily as I did. My gills fluttered to life, my fingers against her skin spreading wide, the webbing cupping her throat, cradling it as the oxygen she needed so badly made its way into her lungs. While I did not have wings like my brothers, what I did have was a very unique body that made me expertly equipped for the water.

And right now, I had never been more grateful to be the way I was. Or for the ability to share it with those I was in direct contact with.

Faye shook against me, her body so small, delicate compared to mine that I barely noticed the soft weight of her against me in the water.

"It's alright. You're alright," I spoke into her mind, my magic translating the low-toned message. My brows lowered as I realized just how hard I was working to not scare this female. It

was instinct, not habit, that drove me to gentle my grip on her body as the darkness of the water surrounded us.

She shook her head, disbelief in every stiff line of her body as I rolled us backwards, my bare feet propelling us deeper into the water. For a breath, I was tempted to magic her to sleep, saving her the fear of the moment, but I wasn't sure how much magic it would take. Frustration burned in my chest. I couldn't risk her safety, not while we were still so far from the Styx and the safety within it. Gritting my teeth, I snarled into the ocean's depths.

I had existed purely on fury alone before, and I would do it again. Anything to make it back to the Underworld. My father and I needed to chat. Soon.

His little trick with the storm had not been helpful in the least. What if I really hadn't been able to get to her and she had drowned? What then? My ire at my father rose in my belly, making my grip on Faye tighten. Her hands rose, fastening onto my wrist and holding there, even as my feet kept us nearly level in the water. I would only need a moment to create the portal that would pull us into the Styx.

"Stay still. I need to open a portal." I spoke directly into her mind once more, an easy feat with her pressed against me.

"A portal? Is he serious? It's so dark. Oh my god, does he have fins? Oh my gosh, he does. That's so cool. Wait—no." Her mind was a jumble of fear and questions, and it made her communication back to me difficult. I pushed more of that smooth, relaxing

healing magic down the connection between her fingers and my flesh until her mind slowly quieted.

"Stay still, please. This will be over before you know it." Raising my now free hand over my body, I let my magic slither down the veins of my arms, making the lines there glow even in the dark water. I could feel Faye's wide-eyed stare as I closed my eyes a moment and called the entryway to me.

The Styx had set points of entry scattered the world over. They were designed to corral and bring the souls of the dead to the Underworld in a more organized fashion than my father's catch-all-dead spells that he had cast for the initial foundation of Hell. Lucifer had whined, my mother said, about how wild and unorganized the souls were, flitting about the Underworld while they had rushed to contain them.

And then one day, thousands of sunsets ago, she had woken up with an idea.

Water. Not just any body of water, but a river.

The source of life in the living world would be the bearer of souls into the Underworld. Water, which had always been a source of magical inspiration, would be the vein in the Underworld's heart, carrying the souls that powered it to their rightful place. And when I was born with powers that thrived in the aquatic environment, my mother and father knew they had been right.

I was born to be its master. And now, as Faye and I drew into the ocean's depths, I called for it. To the portal that would take us to my home.

Magic gathered around us, swirling and pushing and driving until it tugged us along, dragging us into what seemed to be deeper into the sea. But I could feel the change, the way the light shifted and brightened. The brine in the water disappeared just as the pressure in my chest from being in the living world lessened.

We were no longer in any living ocean but coasting through the aquatic tunnels of the Styx. The ancient power was all around us, making my own magic hum with welcome. Any moment, we would drop into the main part of the river.

I curled around Faye, pushing my legs down as the familiar twists and turns greeted us both. I didn't have time to warn her before we were pushed through and out, my feet catching on the smooth sandy bottom of the river with cool, calm efficiency.

She was nothing but a wet, gasping weight on my chest as I stood with her in my arms. The current tugged at me, an overeager puppy, as I trudged towards the edge of the riverbank. Here the riverbanks were covered with heavy stones worn smooth by the Styx as it sliced through the Underworld. Just beyond, a thick rise of shadowy trees covered the landscape. If I paid attention, this was where I could see Arafel's castle in the foreground of the Sleeping Mountains. But I was distracted by the stinging pain in my arm.

"Burning hell," I hissed at the woman in my arms. Faye's blunt nails scored my arms as I waded through the shallows, resisting the urge to toss her from me.

"Put me down!" Her whispered command was said in a way that made me think she might have asked before while I was deep in my thoughts.

I followed her directions immediately, making sure her bare feet were steady in the shallow water before I moved past her out of the river.

"Are you alright?" I asked, watching her shove her curls back and stumble after me onto dry land. She appeared uninjured from our less-than-smooth entry into the Underworld. But I could almost taste the shock and confusion that coursed through her veins. I braced myself for her to run, or at least start screaming, but instead, she climbed onto a rock and did a very slow circle.

"Where are we?"

"You're in my home." I gestured around us. "Or at least close to it."

She blinked at me, her hands smoothing down her wet nightgown again. It was sticking to her, highlighting her slim body and the shivers that had begun to rack her body. My magic curled in my belly, desperate to reach out to her and provide some comfort. I curled my hands into fists, forcing myself to stay put where I was.

Her beautiful face angled up towards my father's false sky. A droplet of water ran down her throat and rested on her collarbone before disappearing lower. The sudden, compulsive need to follow that watery trail with my fingers and then my tongue washed over me. Fuck, I bet she would taste perfect. I shook my head, trying to pull my thoughts back to the situation at hand.

"I'm in the Underworld?"

I nodded, watching her chest rise and fall as she again slowly spun in place.

Suddenly she straightened, pointing her finger my way. "No, no, no. I can't be. Take me back!"

I couldn't help it. I chuckled.

Instantly her pretty face darkened, transformed into one of pure fury. Or as close as she could get. I lived among the darkest souls in creation. Her fury was more of a gnat's buzz than a lion's roar. But all the same, something about her emotional distress propelled me to calm her.

"Take me back, back to the boat. Back to the living world. Back to anywhere but here. You cannot hold me here. I'm a living soul." She marched up to me as she spoke, pressing a finger into my chest and jabbing it with each word.

I cocked my head at her, a bit of my humor returning at her obvious recovery from the shock of our arrival. "I'm glad you're feeling better."

"Better?" She sputtered; her finger paused mid-jab. "I can't be here, unlike whatever other women you bring here. I know the rules. I know I can't be here. You're taking us back, right now."

My temper flared, and I moved to cross my arms, knocking her hand aside. "No, no I'm not And to be clear, there are never any other woman I take here." I hesitated, groaning. "Well, okay, I take women through the Styx, but they are dead ones and not nearly as frustrating as you are."

Faye stared at me, seemingly dumbfounded. Her mouth opened and closed as her eyes dashed back and forth, that lovely brain of hers working overtime. "Well…I'm— You know what, you are still my prisoner."

I smiled at her, letting the move be as slow and casual as possible. I watched her eyes widen, staring at my mouth, at where I knew my fangs flashed. Her scent changed, ever so slightly. My brows lowered, my nostrils huffing in the Underworld air in a vain attempt to catch more of the change.

She had always smelled sweet, but this… My smile only grew. This was utterly delicious, and it was all her.

"Why are you smiling?" Faye asked, brows low. She mimicked my cross-armed pose, but instead of appearing intimidating, it just made her all the more adorable. My muscles bunched, desperate to reach for her.

"Because you seem to be very confused, little witch." I drew myself up to my full height, looming over her on purpose. I needed her to see this side of me too, to understand what confronting a demon would be like. I wanted her to fight me, to fight back, to uncover that well of power that I could sense deep inside her. But even I had limits. Or rather, instincts, and they couldn't be ignored either.

Her breathing picked up, her pulse fluttering at the side of her neck. My teeth bit into my tongue, the desire to taste her there hitting me with the force of a hurricane. Shaking my head, I tried to refocus my attention on our current situation.

"To be clear, I was never your prisoner. Never. I stood inside that spell to humor you, Faye. To keep myself close to what I wanted most. And I did it to protect you. Do you think I'm a fool who would let my soul ma–bound be left alone, somewhere she is terrified, by creatures who serve him? Never." I wetted my lips, watching her gaze track the movement. "I wanted the chance to talk to you. And knowing I was spelled into compliance allowed you to converse with me in a way you wouldn't have otherwise."

"Wait, what you wanted most? Does that mean me?"

I stayed quiet.

"You're lying. I practiced for days—no, weeks," she whispered, her pupils large and dark.

A short, humorless laugh slipped from my mouth. "You are powerful, that's for sure, but I'm a demon, a Prince of Hell. You'll have to work a lot harder to keep me anywhere that I don't already wish to be."

She shook her head, backing away. "No." Reality was a hard pill to swallow, and I could see my little witch struggling with the weight of this announcement. The awareness that what she'd been taught did not begin to compare to what hundreds of years of teaching had done for me.

"Yes," I said, following her, continuing to crowd her. I loved the little huff she gave when I got close. "So allow me to remind you of your newly upgraded status in our relationship. You are now my prisoner, and together we are going to my home so that we can begin the process of removing my soul from your person."

Faye sputtered, words failing her.

"When I have my power restored—and I *will* have my power restored—I will have no reason for you to stay here. I'll take you anywhere you like. Fates, you will be freed to go back to being the Drude's plaything for all I care, although I wouldn't recommend it."

Was that hurt in her gaze? I couldn't tell. My temper was unfolding, wrapping around me like iron-bound arms.

"I can see what you're thinking. Do not run from me." I rolled my shoulders, cracking my neck. "I may look part human, but that part of me is buried far under a predator's instincts, and you, Faye Sullivan, are exactly what my kind hunts. Don't give me a reason to chase you down. The results, while thrilling, may not be what you're looking for."

My words emptied, my lungs felt tight and angry as I stared down at my soul bound.

Faye was panting, her body still shaking as she met my gaze. Slowly, she nodded. "I understand."

The movement sent a spike of joy through me for a moment. This was the beginning, this moment in time when the tide would finally begin to shift in this useless war with the Drude. With this witch's help, I would have the chance to get my soul back. I would be whole. I could protect my home again.

In the next breath, though, everything in me deflated. Her nodding movement had upset a heavy line of tears. They slipped down Faye's face, just until her cheekbones, where nervous hands pushed them away, into the still-wet hair at her temples.

Something hit me low in the gut. More savage than a blade. Guilt.

Shame.

I might have scared her earlier, but just now, fuck, I'd been the monster my father wished I really was. My temper, it was a hungry, ugly thing, and there wasn't a day that passed where I hated how much control it lorded over me.

"Fuck. Faye…hold on."

"Which way?" She lifted her shoulders, looking bravely up at me, even as I could see the damp trail of the tears still drying on her face. My palms itched with the need to wipe them away. To wipe this whole interaction away.

Fucking heaven, this had gone all wrong. Cursing silently, I looked back at our surroundings. This wasn't the ideal drop-in to the Underworld, but I had been more than a little thrown off my game lately. I glanced at Faye, who was still wiping at her tears. In more than one way, it appeared. We had a journey ahead of us, and I wasn't about to call one of my brothers or their creatures to carry us. We would have to walk.

"The fastest way is directly down the river." I gestured behind us. "However, there is a waterfall ahead. We'll need to climb down on our own."

Faye stepped back, sweeping an arm forward, her face pale. "Lead the way, my lord."

I grimaced at the title; it felt all wrong on her lips. "Don't call me that."

She blinked, still deliberately not looking at me. "Isn't that what you're called? You and your brothers? Lords of the Underworld?"

"It's a stupid title," I huffed under my breath before speaking louder. "I prefer Kharon, or handsome, or most powe—"

"And I prefer the living world," she said boldly. Her words may have come across forcefully, but I saw the cost they took on her, the way that she curled around herself, unsure of what I might do or say to that response.

"I know you do." I tried to soften my words and voice at once. The Underworld was lightening around us as my father's attempt at dawn crested over the Sleeping Mountains. "I'll lead the way. There are steps built into the cliff face over here. And my ferry waits at the bottom of the falls."

I moved first, giving Faye my back in a thin showing of trust, as I led the way to an overgrown pathway just to the side of the river. I pushed back the foliage and carefully waited for Faye to join me.

She wasn't far behind, her delicate, lovely features pinched and pale still as we began to follow the curling steps that zigzagged back and forth across the side of the mountain. The path was steep but familiar, and my feet, webs already vanished from lack of need, easily moved downwards. I only made it a few steps before a soft noise stopped me.

I turned back quickly, seeing Faye standing on the stair above me, one leg suspended as she leaned over it, brushing bits of rock and stick from the sole. Fuck, she was barefoot, and I was leading her down a mountain.

Turning, I reached for her ankle before I thought twice. "Can I help?"

Faye lurched back away from me.

I instantly raised my hands. "Sorry, I didn't mean to scare you, I was just going to check your feet." My magic rolled down my arms and into my palms, the droplets brighter than they had been in years. "I can heal them. If you let me."

Her eyes were wild as she took in the swirls of magic, but she leaned on a sapling nearby and let me pick up her foot a little. Not so far as to see what was under her still-wet nightgown, but enough that the soft pads of her foot fit perfectly into my palms. There were scratches and bruises over nearly the entire foot. She had been barefoot since she ran onto the deck in the storm. It was obvious that since the adrenaline was settling into her system, they would now begin to feel as painful as they looked.

I clucked at my own stupidity. "May I?" I held out my other hand, my magic appearing in my palm before running over my fingers and hand like a fountain of water. I held it away from her as she watched the magic drip off me and fall to the ground of the Underworld, where it disappeared instantly, leaving only dry ground.

"Your magic, it's so…" She stopped, biting into her lip, and then carefully nodded. "Go ahead."

I held my hand against the bottom of her foot, watching as, instead of dripping, the water infiltrated her skin, spreading over the injured areas before sinking in and disappearing. Faye gasped; her slender calves tensed just inches from my touch, but she didn't pull away. When I looked up, I was hit with a wave of appreciation for her.

She really was beautiful. Of course, she was. I knew that the moment I met her, but now, as I stared at her, I could see that flicker of intelligence, the stubborn set of her chin, the slight upturn of her slender nose. She seemed fragile now, for the first time since I first caught a glimpse of her. For a moment, I felt my magic stutter, fearful of injuring her somehow.

Gritting my teeth, I called my magic back, letting it sink into her flesh. In an instant, my worries dissolved. My magic moved through her, healing the hurts, and I was unable to look away from her as it did. She met my eyes, chin quivering just the tiniest bit as the last of rocks and dirt fell from her skin.

I didn't need to worry. Faye was like iron inside, the strength of her mind as clear to me as the dark-pink curve of her lips. "Better?" I asked, letting the magic heal the injuries, sweeping away the pain.

Her eyes widened then dropped, realizing how close she had gotten, the way her body had instinctively curled into my hold. "Better," she echoed, still avoiding my gaze.

When I released her ankle, she shifted, taking a small step away from me. But there was a change in the air between us. Not forgiveness, that much was clear, but a step in the right direction. My tongue burned with the need to apologize for my earlier temper, but I swallowed it. She was the Drude's witch, and while every part of her was as alluring and tempting as I had pictured, I still knew little about her intentions. For now, distance would keep us safe from each other.

Straightening, I gave her a half-smile. "I can do a lot of things, but sadly, I don't magic shoes out of thin air."

To my surprise, her eyes lifted to mine, the tiniest hint of a curl to her mouth distracting me. Confidence roared through me.

"But what I can do is offer you my back." I jerked a thumb at the body part in question.

Faye's eyes followed my movement. "What?"

"I will carry you; it will take us half the time, and you will end up at the base with no injuries to your poor little toes."

We both looked at her feet in unison. I could practically taste her indecision, but when I saw her fingers tugging at the edge of her nightgown, her concern became clear.

I tugged my shirt over my head, handing it to her.

Faye started, her mouth hanging wide open. "What are you doing?"

"Your nightgown is short. You can wrap this around your waist. It will hang down like a skirt and hide anything you're worried about until we get to my home."

Her brows rose.

I rushed to explain. "No, I cannot read minds. I just saw…" I glanced towards her nervous hands, which immediately went still.

Silence fell between us, the tension slowly rising.

"If I say yes, will you…will I trigger any of your…instincts?"

I cursed aloud, rubbing my face with my hand, wishing I could take my temper tantrum back. "No, Faye. I just want to get you safely down the mountain."

She moved an inch my direction, but it felt like a mile. "And am I still your prisoner?"

Sighing, I shook my head. "That's not the right word. I shouldn't have used it like that. You are my guest. But remember, you have to stay with me, for your own protection."

"So only a little bit of a prisoner, then," she hedged, moving closer and then edging around until she was on her tiptoes at my back.

I gritted my teeth at the feel of her curious fingers at my shoulder. Electricity burned through my body at her touch. Turning my head, I looked over my shoulder at her. "You are mine." Her eyes widened, and I rushed to continue. "My soul bound. I will not let anything happen to you."

Faye nodded and then, with a rush of breath, pushed down on my shoulders. I yielded in an instant, feeling the surge of her body against mine as she climbed onto my back. As I stood, her legs wrapped as far as they could around my waist.

Faye squeaked when I reached my full height again. I halted, my breathing coming rapidly as I felt her weight against me. Everywhere we touched, my being went wild. My magic was a hurricane at my chest, a thick cloud of lust wrapping around my mind.

This was a horrible, horrible idea.

"G-Good?" Her voice caught.

"Very," I forced out, turning back to the stairs and focusing very hard on not tripping and falling. If I were to fall now, there was a very good chance I would injure her, and that would simply not be acceptable. I couldn't take my earlier words back, but I could give her new ones. More chances to trust me.

I cleared my throat, turning to catch her eye. "How about we play a game?"

"Are you serious?" she whispered, but somehow, I knew she wasn't talking to me, maybe because a moment later, she asked me, louder, "Do we have to?"

"We don't. I do. It'll keep me focused." On something other than the rising need to run my hands up her slender legs.

Faye gave a breathy sigh, which I felt against the back of my head. "Where are you in the birth order?"

"Hmm. I'm the middle."

"I wouldn't have guessed," she said softly.

I ignored her, forgetting my earlier ambition and allowing my hands to caress her legs briefly before locking on her ankles and holding her tightly as we descended the first stair. She rocked against me, and I knew she heard my sharp intake of breath. I coughed once then pressed onwards.

"What's my favorite movie? Let me tell you all about it. My favorite is probably *The Lion King*, followed up by *Rear Window*, which admittedly don't have a lot in common, other than a plethora of trauma for our male main character, but they're both entertaining, exciting and gave me, in the human sense, 'butterflies.'"

She huffed against my naked shoulder. I wasn't sure whether it was a laugh or a curse, but either way, I knew she was listening. That only fueled me.

"What's my favorite meal? That's complicated since I don't technically require food to live, but somewhere over the years, my brothers and I discovered the joy of food, mostly since the eighteenth century, I mean, no one was really eating that shit that the English were first making, but when the French first figured out a truffle, everything took a major turn for the better. And at my core, I'm just an all-American wannabe, so I'd say burger."

"You must be insane," she said, but I could hear the lightness in her words, feel it in her grip on me.

"Not quite, Faye. I'm just very, very old, and while you have been surrounded by people, albeit horrible ones, I have been largely alone. So, I've found ways to entertain myself. Otherwise, I might've gone crazy in a less fun way."

"Less fun?"

I angled us around a tree growing in our path, making sure to duck far enough the branches wouldn't brush over her. "Yes. You've met Nephesh. He's a prime example of what happens to our social skills when we're left alone too long."

I thought she might laugh, but she was silent for a breath. "I hurt him," Faye said then, her voice soft. "I'm afraid I hurt him badly."

"We are quite difficult to kill, I'm sure he's fine." I continued down the path, rocks loosened by my feet tumbling down ahead of us. "I guess I'm not sure that's what you wanted to hear, but that's the truth of it. We're part witch, part whatever my father is now, and part cockroach."

"But the Drude, he said he can kill you."

I stepped down a particularly steep step with a grunt. "I imagine that he has found a way to drain us, which is different than killing us. In our eyes, worse. No magic, no soul, no life, save the stupid immortal heart that would beat for eternity in our chest."

I could feel her push back, separating her body from mine for a moment. "I don't know what he was planning, so I can't tell you anything."

I shrugged, moving her slightly with the movement, encouraging her to go back to how she was before. I missed her warmth. "I wasn't going to torture it out of you, Faye. What I need from you isn't information. It's more delicate than that."

I could feel her as she nodded against me. "You want your soul back," she answered.

"Yes."

"Will it hurt?"

I gripped her ankles hard. "No, witchling, I would never hurt you."

We moved on, my chatter coming easy and light between us. I wasn't sure if it was the recent turn of events or her presence, but I felt like the words just kept spilling out of me, filling the Underworld air as the sky above us lightened to a bright daylight. At one point, I paused, honestly curious. "Am I bothering you?"

Her chin bumped against my shoulder blade as she shook her head. "Everyone at home is terrified of me—or of what will happen if they talk to me. So, they just don't. Having you…fill the space is rather soothing."

I felt her duck her face then, pressing a cheek against my back. She'd been embarrassed by her answer, which somewhere deep inside made me realize that she'd been honest.

My shriveled heart glowed with the truth of it. She was scared, she still wanted to give me to the Drude, but she also liked my chatter. At least a little. It could be the soul bond between us helping to forge this connection, but I wouldn't look a gift horse in the mouth. Especially as we ventured farther into my realm.

By the time we reached the bottom of the stairs, Faye was a limp weight on my back. One of my hands held hers below my throat. The other looped back to support her thigh. She had been nodding off, falling asleep as we moved, and I couldn't help but feel the soft wave of pleasure as I reached flat ground and reached back, shuffling her to the front of me so I could safely deposit her onto the flat-bottomed ferry.

Faye roused as I set her down against the benched seating. "Is this…" She gulped, the sound loud against the muted sounds of water around us. "Is this the Ferryman's boat?"

I sighed. "I actually have several. The Styx is a large river, and I have to crisscross it at several points, so it makes more sense to have multiple ferries set up."

She looked to me, blinking, more awake now.

"And if you're thinking of asking, no, Cerberus does not guard the river anywhere, unless he's specifically asked to do so. Usually, he's at the courthouse begging for snacks from the Brotherhood."

She merely nodded, looking a little shocked as she turned to the water.

"The river… We've already been in it, so this feels like a stupid question, but does it…hurt us? Like drain our lifespan or something?"

"Not when you're with me. The river is a part of me, and therefore it does what I ask." I paused. "At least, that's what's supposed to happen. With the corrupted souls and the battle across the Underworld, there is less order to our processes as of late."

She didn't speak but moved to the edge of the ferry. I almost warned her but then held my tongue, remembering how she'd reacted when my magic touched her. She was iron, forged in fire and bathed in ice. There was a reason my soul had chosen hers to bond with. And I had a feeling it only started with the immense well of power that had been waiting just below the surface.

Carefully, she eased to the edge of the water.

I forced my hands to stay at my side. "It's only a few feet deep here, but the current is strong, especially if you're not a good swimmer."

Faye didn't look at me, didn't even acknowledge that she'd heard me, but I knew she had. Her breathing picked up, her shoulders moving as she leaned farther, her face mere inches from the water.

I knew exactly what she was seeing. The same sight that greeted me every day. Faces. Souls. Those who looked to me for protection and safety and healing.

The same souls that she and her master threatened with every move of their sham of an army. I wanted her to see them as they were supposed to be. For the first time, I wanted her to understand the real story of what the Underworld was for these souls. They were not currency. They were echoes, ripples of a human life that deserved a place to rest. And my family, we wanted to give them that.

Her fingertips reached out, hovering in the air, before gently lowering, barely brushing the top of a small ripple of water.

A soul's hand, transparent and pearlesque in the light, reached towards her, mimicking her pose with just a single index finger pointed out. It brushed against hers. With a gasp,

Faye tensed, but to my surprise, she didn't jerk away. She stayed there, her finger brushing against the soul's until they sank back into the Styx.

"Beautiful," Faye whispered, her voice shook slightly. The souls, drawn by me, were moving closer to me, ignoring the living soul at that end of the ferry. She sat back, turning to watch as I paused, reaching down into the water at the back of the ferry. Immediately, hands, whole forearms, reached for me, brushing over my skin, my hands, any part of me they could reach.

My gifts may not appear important to my father, the King of Hell, or to my brothers, who harvested and collected the souls, but to these lost beings, I was the only thing that made sense. My touch was a calming balm that, without their physical forms, they searched for endlessly.

The only healing some would ever receive.

"You heal them," Faye said suddenly.

I looked over to see her standing right by me, her eyes wide open as she looked at the clustering forms. "But how…what are you healing?"

Breathing out, I released my magic in increments, reaching into the waiting souls. "Healing isn't just closing a wound, witching. It's an understanding between body and mind. And while these souls no longer have a body, they linger, trapped in pain, trapped in grief, trapped in loss."

I'd looked out across the river as I spoke, but the silence that followed was too heavy, and I broke, finally looking to her.

Faye's eyes were wide, staring at me, her entire form quivering as she took me in. Our gazes met and held, a moment, two. I couldn't read what I saw there and became afraid of what she might see in me.

I stood quickly, and Faye retreated a step, asking, "How do you do it?"

I couldn't answer that, couldn't share that part of me with anyone. And so, I ignored her, moving back to the chains. "We'll be landside in a moment. Let's find you somewhere to rest."

She didn't move, but I could feel her fear skyrocket. "And then?"

"And then, little witch, you get to meet the family."

5

I stood on a very different dock than I had just days ago in Florida. This one was immense, stretching alongside the smooth curve of the River Styx, before disappearing as the sleek water angled away. Just beyond, a thick forest rose from the fine pebbled peach, crawling up the nearby hills with dark-green foliage.

And to top it off, a thick silver fog wound its way through the forested surroundings, the cool air making my skin tingle as I stared around us. The Underworld was not what I expected. This world teemed with power, that much was clear, but it was beautiful, thrumming with a gentle pulse of life that seemed to crawl up my legs.

I closed my eyes, a weight sliding from my shoulders simply from being in this place. My power, always reminiscent of a sleeping tiger, stretched in my chest, sending curls of heat through my body. God, it felt good. And not just good, but controlled.

"Faye?"

My eyes flew open.

"You alright? We should head in and see what kind of disaster is awaiting us," Kharon said. His immense form was warm at my side, a hand gentle against my lower back as he guided me down the slender bridge leading to the two-story home built right up against the docking. Blinking, I stared as the rippling waves passed under the house's main entrance. A house over water. Perfect for the River Lord.

His home.

The door was sealed with a simple doorknob, but I could feel the haze of magic and spells that slipped over us the closer we got to the entrance. Not just any magic. His magic. And the message was clear. This was his home, guarded by his magic, and while he had stepped right through my spell earlier, there was very little chance of an amateur witch like me breaking any of these ancient spells.

By the time we moved through them and into a comfortably furnished living room, I was sweating lightly, my body aching and my mind drained. I needed a break. I needed a breath.

Alone. God, I needed to be alone, to take a moment to try to reorient myself to what I should do next.

Kharon left me by the couch, stepping through the house with casual ease, before disappearing around a corner. Out of habit, I looked over my shoulder at the wide-open door. But once again, I didn't bother to run. Where would I go? To the river where souls waited for him? I had touched only one soul, and I had nearly lost myself to the magic of it. I'd been able to feel that soul's pain, his heart-rattling confusion. The way that he longed to go home and check on his family. That feeling had warred so harshly with the overwhelming love and joy packed into his memories. Of a lifetime of joy and pleasure, loss and pain. All transferred to me in a single brush of fingers.

I could never survive being in a river surrounded with those emotions. I barely understood my own feelings for this situation. No way was I capable of absorbing theirs. And yet Kharon, he'd been able to let them seek him out, touch him. And he'd returned their feelings with a healing of his own. And it had been natural for him. Completely normal to give himself over to these souls who took from him.

So, no, I couldn't run. I would stay here. Nicola said Kharon could be trusted, and while I had no idea how this was going to help my case with the Drude, I was willing to see what happened. Especially if that meant that I could curl up on this sofa for the foreseeable future. I didn't even know how long I'd been awake at this point, but it felt like forever.

I had just started to sit on the couch, when a ghost—or a spirit or something—came coasting through the wall closest to me.

I screamed, leaping up. "Kharon!" I shouted, my hands flying out. My magic, or what pitiful amount seemed to exist here in the Underworld, bloomed in my palms.

At the same moment as my scream, the soul jerked away and pressed a hand to his translucent chest. "Kharon!"

Kharon came bursting back into the living room, sweeping an arm around my waist and shoving me behind him before turning to face the attacker. I cowered, confused and exhausted as his back, freshly covered in a new shirt, expanded and collapsed against my chest.

Instantly though, Kharon relaxed. "Fucking hell. Chris?"

"My lord, you've returned. Thank Hades." His voice was strange to my ears, a little rough and hard to decipher.

Kharon straightened out of his bent-kneed attack pose. I peeked around his side at the ghost—no, not a ghost—the soul, who hovered closer. He was a male, dressed in what clearly used to be some kind of naval uniform. His face was gaunt, eyes dark and hollow as he observed me as well. After a long moment, the man's face brightened, the ghostly pale form solidifying as he shot me a small smile.

"Calm down, sailor. While I appreciate the sentiment, I wasn't even gone that long."

"Haven't been gone long?" The soul shook his head, the effect a little dizzying. "No, my lord, you're wrong. It has been weeks since you left."

Kharon paused, looking over his shoulder at the interior of his home. I followed his stare, noticing the multitude of items that were pushed around, overturned. Against one corner, a desk was covered with strewn-about papers. It looked like someone large had paced around it with little care to the furniture or the accessories.

"This doesn't make any sense. No one else could get past my wards. Only I can…unless…" Kharon's handsome features were full of thought as he stared down at me. For whatever reason, I shrugged, a little confused why he was staring at me. I had no idea where he had been before he appeared to pull me from the ocean the first time yesterday.

"I need to see my father. And Nephesh. Immediately."

The soul sharpened, became clearer as he saluted Kharon. "Should I tell the reapers to fetch them?"

Kharon stepped away, leaving me for Chris's strange transparent eyes to roam over me in another quick perusal.

"Give me a minute to think." Kharon leaned over a desk in the corner, his face tight, eyes trained on the wide window above it, the one that started out over the river.

"Reapers?" I found myself asking softly to myself. But I forgot who I was with until two heads swiveled to meet my gaze.

Chris and Kharon shared a loaded glance that worried me, and as if in mutual agreement, neither spoke.

I rubbed my eyes, climbing back over the sofa and settling myself on the cushions. I could feel Kharon watching, but I didn't care anymore. I was too tired. My mind hurt from trying to take in all this information. Not to mention trying to decipher the complexity that was *him*.

I closed my eyes.

Kharon's voice, low and soft, spoke again, to Chris I assumed. "I have to go to see my father. Please, can you stay here with her?"

"She's tired. I will let her sleep," Chris commented in his rough voice.

I clenched my eyes shut, desperate to shut everything off. "I want to come with you. Don't leave me here," I whispered into the cushion. "Please."

Kharon grunted, and I heard him rummaging in a drawer or something. "You do not want to come where I'm going. You will be safer here."

"But…" My exhausted brain scrambled to find the words to make him understand. "You are my prisoner. You must stay with me." I forced my eyes open to look at the male across the room.

Kharon turned to me with a curl of his lips. They were soft looking and so prone to that smirking smile. Distracting in a way that my sluggish mind couldn't deny. "Your prisoner? Oh, my sweet, sweet, little witch. In case you don't remember, we already addressed this. I was never your prisoner. You have always been mine."

I stuttered, my tongue thick in my mouth. "What? But you…"

"And you will stay here, where you will be safe. Where you will keep my soul safe." His finger pointed to my ankles, and a moment later, a delicate line of pearls appeared around one foot. I immediately moved to touch them but reared back in surprise. They were real pearls, but they were doused in magic. His magic. And just like his home, their purpose was clear. Stay here. Stay where he put me.

Tears welled as he once again resumed searching the drawer as if it was a done deal. "You are going to lock me in here?"

"Lock?" Kharon didn't even look up at my words. "Never. That bracelet will keep you here, for your own protection."

Those words. How many times had I heard them? My every muscle quivered, chills racing down my spine as my fingers brushed over the pearls.

"My lord?" Chris was looking at me, then his master, and back again, clearly unsure.

"Chris will stay with you, Faye. I'll be back as soon as I can. I need to talk to Nephesh, my oldest brother. He's…ugh. He's the angry one."

I nodded, my body still trembling with the effort to hold in the sobs that threatened with every thought.

For your own good. How many times had I heard that?

Kharon moved to the door, passing straight through Chris as he did. The transparent male cringed but didn't say anything as Kharon marched straight to the door, only pausing for a moment to glance back over his shoulder at me. Every part of me screamed to go with him. To stay close to him.

"Please," I said again, hating the desperate way my voice trembled.

Kharon's entire body tensed, and then, without another word, he disappeared into the Underworld.

I wasn't stupid. I carried this soul. He wouldn't hurt me, at least not yet. And while I was frustrated with the situation, Kharon had been nothing but gentle with me since his little shouting session at the top of the river. And even then, it hadn't really been about me.

Watching him walk away felt like a slice straight down the core of me. My magic rose, emotional and vibrant, to pulse under my palms. I didn't know what to say, though, or what to do. He had said it already. I was his prisoner, and I was a danger to others in his family. Of course, he would never take me anywhere near them. I couldn't blame him. I had people to protect too.

But that didn't change how much I hated being left here.

My temporary home and jail cell all rolled into one. I flopped over, my cheek against a cushion. It was comfortable, and the entire couch smelled of Kharon's clean, salt-breeze scent. It shouldn't have appealed to me, but my body didn't care. Every breath calmed my racing heart and mind more.

I tried to focus less on the comforting scents of this place and more on the reality of my situation. I knew that even the most decadent of homes could still be a jail cell when the person holding the keys also held your freedom.

Nothing had changed.

Brushing an errant tear from my cheek, I ignored Chris as he moved into the room and hovered by the chair opposite me. I could tell he was hoping I would talk to him. Or maybe he wanted to say something to me. But after consideration, he opted to remain silent. I was glad. If I opened my mouth right now, I had no idea what might come out. Truth, lie, magic, and mayhem all waited on the back of my tongue.

I swallowed them back, closing my eyes.

I would rest, let my magic rebuild. Learn the ways of this place, just as I had before. And when it came time to prove myself to my master, I would. This time, unlike when Nephesh and Justine escaped the Drude, no one could deny what I brought to the table.

A demon prince.

The Ferryman himself.

He may think me a prisoner, but my lifetime had shown me something else. That the keys to that cell weren't often literal. They were leverage and power that could be shifted, held, hoarded.

And I had the greatest key of them all.

The one thing he wanted.

My lips curled as I began to drift away.

If he wanted his soul, he would have to give me something else.

And I had just a few ideas.

***

Kharon

Time. We were losing time. I wasn't sure when it had started happening, but based on what I had just deduced from the reapers I had called to my aid once I hit the water, it had been weeks since I'd last been seen. As I'd always trained them to do, they had gone to Nephesh for orders. Since my brother had been missing for nearly as long as I had, they inevitably turned to the Court of Hell for orders.

Nephesh had returned recently and had been running amok around the Underworld with my reapers, in his monster form of all things, hunting the souls that were continuing to get loose before and even after they were judged.

I huffed out a short breath. My eldest brother and I had a complicated history, made only wilder by me stepping in to stop his attempt to rescue and return his first soul bound soul to her body after she was killed in an automobile accident.

We had not spoken much since then, save the odd dinner that my father forced us all to join him at his home at the Court of Hell, located centrally in the Underworld.

The last time we'd all been together had been the night that Arafel, the Lord of Dreams, had brought his own soul bound to meet our father. They had wanted to uncover a way to remove Arafel's soul from the human woman, Lucia. None of us had known how, but that wasn't the important takeaway from that meal.

It had been that Arafel was deeply and unapologetically in love with a living human Not just any human—his soul bound. The human who carried the missing half of his soul.

Fated, he'd said, the enormous shape of him nearly gushing at the sight of Lucia. I'd admit, she was a lovely woman, all quick wit and pretty smiles. And I had been envious, but not nearly as much as my two younger brothers, Kadmiel and Elon.

They, of course, would never admit it. Not like I had.

But none of that mattered now. Lucia was here, sharing her soul with Arafel in order to restore his realm within the Underworld. The first of my brothers to return his soul to the Underworld. When my mother and father split our souls to protect us from danger, I didn't believe they had intended to create us mates. It seemed even the Devil and his queen could be victims of a powerful, unreliable magic.

But I couldn't deny it. Faye intrigued me. Even now, a short distance from my house, my heart raced with the need to return to her. To check on her. I worried, perhaps for the first time in hundreds of years, what she thought of me. Had I been too rough in my words? I needed her to stay where she could be safe, so I'd been aggressive. Maybe too aggressive.

But now, I could only hope she stayed where I left her. I didn't want to leave her there, my home turned prison, but she couldn't be trusted to not get into trouble while I was gone. Not while she believed so strongly in the Drude and his plans to take over the Underworld.

I cursed, pulling magic from the Styx with one hand as I realized that going to Court meant that I was going to have to tell my father about that part too.

"Fuck me."

A reaper, still lingering by the shoreline, cocked its head at me. I swallowed, raising the hand not cupping the water to the creature, willing them away. Reapers were mine, a subset of creatures composed of the souls from Tartarus who had graduated from my brother Elon's punishments. Whatever was left after that, I brought into my realm and held them to my own standards. They were rehabilitated but untrustworthy. I worried what they had gotten up to without my control in these past weeks. They were hungry and fed on the magic that leaked out of my family and into the Underworld itself. A parasitic relationship based on a mutual understanding.

The souls must be contained.

Alone now, I turned my hand over, letting the water drip over my palm before dripping down into the Underworld soil. I let my magic take me over, thinking about my suite of rooms that my father always kept us at his home in the Court of Hell.

A moment later, I was there, but not in the room I'd asked for. Instead, I stood in Lucifer's throne room. The sound of chatter and guttural demonic phrases ceased immediately. At one end, my father stood. The picture of masculine power and beauty, Lucifer's snow-white wings, so like Nephesh, swept wide.

I rolled my shoulders, squaring myself up as Lucifer stepped down from his dais. As if sensing danger, most of his soldiers and servants were already slipping away, like water through cracks in the walls.

"Out," Lucifer said, his voice booming through the room, filling every high bit of the vaulted ceiling.

I glanced up, listening to the slight echo. Above me, the ceiling was painted a vibrant battlefield, with the seraphim and demons locked together, a battle raging around them. And at the center, my father and mother, back-to-back, their magic a dark swirl against the crystal-blue sky.

The tearing, we called it. The final battle where the Underworld was created, torn from the living world by magic and sheer willpower. The painting was beautiful, intricate, but could hardly be called accurate. After all, it had been the three fates who had dealt the final blow to the seraphim general and freed the lesser Others—demons and harpies, minotaurs and incubuses—to join us in the Underworld.

By the time I looked back at my father, the real one, not the painted version, the room was empty save the two of us and his tried-and-true right hand and his most trusted valet and assistant, a demon named Hiram. The male scuttled along the walls, barely distracting me.

"Father." I bowed with both respect and irritation.

"You're back," Lucifer breathed out hard.

I looked at him, curious. He sounded almost…relieved. That, however, could not be possible, since my relationship with my dominating, all-powerful father had always been just as complicated as the one I shared with Nephesh. Except this one had real venom behind it.

Shaking myself free of the old memories, I spread my arms wide. "I'm here."

Lucifer moved ever closer, but before he could get close enough to hit me—or worse, embrace me—I stepped back, a hand in front of me.

"And I have bad news."

Lucifer's face darkened. He looked nearly human these days, just like our distant cousins the seraphim. Which made sense, because every soul stolen by the Drude was one less soul that fed the machine of my father's world. He replaced that soul with his own power, but seeing him today, something twisted in my belly.

He was tired.

The pallor of his fair skin was not glowing with that usual smirking pleasure. It was dull. Tired, even more so as my words landed. I could actually see his mouth tighten. "Shall we go to my private office?"

I nodded, and tucking his wings away, Lucifer led me out of the throne room and down a narrow, red-lit stone hallway to his office. The room was covered in books, shelves from floor to ceiling, with an immense fireplace dominating one entire side of the wall.

My mother had always loved this room. I had spent many days with her here, curled up on that sofa as she schooled me, or we simply talked about our plans for the realms. The furniture was the same, the scent of the leather-bound books identical, and yet nothing was the same.

The door shut behind me, and my magic twitched to life. If my father noticed, he ignored it, moving to sit on an overstuffed navy chair closest to the fire. He gestured to one at his side. "Would you like to sit?"

His manners, which should have comforted me, only felt abrasive after so many years of uncomfortable conversations. "No, I'd rather stand."

Lucifer nodded then gestured for me to begin.

"I was called to the living world," I said, jumping straight to the subject. I didn't want to leave Faye longer than I had to. I wanted to get this information out and relayed, and then I could return to her, make sure she was healed and rested and begin the process of rescuing my soul from her person.

"The living world?"

"Yes. I felt a call—I felt *her* call to be more precise." I started to pace, needing to do something with my feet. "My soul bound was drowning, in the ocean no less, and so I saw no other way to stop things. I went to her."

My father made a sound deep in his chest but didn't say anything.

I continued, twisting around to pace the other direction. "I brought her to her vessel, got her safely up on deck, and then…she trapped me."

My father leaned forward, his elbows on his knees, eyes fast on me. "What did you say?"

"I mean, not very well, but she threw a hell of a caging spell on me." I thought back to the familiar feel of her magic against my skin. "Other than us, I'm not sure another demon would've been able to ignore it like I could."

"What did you do?"

"I let her think I'd been captured. I dropped the glamor. But I hadn't expected the others. There were three Corrupted who acted like soldiers, plus a spelled captain who was driving the boat."

Lucifer was nodding. I could only assume he knew about this portion, after all I had smelled his magic on the storm and knew it was another of his misguided attempts at parental support. I pointed at him as I paced past. "This is where you came in, right? You sent the storm."

"I just altered a few weather patterns. I felt your distress but was unable to isolate what was happening. I figured of all my children, a little rainstorm would never hurt you."

"You're right, but it nearly killed her." The last part came out a growl, surprising us both.

Father rubbed a hand over his jaw. "What is her name? Your witch?"

"She is not mine, not in the way you're thinking. She is my soul bound, though, that much is clear. I can actually feel the pull of my soul when we're close, and my magic, it's attached to her.

Nodding, he stood, taking his place by the fireplace, where a fire burned without fuel, probably held there by his magic. "And how did you get back?"

"I called for a portal—when the storm tossed us into the ocean, I took her and myself down the portal straight into the Styx." In case he was concerned, I clarified, "No one else came through. The way remains secure."

Father sighed, his face turning to the fire. "And the witch? Her name is Faye, right?"

I was startled that he knew but tried to hide it. "Yes."

"She is the Drude's witch, then?"

Something in my chest twitched, and I wished I had left more of the reapers around my home with Faye. They served me first. They wouldn't be able to stop my father's advances if he took his soldiers to my door, but they sure as fuck would slow them down.

"You can't hurt her."

Lucifer turned his face to me. "You think so little of me that you think I mean to hurt her?"

"I think you are a king who is—"

"I am a father too, Kharon, and I would never put you through the pain of losing your soul bound. I saw what it did to Nephesh…"

We were both silent, the fire crackling on its imaginary firewood.

"Besides," my father continued. "If she is the Faye that Nephesh's mate knows, then there may be more to her story than meets the eye."

I raised my eyebrows but didn't speak. "You've spoken to Nephesh already? I heard he had returned."

"He has." My father didn't elaborate, and it made my skin itch. I was loath to ask about it in case he did something so stupid as tell my brother that I'd asked about him. No sense letting Nephesh know I cared about him, assholery and all. We may work together to run this world, but we weren't really big on family group hugs or anything that stupid.

I grunted. "So, you already know about the time slipping?"

That drew his attention back to me an instant. "Time slipping?"

"Yes. I left yesterday from my home to save Faye. When I returned, a soul informed me that it had been weeks since I left."

Lucifer was nodding slowly, dark hair slipping forward before a hand pushed it back off his forehead. He must've already had some suspicions. "Nephesh said something similar, but not to that extent. He was gone for two or so weeks but was missing from the Underworld for much longer. We couldn't get a clear timeline because of how isolated he'd been before."

"I don't understand. How is that happening when the boundaries are still intact? The Underworld should be a mirror to the living world." Our world was built with the strongest boundaries magic could provide. It was the only reason we could exist here, a world within a world. But if they were weakening or failing… It would mean disaster.

"I don't know. But there must be some reason for it to be happening now."

I stopped pacing for a moment to stare at him. The question burned its way free of my chest. "The other spells protecting the souls are failing, aren't they? The ones who guard Kadmiel and help judge with Nephesh?"

My father stretched his back, and I could tell that he wished he could let his wings loose. My mother had once claimed that this dignified, business-like appearance that we often saw him in was only one edition of our father. I wondered if in these moments, where I could feel the frustration rolling off him, that he wished he could go back to a more primal time, when he first carved our lives from this world, using only his pain and grief. When claws and wings and fangs were his biggest assets.

"Do you really want to know?"

I snorted. "Of course I do. What kind of question is that?"

He sighed. "You must admit, Kharon, that you prefer to live in your own bubble. Each of you do."

"Shouldn't that be more of a reflection on your parenting than my interest level?"

To my surprise, my father chuckled, just once. Then the smile slipped from his face. "She would've known what to do. She always did."

I blinked in surprise, ducking my chin rather than let my father's laser-sharp gaze read my expression. He typically avoided talking about my mother at all costs. The fact that he had brought her up now was unusual.

I took a step back. "Tell me about the shields." The Underworld existed within a realm of its own, but it was a parasite on the living world, mimicking it in so many ways but powered by the souls that flowed through our lands. No souls meant no power.

My father's abilities, which had never been recorded or shared in my five hundred years, seemed to make the souls' energy into something that resembled the living world above. And over the years, Others had come here, molded out of need and pride by my family. The Brotherhood—my family's private, specialized military—were souls who volunteered to stay behind and work within the Underworld. The mahrs who sought out my dream king brother's protection as they were pushed into creation by the clashing of powerful curses generations ago. Even those who toiled among Tartarus, helping my youngest brother, Elon, to rehabilitate the worst souls that came here, were some versions of a soul. Many imbued by our power or ability or, even rarer, my mother's powerful magics.

Elon's creatures, the Nameless, had never left Tartarus, and he guarded them fiercely from our attention. The other demons who lived here, in family units and small cities, were as much citizens as the souls who chose to stay awhile in Elysium.

We were a world within a world.

But we were dying. What would happen to all of this if the shields gave way? Would that push our world into the living one? Would the incubus tribes have to walk down the streets, holding Starbucks cups and mingling over cocktails? Or would we simply cease to exist, and the cycle of souls would crank to a halt?

"They are struggling," Lucifer said finally, giving up on me meeting his stare. "While Lucia and now Justine…"

"Is that her name? Nephesh's mate?"

He nodded. "Shrewd little thing. She hates me."

That surprised a laugh out of me. "Does she? I like her already."

Lucifer and I shared a short look, and then I dropped my gaze again, resuming my pacing, but this time at a more sedate pace. "Their souls, Nephesh and Arafel being home, has strengthened us. The jurors at the gates are awake. They are able to pull more souls in every day. But I don't understand why the shields are causing a time slip. We still seem to be losing power. I thought at first that too many souls were remaining here, using our resources, but I spoke to Kadmiel. They are leaving for the living world in huge batches, as if they can sense the change too. None of them have any reasoning. Just an instinct to go, to—"

"To run," I finished for him.

Lucifer moved to stand in front of my path. I stopped, watching as he reached a hand out to straighten the collar on my shirt. "But the question is, Ferryman, are they running from someone…or to someone?"

Fuck.

His face curved in a slow, sad smile as he patted my chest with his hand, the jewels on his fingers winking in the firelight.

"What do we do?"

"The only thing we can do. We need your soul. You control the river; you and your reapers can pull them back into the water if we need to."

I nodded. "How did Nephesh take his back?"

Lucifer startled. "Take it? Clearly you have not met Justine."

I barely resisted rolling my eyes. "A social call has not been on the agenda in the few hours that I've been back."

"I only mean to point out that there's no way Nephesh could *make* Justine do anything." Lucifer moved to the door. Hearing his footsteps, Hiram, opened it from the other side. They stood together, demon and king, watching me. "She offered it to him, Kharon. Which means that you have an even bigger task ahead of you."

I shook my head, disbelieving. "She gave it to him… You're saying that giving is the key? That Faye has to give it to me? She's never going to do that." When did my voice get so loud? Even now, it echoed across the walls as I stared at the pair of them. I could've sworn that Hiram was laughing internally as my frustration boiled under my skin.

"It must be willingly given, Kharon." Lucifer shrugged. "That is the only way we know of so far. You are welcome to pursue other methods…while you charm her."

He wanted me to charm our enemy's primary weapon into giving me the one thing that she knew kept her alive. There was no way. "I don't have time for this."

Lucifer turned back to me. "I suggest you make some, or we will all be out of time in the very near future."

He stepped through the door, and Hiram closed it behind him, shooting me a wolfish smile as he did. I slammed my fist into the nearby wall, delighting in the crackle of the stone and the ricochet of force that slithered up my forearm. "Fuck!"

I shook my arm afterward, wishing I was regretful of that show of power, because I had no power left to waste, no time either. I needed to convince the Drude's witch that not only did she want to give me her most valuable bargaining chip, but she had to do it quickly.

My family's time in the Underworld may be coming to an end, but as a living soul not attached to a mate bond, this world was already hard at work killing her.

I groaned, closing my eyes.

This was going to be a fun conversation.

6

Faye

I knew I had only slept a few hours, but when I startled awake, still lying awkwardly on Kharon's couch, I already felt better. Blinking, I curled my fingers closed then opened them again, a soft welling of magic growing in my palm as I watched.

My magic felt stronger now, less erratic. Even now, it danced on my palm, the droplets catching the soft light that filled the room.

"Pretty."

I jerked away, the water dancing in my hands immediately solidifying into sharp iced bullets that hovered, waiting on my aim and release.

The soul hovered close to the front door. He raised his hands. "Don't! You'll ruin my outfit."

I was so shocked that I actually paused, my bullets melting back away. I swallowed, asking, "Your outfit?"

The male moved his hands into a shrug. "It was the first thing that came to mind."

I looked him up and down, trying to make my brain register the fact that while he didn't have completed legs, he was wearing a very jaunty, neat, if not translucent, uniform. I closed my hand entirely, the magic sinking back into my skin. "I'm sorry. You just scared me."

"I tend to do that."

I smiled at him. "It's not you. I tend to be a jumpy person." I looked away, straightening a pillow. "Product of my upbringing, I guess."

"I'm not offended, my lady."

I ran a hand over my curls, cringing at the sheer size of them. "My lady?"

"Old habits die hard, I hear."

I straightened my legs and swung them off the sofa to stand. "I guess so." Since we hadn't yet been formally introduced, I said, "I'm Faye."

His features brightened immediately, and he swooped closer as I held out a hand. His own pearl-toned fingers brushed mine, leaving a sort of cool caress as he moved. "I'm Chris." Thankfully he didn't have the same emotional roller coaster effect that the soul from the river had had on me earlier.

I stared at the uniform, recognizing several flags that didn't exist anymore. Unless you were in a museum. "How long have you been here, Chris?"

"Probably too long. But Lord Kharon puts up with me better than the Others, so I stay here."

"You're a spirit, then? A ghost?"

"I'm not sure they have a name for me yet. Not really. See, I'm still a soul, a shadow of the person I was in the living world. Just like those ladies and gents in the river, but the more time I spend out here, around the lords, the more stable my soul is. Resulting in what you see now before you."

"Don't you want to…I don't know, move on?"

"To Elysium? Maybe someday." Chris shrugged. "I'm in no rush, my lady."

"Is that…" I wasn't sure if I wanted to know. "Elysium… Is that like Heaven?"

Chris looked at me sharply, his strange eyes wide. They held mine captured, as if trying to read something in my face. Whatever he was looking for, he must not have found it, because a moment later, he ducked his chin, moving back towards the door. "You have much to learn about Heaven, my lady. And I am not the correct tutor. How long have you served the Drude?"

Feeling a little stilted by his sudden cool attitude, I began to finger comb my hair. "Nearly my whole life, or all the parts I can remember."

Chris wasn't looking at me anymore. "That makes more sense, I think. You look like a completely normal person, other than all that magic. Why else would you serve someone like him?"

Shame and something like anger simmered along my veins, making my voice snap when I responded. "Like him? You are friends with a demon. I'm not sure you have much room to talk."

Silence fell between us, stiff and unwanted.

Restlessness took over as the soul continued to stare away from me. I walked the length of the room once, and then, flushing, I realized I have no idea where I was going.

"I serve a healer," Chris said from where he appeared to lean against the wall. "I serve a family intent on giving souls the chance to be more than a memory. You speak of Heaven when you have no concept of Hell either. Start with that, Faye. Start here, because that witch blood in your veins says that you were always destined to be tied to this place. And these people."

"I know everything I need to know."

Chris's smile was sad. "But why limit yourself to what you need to know—or what you *think* you need to know—when there is so much more out there?"

I bit into my bottom lip, frustration a living thing in my belly. "I am doing what I have to do."

The soul was nodding, his face relaxed, "And so will he. I just hope you can see someday that those two paths are the same."

I huffed and moved to the window, where I stared out at the river. "I find it fascinating that a dead man believes in fate."

Chris shifted, and I knew he was about to begin speaking again, when I turned to face him. "And I find it even more fascinating that you, who is fate defined, have such little faith in it."

Something about his words stole my breath and made me feel even worse about what I was about to do. "I gave up defining my own life a long time ago."

His smile was dark. "We are not responsible for the current that drives us, but how we steer into waves is what defines us."

My magic flared at the first thought. "I don't like the water." But I knew a lot about it. Including the fact that Chris had said he was imbued by Kharon and his power. I was convinced enough to gamble on this, because I had no other option than to believe it.

And water, water in any shape or format, always froze.

Chris never saw it coming. The spell shocked me as it burst from my palms, wrapping Chris up in an instant. Capturing him. Freezing him in place.

I was out the door in an instant. My ankle burned only for a moment for the pearls to slip to the ground.

"You're my soul bound; I could never really hurt you." I had taken his words for what they were. A peek at the truth of our bond.

No spell would hold me, because as much as he hated it, his magic would recognize the other half of his soul in me. I may not have been able to get back to the living world. But I could get farther away, to a place where I could send a message to my master.

And to let him know that absolutely nothing had changed for me. The plan to capture Kharon was still in action. I could not let him think I had failed.

Kharon

I tilted my head, staring from my home to the embankment just beyond and back again. What was that? I felt more than saw the moment something moved through my home's wards. The flash of bouncing curls and bare feet was enough to tell me my greatest fear was quickly coming true.

"Fuck," I hissed, taking off after Faye as she sprinted off the dock sand into the surrounding field.

Chris hovered by the door, his face shocked as I blew past him.

"You were supposed to watch her!"

"I *was* watching her. She spelled me, and it took me a moment to recover," Chris retorted. "She went straight through the wards, right through them."

I growled, watching her slim legs carry her across the ground. For a human, she might be considered quick. But she had nothing on me, a demon hunting its prey.

Instinct roared in my brain, to chase, to tackle, to take… I could almost feel the sweet texture of her body underneath mine.

My legs picked up speed, eagerly eating up that space between us. And yet, somehow, I felt like I should slow down, I almost wanted her to run again, to prolong the chase between us.

"No!"

Yes, I chanted internally, drawing level with her just as a flash of black caught my eye from the side. My reapers had seen me, or maybe even Faye, and joined in on the chase.

Something lit the air between Faye and me. No longer was her run fueled by anger or even frustration. Fear filled the scent of her, replacing my interest with anger as the reapers swept in around us.

I hurled myself forward, wrapping my arms around her middle and taking her to the ground. I rolled, taking the blunt of the impact on my spine, her spender body pulled atop mine. For a moment, Faye lay quietly, and then with a curse, she sat up, braced over me as she pushed at my hands.

"Let me go! You can't keep me here!"

I tried to catch those angry little fists. "Faye, stop."

"I'm not your prisoner..."

I sighed, letting her get in a few good hits before stopping her once again. "There are more things at play here than just who is in charge of whom."

Faye stopped, chest heaving, to glare down at me. "Take me back."

I swallowed the apology that begged to emerge. Choosing to instead say, "I can't." That was the truth.

"You are Lucifer's son. Don't lie to me about what you can and cannot do." She gestured around us. "Your family built a world. You are practically gods."

Quick as lightning, I covered her mouth with my hand. "Don't ever say that again. Never, Faye. Do you understand? I can't take you back because that kind of power is immense, even for someone like me. Bringing us here cost me greatly, and I need to recover before we do anything close to the living world again."

She paused, my words sinking into her mind. "Before we do anything?" Her slender throat bobbed, and I wondered what her skin there would taste like, right above the thrumming pulse. "You mean, you would think about taking me back?"

"Let's say that I'm open to negotiations. But first, you have to stay close to me."

She huffed, leaning back and looking to escape once again.

I stopped her with a hand on her thigh. "Faye…"

She was sitting across my lap, her hips directly over mine. And the way she squirmed, the sweetness of her skin against mine, sent brilliant heat straight to my cock.

"What?"

"Stop moving."

She obeyed, her eyes wide as she finally took the time to look around us. The reapers had joined us, circling us slowly, their eerie black cloaks floating with their movements. From my position on the ground, I could actually see the pulse in Faye's throat begin to pound.

She swallowed, her little fingers curling in my shirt. "What are they?"

"Reapers."

"Reapers?" she repeated, her fingers slowly releasing the fabric. Deep in her chest, I could feel her magic unfurl, rising to the surface as she watched them. "Whose are they?"

"Mine."

Her head snapped down to mine. "You sent them after me?"

"No, I went running, and they assumed you were a corrupted soul." I shifted up onto an elbow. "But understand why they are frustrated. You were running…from me. They are my creatures and will always side with me."

She nodded, so slowly it was barely a movement. "I get it."

"You have to stay with me, Faye, not just because you want to feed me to the Drude. There are things here in the Underworld that you can't even imagine."

She nodded again, this time dark spots appearing on her cheeks.

"Okay. Let me help you up."

I pushed her to her feet as I rose, summoning a reaper forward as I did.

The reaper regarded me warily. I didn't interact with them often. But when I held my hand out, he knew what I wanted. I felt the weight of the soul chains before I saw the glimmer of the magical devices. Reaching for Faye, I slapped a hand over her wrist, slipping the handcuffed edge quickly over her hand.

"What? What is this?"

Not answering her, I did the same to my wrist, my left to her right. Then with a flourish, I held them up. "Not all souls come willingly. These are something my mother made—a soul chain. The reapers use them to guide the souls to the river's mouth."

Faye's mouth dropped. "You put a handcuff on me?"

I huffed at her. "Not a handcuff. A soul chain. It's special. Don't worry. As soon as we talk through our options, I can take them off again." I held up a ball of my magic, letting the glowing mist around my hand illuminate the delicate silver links that were not only on my wrist, but on hers. "No running, witchling."

She sputtered up at me, but I ignored her now, suddenly very tired of all of this. I wanted to go to my room, to collapse into my bed, and to forget that I was now a major player in a game that my father and the Drude had begun a long time ago.

Ignoring Faye, who was still yanking on the silver bracelet, magic glowing at her fingertips, I turned for home. The soul chains between us gave her plenty of room for her to curse my name for another full minute before they tugged on her wrist. Still hurling insults, Faye followed me back towards the docks.

A moment later, she tried a new technique, her magic slamming into the back of my shoulder. I paused, looking back at her. She blinked, looking down at her still-open palm as if surprised by her own attack. I would've laughed if I had the energy to do so.

I put a hand on my hip. "Did you just try to spell me?"

"No..." Faye swallowed, raising her chin. "I just threw some of my ice at you."

I closed my eyes with a sigh. "And how did that work out for you?"

Those pretty lips pressed together hard. "It didn't."

"Alright, so let's please be done for a bit. I'm tired."

"I had to try," she whispered under her breath. And it made the corner of my lip curl. Restarting my path, this time with Faye trailing directly behind, I set my eyes on the softening light of the Underworld. The river bubbled quietly, and with the witch at my side quiet, even if it was sullenly, the world seemed to be at ease. I knew it was a lie, but I took it as the gift it was.

"I would've been disappointed if you hadn't," I whispered back to her.

The reapers were melting away, disappearing back down the riverbanks and into the rise of woods that signified just how close Faye had gotten to the beginning of Arafel's realm.

Chris was nowhere to be seen and must've gone to hide. Smart soul. I had trusted him to keep her safe, and that meant keeping her inside of my home, where my magic remained strong. Passing through the door, I swept a hand over the entryway.

"You must have some experience breaking wards?" I said, knowing she was watching me.

Faye didn't answer for so long, I almost gave up her responding, but then, just as I stepped forward, she said, "I

wanted to be sure no one could ever keep me somewhere I
didn't want to be."

The frustration boiling in my veins vanished in an instant. It
was easy to forget that while she may still believe in the Drude,
it was because she had spent her life a prisoner of his. No matter
what she claimed about working for him, I knew the truth of it.

I sat down at my desk with a heavy clomp of boots and
stared over at the couch.

"I know you don't believe me, but you're safe here. Until I
can convince you of that, we have to…" I groaned, already
second-guessing my decision to use the soul chains. "We have
to stay together," I said, echoing my earlier comment. Rubbing
the palms of my hands over my eyes, I waited to see how she
would respond.

Faye had hesitated, hovering at the end of the twinkling
chains near the warded entry. But after a moment, she must've
made a decision, because I first heard a tiny exhale, just enough
to make the hair on my arms lift. And then her feet were nearly
silent as she skittered across the room and began to situate
herself on the couch.

"Luckily, Father was talkative today," I said. "Unfortunately
I didn't find out a lot, but there are a few things that might
pique your interest." I could nearly taste the anxiety coming off
her, and it turned my mouth sour. When I opened my eyes
again, she was perched at the edge of the cushions, her face
downcast. Anxious fingers ran over the soul chain at her wrist.
Everything about her screamed sadness, from the soft way her

shoulders were rounded over, as if somehow preparing to shield herself from me, to the way her chest still rose and fell quickly, even though I knew she was recovered from her runaway attempt.

I growled, my confusion warring with the overpowering need to go to her, to comfort her. Faye was the fucking enemy, but right now, here in my home so far from everything she knew, she looked too vulnerable. I hated it.

I had seen her that way before, on the boat when those Corrupted had first talked to me. When they had spoken about the Drude being disappointed in her. I'd seen it then, the way she had shrunk into herself. I'd instantly hated seeing her like that, so small and scared. No traces of that iron core that I knew she contained.

I much preferred when her eyes sparked, that glowing power in her swirling to life as she threw exasperated looks my way. I wanted her that way again. I wanted it more than my next breath.

"It's not going to kill you, you know."

Faye didn't raise her head. She didn't even look at me.

"The Underworld will, though, so time is of the essence."

That got her attention. She raised her chin slightly, leveling a wary stare my way.

"What do you want? I'm here. I'm trapped. Just take the soul and go." Faye gestured at her chest.

My eyes jumped there as well but were decidedly more interested in what was on her chest than what existed inside her.

I groaned, leaning back and away from her. My arms still tingled from the magic she'd thrown at me a few minutes ago. It may have just been ice, but when it broke across my shoulders, it was as if the magic itself got wound up in mine. I felt it now, cool and sharp against my core.

"Thank you for the segue, my little pessimist. But you have actually uncovered the problem. I cannot just take the soul from you. It is not possible."

Faye continued to pick at the invisible chain.

Something just north of my belly tugged hard. "Faye…" I waited, biting into my lip hard enough to make it bleed. But finally, she slowly looked up. The tears shining in her eyes nearly undid me, and suddenly I was on my knees in front of her on the couch, my hands clenching, my arms reaching out like I had the right, the privilege to touch her. Breathing hard, I made sure she was looking me in the eyes when I spoke next. "Witchling, hey, look at me. I cannot be sorry that you're here, I'm sorry I tackled you. I'm sorry that my reapers are scary."

Faye sniffled but still remained silent.

I continued, barely resisting the urge to brush those curls back from her face. "And I'm sorry that you didn't get to sacrifice me for a promotion with your asshole boss."

A watery chuckle surprised me but also seemed to surprise her. Blinking rapidly, Faye wiped at her cheekbones.

"He's not my boss. He's…" She trailed off, taking a long breath in. "Is it going to hurt?" She put her hands on her lap, so close to mine that my fingers actually twitched with the need to slip them around hers. To feel just how small she would be against me. How breakable. How precious.

Fuuuuuuuuuck.

"Is what going to hurt?" I wouldn't let anyone hurt her ever again.

"When you take my soul…or I give it to you. Whatever you said has to happen. I know that you need it, and I don't know why I have it, but at this point, I'd rather we just get it over with."

I immediately leaned forward, my chest hovering just inches from her folded legs. "Wait, hold on. Faye, I'm not going to hurt you."

She huffed, her bare feet curling around each other as she shrank down on herself even further.

"Again, I'm sorry if I hurt you when I tackled you. But I don't want to hurt you. Ever. And it's not like that. I can't just take the soul from you."

Faye blinked. "What?"

"And for the record, it is *my* soul, carried alongside yours." I rose and moved towards the kitchen. "I don't want *your* soul, witchling. Even I am not that evil."

Something lightened between us, and when I returned, carrying a plate full of fruit and a crusty loaf of bread with an enormous pat of butter on top, Faye was sitting up straighter on the couch. Suspiciously, Faye eyed the plate.

"I blatantly refuse to taste test this. The texture of bananas is one of the world's worst, so you'll just have to trust me that they aren't poisoned or something."

Faye blinked at me. Then slowly she reached for the bread, her slim fingers tugging the chunk free before putting it carefully on her tongue. She met my eyes for a long moment as she chewed. I saw the moment the sweetness and salty taste broke across her tongue. Eyes brightening, she reached forward, pulling off a larger piece of this time.

"All yours." I gently placed the tray onto the couch beside her.

Faye flushed a little but didn't stop chewing.

I watched her eat, a strange satisfaction growing in my gut as she enjoyed something so much that I had provided. The demonic side of my lineage practically shouted in my mind that I had done well. I had tackled my prey, I had brought her back to my home, and I was feeding her.

A proper little demon male these days, with my fucking soul chains and primal chasing techniques. Groaning, I rubbed my hand over my face. This was not the time to fall back onto very, very old habits. Even if I suddenly found the hum in my demon blood very tempting.

I couldn't wait any longer. Watching her eat wasn't a good use of time, even if I loved it.

"I meant what I said earlier. I can't take anything from you. Not while you're living." Faye stopped chewing, casting me a wide-eyed look. I pointed at her with a long finger. "And you *will* remain living. You have my promise. And as long as you are breathing, you are in control. It is you who has to give me my soul."

Faye slowly resumed chewing. The look on her face told me everything. She didn't believe me.

"You have to willingly give me my soul. As in, I cannot remove it from you or coerce or alter your perspective of our situation so that you may want to. You have to legitimately want to give it to me."

She swallowed, teasing me with a peek of her pink tongue as she swiped her tongue over her lips. "What happens when you have it back?"

I sighed, resting my head on my elbow as she selected a banana and began to peel its skin back. "To put it lightly? All the things your master doesn't want."

Faye paused, the fruit midair. "But what exactly though?"

I studied her. This was a test, disguised as a simple question. One I refused to fail, especially considering I would not fail. There was no harm in letting her know what the next steps in this war with the Drude would bring.

"I will have my powers back. If you think my brothers or I are powerful now, this version of us is a mockery of what we used to be. What we have to be. And with my soul, I will be complete again for the first time in hundreds of years. As such, I imagine the River Styx will be safer, faster, and the magic that runs in those waters more powerful. More souls. More power." My eyes cut to hers and held. "No more Drude."

Appearing thoughtful, Faye nodded. "And you think you will fight the Drude. To win this war?"

I gritted my teeth. "I will keep him out of the Underworld. At whatever cost it requires."

She ate a small bite of the banana, taking her time to swallow, and then looked back at me. "And after, will you be more powerful than him?"

"Than the Drude? None of us have faced him directly/ I'm not entirely convinced he's more powerful than me today."

"He is," she answered, looking away from me. The truth— this was the truth. I hated to hear that but was relieved that she was engaging with me after my fuck-up in the woods.

Faye slowly put the banana down. "I'm sorry. I don't know how to feel about this."

Standing, I felt the soft jangle of the invisible cuff against my own skin. "I won't rush you, witchling. It's been a shit few hours for you, and I can't imagine how this feels."

She paused, watching me as if waiting to see if I might go back on my comment or follow it up with sarcasm. But I meant it. I was surprised that I did, but it was true. I wanted her to think about this. Because if I could convince her to give me my soul, it would change the world. If she chose to keep it, she would doom mine.

"Let's find you a room," I said brusquely, clapping my hands together. "The kitchen will be open all night, and don't worry about the reapers. They are spelled to stay out."

Immediately, I turned, intending to stride down the short hallway to my room and the guest bedroom just beyond. I only got a few feet before there was a soft squeak, followed by the sound of something hitting the floor. I turned to find Faye glaring up at me from the floor.

Wordlessly, she held up the wrist I'd slapped the chain on.

Heat crawled up my neck, surprising me again. "Oh, I'm sorry about that."

Faye pushed away from the sofa, untangling her legs and righting herself just as I reached her. When my hands skimmed up her forearms, offering my assistance, she let out a sharp intake of breath. I recoiled as well, shocked by the spark of power that lit up the moment our skin touched.

We looked at each other, her gaze confused and wild. I wondered what she saw in mine. She licked her lips, and I watched, entirely transfixed by the simple motion. "It, uh… It must be something about the chains. I'll be more careful."

Turning, I forced my steps to be slowly measured as I combed my mind desperately for why I'd just lied to her. There was no way that spark had been from the soul chains. It had started somewhere else, deep inside my chest. It didn't seem likely that it had been my soul. But I had no other options currently at hand. Whatever it was, it had made my heart pound. And worse, I had been nearly overwhelmed with the need to do it again. To see if that zinging pressure between us was built on more than just the spelled chains.

How long had it been since I'd been truly interested in a female? Like my brothers, I'd dabbled in pleasure through my entire life, both in the living world and the Underworld. But it had been so long. I couldn't even remember the last time someone had tempted me.

But those lips…

I ducked my chin, stealing a glance at the profile of Faye's face as she moved to my side in the hallway, our shoulders bumping gently in the close proximity. Heat infused my blood, and I knew she felt it too. Her heartbeat sped up, her breath coming short as we bumped against each other in the short hallway.

The very short hallway.

Fuck. We were already in front of my bedroom. And suddenly, I was violently aware of my mistake. I actually felt the moment Faye realized it too, her body tensing, a combination of fear and confusion pouring off her skin like poison. I hated it. I wished that I could take her into my arms, explaining that I never again wanted to be the source of her fear or distress.

But right now, I wasn't sure that would solve anything. Besides, when had anyone sought out me as a source of comfort?

"The next room will be yours while you are here, but tonight, because of the cuffs—chains—because of the chains, you will need to sleep in here."

Her tongue wetted her lips once more, making my stomach twist.

I looked away, cursing this nonsense arousal that seemed to lurk at every corner. "Don't worry. I'm more than comfortable sleeping on the floor. You can take the bed, and tomorrow, the chains will be gone."

Faye hesitated for a breath then slowly nodded. "Alright. But I'll take the floor."

"You absolutely cannot."

Her head jerked, looking up at the rough tone of my voice.

I shook my head. "I may be a demon, Faye, but I would never put you on the floor while I had the bed. You will take my bed, sleep in my sheets, and I will be close by the door so that we are completely certain no one comes to us before we figure this out."

Her mouth formed a soft *O*. But she nodded. "Thank you."

I blinked at her. My prisoner saying thank you was not on my bingo card, but again, it seemed every word that she offered me loosened a knot so viciously tight in my chest. "No need to thank me. Let's get ready for bed."

Faye nodded eagerly, her hand moving to the soul chains as she swayed on her feet. "How do we do that?" Tired eyes searched the room, eyes catching on the bathroom off to one side.

I hid my smile. While the Underworld was only a reflection of the world above, that hadn't stopped us from borrowing features and technical advances. A hot shower was one of those.

"Would you like to get cleaned up?"

"How can I?" She raised her arm, the disappointment evident in her voice.

"The chain is long enough. The curtain is very dark. I will stay outside of the shower, let you get cleaned up."

She glanced down at her clothes, and I hurried to supply a solution for that. "I have clothes too, ones you can borrow." Her gaze landed on me, so relieved that it nearly made me glow with pleasure. Visions flew across my mind, of Faye in my clothes, her scent sinking into the fabric.

I growled softly. These fucking demon instincts were getting way too close to the surface. I cleared my throat, shoving those wants, the pull of this female, to the back of my mind.

Faye took a deliberate and slow step closer to me. In response, I guided us over to the wardrobe along the far wall and drew out a plain white shirt. It was soft, clean, and long enough that it would nearly be a dress on the witch's petite frame. My mouth was dry as I held it out to her.

"This should work. No comments on style. My ego can't handle any more direct hits tonight."

She took it without saying anything, tucking the clothing against her breast and waiting once more. Something in my stomach twisted again. Was she scared? I smelled the air but sensed nothing other than the usual pleasure of her scent.

Clearing my throat, I pointed at the bathroom. "I would like to shower too. Do you want to go first?"

She was already shaking her head before I was done speaking. "No, no, you can go first."

"The chains won't let me go far," I confessed. "I'll have to stay close."

"Then we'll have to trust that your mother raised a gentleman," Faye said, her words a little breathy, "And that you'll turn around or close your eyes or…"

"I'll do both," I promised easily. My cock throbbed at the promise of even being close to her as she let water slip over her body.

"Good," Faye responded with a little jerk of her chin. When she turned away, I palmed my dick hard, tucking it into a safer position. Or at least a position where it wasn't as obvious where my thoughts were heading.

"Good," I echoed. Unsure of what else to say, I led the way into my bathroom, ignoring the way that the smaller room forced us close once again. Something in my mind complained that I hadn't built a fucking fort like Arafel, but instead had chosen this cottage-style home. I loved my home, the warmth, the quiet comfort, and the access to my river. But at least with the fort, I would have spread out, stepped away, been able to have taken a breath that wasn't completely lined with the sweetness of her.

Turning the water on and watching the steam begin to rise, I braced myself for what I knew would come next. I was reaching for the hem of the soiled shirt that I'd worn since I'd entered the living world, when Faye gave an indigent squeak and swiveled to show me her back.

She clung to my shirt. "Kharon! You could've warned me."

My chin dropped, and I hid my grin as I stared at her back. "I'm not shy, Faye."

"Well, I am," she sputtered, her curls bouncing in her self-righteous fury. "Please hurry up and do it, then."

I chuckled, the tension in the room gone. "I think this is the first time I've ever had a female tell me that."

I quickly shucked my clothes and hopped into the steaming water. The soul chains only tightened a moment before Faye stepped closer again, standing on the dry side of the curtain as I rinsed my body, letting the sandalwood soap that I loved so much fill the room with its soothing scent.

"Are you ready to switch?"

"No, not yet," Faye responded, followed by quick sounds of fabric being removed. A bolt of heat laced my gut. She was undressing. Right there, just outside of this shower. It would take nothing to reach out, to run my fingers down her throat. To press my mouth against her pulse as I tucked her in close…

"Okay, I'm ready."

"Fuck," I whispered, reaching down to palm my rock-hard cock for a moment before realizing that tightened the chain on us once again. These really had been the worst fucking idea I'd ever had.

Faye responded to my tug, one slender leg stepping into the water with a sharp gasp. "Kharon!"

Fates, I loved the way she said my name, even when she was pissed. Which was right now. She stepped in, tumbling under the water and into my body for just a short moment. I caught her and the flash of smooth olive skin she'd revealed before I quickly slammed a hand across my eyes.

"I'm not looking!" I actually turned my other hand to shield my cock and balls from her in case she retaliated.

But there were no angry fists, no quick knee to the crotch. Just her voice, soft and a little high with nerves. "You better not be."

"I'm not."

One bad part about this particular pose was that while I couldn't see a freaking thing, she could probably see all of me. My hand wasn't big enough to hide everything. I had never been shy in my life, and while I found the idea of her staring at my body intoxicating in its own way, I was trying hard not to focus on our situation. Or on the water that still rained over us.

Was it drenching her curls like the ocean had? Was it pouring over those pouting lips? Did it drip down her collarbones?

Did it outline those breasts?

I groaned, pressing harder against my eyes as if I could pretend I wasn't visualizing every inch of my soul bound's body.

"Kharon?"

I needed to get the fuck out of this shower. "I promise I'm not looking."

She gave a short laugh that ended in a snort.

I frowned, nearly dropping the hand I had covering my eyes. "Are you laughing at me?"

"No, I'm laughing at this. How did we end up sharing a shower? I figured that you would step out or something when I got in. This whole thing, it's just ridiculous." She was laughing again, but now I heard the barely restrained hysteria there.

Realization dawned, and I lurched backwards, my free hand feeling for the towels I'd left us. I immediately knocked them to the floor. Cursing, I twisted my body around to try to reach them without exposing my still-hard cock to her. Faye let out a soft chuckle, and I rolled my eyes.

"Only you would find this funny."

"Maybe a little. I pictured the son of Lucifer a tiny bit more…collected."

Grunting, I stepped out of the shower, the towel secured firmly around my hips. "As I've mentioned, witchling, your references are giving you bad information. You should know my family is nowhere near being collected."

The sound of the water changed, and I pictured her shifting under the spray. A moment later, the scent of my shampoo filled the room. She was using my soap on that lovely skin. Goose bumps raced along my arms, pleasure hot enough to make my throat ache settling over me.

"Would you tell me about them? Other than Nephesh, what are they like?"

"Why? Going to tell your boss about them?"

Silence fell, and I could tell that I'd pierced this bubble of peace we'd temporarily set up around us. I took a breath. "Elon's favorite food is sushi. The male once heard that a famous sushi chef had passed and came to the Styx himself to offer him sanctuary in return for showing him how to make his own sushi rolls."

I could almost feel the soft smile on her face.

"Kadmiel is in everyone's business; he can't help himself. Sometimes I think too much human and witch blood went into him. He can spend copious amounts of time in the living world without ramifications. I wonder if he feels more at home there than here. And Arafel is the best of us, the combination of demon and human that I think my parents wanted. He's a devoted male to his mate—she's human and a witch like you. They're holding the worst of the destruction at bay."

"And what about you?"

"I'm the middle child; unimportant and uninteresting when compared to the rest of the lot. But all the same, a useful cog in the wheel."

Her breathing picked up, and I could smell my soap as she no doubt used it on her body. Heat infused me, harsh and desperate as my soul bound cleaned her naked body. That heat only rose when I thought about how she would smell like me too tonight. It eased a need inside me, to lay claim to this witch in the most primal of ways.

"That's rather critical," she answered after a moment.

"That's reality, witchling. I understand my part, even if no one else does. I am in the middle, the push that keeps the machine of our lives in motion." I paused. "Your boss would be thrilled to get one of my brothers, but me? I think he'd toss me back."

"Don't be so sure," I heard her whisper, but I didn't think she meant for me to hear it, so I remained quiet another minute.

The water turned off. "May I have a towel?"

"Here," I said, pushing the towel around the fabric curtain.

"Don't look," Faye cautioned, and I snorted while I resumed my earlier pose, one hand over my eyes, another at my waist.

"I can assure you, witch, I do not take what is not willingly given." I inhaled, tasting her on my tongue, the flavor making me dizzy.

"Excuse me if I have a hard time believing that. You are a demon, Kharon."

A soft growl rumbled out of my chest. "I can't make you believe anything, but know that while my kind might enjoy the more visceral things in life, I find there is nothing sweeter than the sound of a female begging for my cock."

The towel stopped moving against her. "Begging?" she echoed, her voice a rush.

"Begging."

"I don't beg," Faye said.

I smiled, turning back to the pile things I'd brought into the shower with us. "Not yet you don't."

Her heart rate was wild as she continued to dry herself off. I handed her my shirt next, watching as her hand snatched it back into the privacy of the curtain.

"I'm sorry that it's a little big. It's the best I could do…" I trailed off as Faye's slender hand reached up and pushed back the curtain between us. She smelled like me, her skin glowing with warmth and cleanliness from underneath the soft white shirt that draped over her slim shoulders before dropping to mid-thigh. As my eyes tracked her fingers there, she tugged at the end, as if aware again of being in such revealing clothing around me.

She was beautiful.

"Thank you," Faye said, ducking her chin to her chest.

I blinked. Had I said that out loud? Fuck.

"Let's get to bed," I said gruffly, quite sure that I needed to get out of this steamy warm bathroom and into my bedroom, farther from my soul bound. Everything would make more sense in the morning.

Faye followed me back into my bedroom, stopping only when we faced the broad footboard of my bed. She was biting her bottom lip, her fingers twisting in her borrowed shirt.

"I'll just sleep right there, by the door."

She was going to bruise her lip if she kept chewing it like that. "You don't have to do that."

I froze. "What do you mean?"

"It's a huge bed, I sleep all curled up. You can have this half." She gestured at the side of the bed closest to the door.

"I don't think that's a good idea."

She looked up at me. "Why not?"

"Because if we are both in this bed I won't be able to stay…on my side."

"What?"

I huffed, leaning down enough to brush my nose over hers before she could pull away. "I can't be the only one feeling this connection. And when I'm asleep, then…"

Faye reared back, but no fear tinged her scent. Only a sweet, heady one that pieced my skull. "What? Then what?"

I stepped closer, suddenly unable to stay away, "You, little witch, are made to withstand everything I can throw at you. Everything. So unless you want to test those boundaries starting tonight, I suggest you get your cute little ass into my bed and stop asking questions you already know the answer to."

Her eyes were wide, but after a long breath, she turned and simply climbed into my bed, folding the sheets over her body with quick, efficient movements.

I breathed in, needing to calm the soul in my chest screaming at me to do something, before I quickly reached over Faye to grab my pillow. Throwing it to the ground by the bedside, I prepared to lie down.

"Wait!"

I halted, cringing at the ringing in my ears. "You do a lot of singular-word shouting, woman."

"I just…" She held out the top blanket of the bedding. "I won't need all of this. You take this so it's not so hard."

I took the blanket with a frustrated swing of my hands then threw it down on the ground. Planting my hands on my hips, I faced her. "Thanks. Now, anything else?"

She crossed her arms. "No."

"Good."

"Fine."

"Goodnight."

And then there was nothing but silence and the lingering draw of something just out of reach that tingled and burned between us. Closing my eyes, I begged sleep to take me. I needed my rest. In the morning, I needed to convince the Drude's witch to save the Underworld.

7

He snored.

Not like Paul had, or even some of the other Corrupted whose bodies still rested as if they were still human. Kharon snored lightly, more of a soft whistle of breath between his lips as he slumped on the floor, one hand thrown over his head, nearly touching the door. The other crossed his belly, curling and relaxing reflexively.

His breathing changed, and I realized for the first time what a creep I must look like, leaning over the edge of the bed and staring at him. A hot blush stole up my cheeks, making my hands jerk back quickly as I hid them in the blankets I'd slept in.

But he didn't wake. Just shifted a little on the pallet he'd made, moving the blankets farther down his torso. More of that beautiful blue skin was on display now, not to mention the wealth of muscles that seemed to wrap every inch of his lean frame.

He really was alluring. No wonder demons had no trouble capturing their prey. If I hadn't known what he was, what he was capable of, then I, too, would've been drawn in, desperate to know more. As it was, I was drawn to him even knowing those things.

Was it because the soul that burned inside of me was his? Did it long to return to him? Try as he might, the Drude hadn't been able to find a way to explain the soul magic away. It was something unique only to Nicola and her sons.

Oh God… Nicola.

I buried my face in my pillow. After everything she had done for me, I was now drooling over her sleeping son as he kept me chained to his side. What a monster of a problem this was all turning into.

What would she say to me about all of this? I had so many questions for her. When she disappeared, I'd been completely at a loss. My first and only teacher, she had practically raised me at the Drude's first compound, long before he'd begun to grow in power. Back when Nicola was the only thing keeping him alive in the living world.

She'd kept me safe. Taught me things even he could not do. Even when she knew we would never truly be on the same side.

It was clear now that we still weren't. I might be drooling over her son, but I still fully intended to turn him into the Drude the first chance I got.

He might not be as bad as I pictured, but that no longer mattered. Too much was on the line.

"You are thinking so hard, you woke me up," a deep, rough voice grumbled.

I rolled over, pinning him with the best glare I could come up with. "And you were snoring loud enough to wake me up. So who's fault is it really?"

Kharon grinned, running a hand over the smooth plane of his skull before moving down over his face. "You're spicy in the morning. I like that."

I gave a halfhearted grunt and rolled back onto the bed.

Kharon sat up, his head even with my eye line.

"Must be a nice change from all the oohing and ahhing that you typically get from the women you wake up beside."

Kharon's smile only broadened. "Maybe it would be if I woke up with a woman often, but you, my little witch, are the first."

My heartrate picked up, heat curling in my core as I met his gaze. He was telling the truth. Why did that make me so happy?

"I'm not your little witch." I sat up, stretching a beat before triple checking that my borrowed clothes were all still in place. "And how is that possible? Aren't you hundreds of years old?"

A blue shoulder raised. "At least."

"And you still haven't woken up beside a woman?"

Kharon's brilliant blue eyes narrowed, and I saw an opening. "Oh," I said, tapping my chin. "I get it now."

His smile faltered. "Get what?"

"Your charming personality must keep them all at bay."

Kharon smirked, and it did dark, twisting things to my belly. "Perhaps."

"Well, I'm glad we can agree on one thing. Or rather two. Number one, you snore, and number two that women don't like to have sex with you." I ticked them off on my fingers, ignoring the flutter of my heart as his eyes darkened. "What?"

"Nothing. I was just wanting to clarify a few things." Kharon slowly stood until his body was arching over mine, each hand on the bed alongside my hips. I tried hard to stay still, to not let him intimidate me into leaning away, but it was hard. Especially when the soft smell of sandalwood from our shower last night washed over me. My eyes fluttered closed.

"And what are they?" My voice had lost its confidence, coming out barely a whisper, yet still managed to fill the ever-diminishing space between our faces.

"Women love to have sex with me, witchling. Don't make assumptions that I'll be forced to disprove."

My cheeks were on fire. "I...uh..."

"Unless you would prefer a demonstration as to why?"

"Why what?" What was I doing? My lips were dry, my throat hotter than the desert.

"Why they are completely willing to fuck me but not sleep with me."

"Oh, no. No thank you." I swallowed, trying not to squirm. "I believe you."

He leaned in, close enough the tips of our noses brushed. "Good."

His eyes caught on something to the side of my face, and without backing away, he gave one of my curls a soft tug. "If you ever do need a demonstration, all you have to do is ask. And as for the snoring….” Kharon’s eyes crawled slowly up my form. “I had to have one flaw. Otherwise my brothers would be jealous.”

I huffed at that, letting my body fall back to the mattress as I shoved at his arms. “Get out of here, monster.”

Kharon retreated but only a few steps, raising his arm in my direction. “Don’t forget, I’m not going anywhere without you.”

The soul chains. I’d nearly forgotten. I groaned, grabbing the blankets to tug them over my face again. “I thought you said those would be gone today.”

Kharon glanced at the window. “A few more hours, and then we can plan on chasing you down again. Sound alright?”

I grunted noncommittally. My legs were sore, and while the night in Kharon’s bed had refreshed me, I really wasn’t in the mood to try to run away again.

“Perfect,” Kharon said, rubbing his hands together eagerly. “Now, do you want to borrow my toothbrush?”

For that, I pushed the blankets down to glare at him. The male leaned close again. “Based on that look, I’m guessing no.” He moved back, swatting at my legs. “Get up, lazybones. We have some negotiations to start.”

“I’m not negotiating with…” I paused, considering my options. “Without breakfast.”

Kharon’s gaze warmed. “I love a woman with an appetite.”

My traitorous heart thumped in my chest at his words. I knew it was a joke. I knew it meant nothing. But once again, my body had other thoughts on the matter. "An appetite for pain, clearly, or else she wouldn't be here. I was thinking more along the lines of real food. Human stuff."

One side of his mouth rose, and the white tip of his fang was visible. My thighs tensed, a steady throb between my legs making it hard to focus.

"What do you think I live on?"

"You aren't able to sustain yourself on your own ego?"

"Enough," Kharon held up a hand, but couldn't hide the soft laugh that slipped out with the word. "Get out of my bed, and I'll feed you. Then we'll talk."

I carefully got out of bed, making sure his shirt covered all my important parts as I moved. Glancing up, I found him watching me again, a soft green glow in his eyes.

It was gone a moment later. With a flourish, Kharon offered me his elbow. I took it, sliding my hand against his skin as he ushered me out of the hall back towards the living area of his house.

Fear struck me like a punch to the gut. Our banter had been fun, light, and deeply enjoyable. But every step I took was taking me closer to the moment I had to decide what his soul was worth. And what my loyalty to the Drude looked like under pressure.

A hell of a lot of it.

I hadn't thought that I'd been able to eat—the nerves were already settling hard in my stomach. But the moment Kharon whisked a plate of food out of literal thin air, the smell of scrambled eggs and bacon changed my mind.

I ate the whole plate and then most of another. My stomach slowly filled, and my pulse slowly rose until I could barely sit still.

Kharon sighed when I pushed back my plate, his eyes on my face as he sat. "Better?"

I lifted my wrist, the delicate chain slipping down my forearm. "Better. Can these come off now?"

Kharon's brows lowered, the muscular line of his shoulder tense. "It's odd they haven't fallen off yet. Elon also uses them in Tartarus. I will contact him after we talk. Or what did you call it last night? Negotiate?"

I knew I was gaping at him but couldn't stop myself. "Tartarus?"

"Yes." Kharon folded his hands across the polished surface of his countertops. They were so clean and new, I couldn't believe anyone had ever used them for their intended purpose. But then, seeing as he'd just whisked the food from someone there, there was a good chance he didn't need to. Kharon's voice was soft, the words rushed, as if he were suddenly less comfortable talking about this subject. "While much of this world is a mirror of the one above, there are elements of it that are truly hellish. Elon's realm is one of those."

My stomach rumbled nervously, and I wished I hadn't eaten so much. "Do we have to go there? To Tartarus, I mean."

"I hope not." Kharon was serious, watching me carefully.

Wrapping my arms around myself, I suddenly had a horrible thought. That was where I would end up at the end of this pitiful living existence that I was fighting so hard to maintain. My lips quivered, fear spreading through my body.

"Witchling?"

I blinked, trying to calm down my emotions, but still, they writhed under my skin, desperate for release after the stresses of the past days.

"Faye," Kharon said, louder now.

I looked up at him, shocked to see the dishware, the cookery, even my still-dirty plate suspended in the air, hovering, held there by my out-of-control power. Horror sliced through the fear, but that only fed the power, making the very floor under our feet move.

I looked down, staring at my bare feet against the floor as my toes curled, my skin tone garnering a soft glow as my power slowly took on its own life.

"No, no, no, no." I pressed my hands to my eyes, trying to remember what Nicola had taught me, trying to remember how to calm down, to pull that great power back under my skin where it always lurked.

"I need my master," I whispered, hot pinpricks of power continuing to race up and down my spine. My hands twitched where they pressed against my face. If he were here, he would know what to do. He would siphon off the power until I could gather the control back. I would be safe then. I wouldn't hurt anyone. But I couldn't be trusted like this.

My parents' faces flashed across my eyelids as I swallowed down the scream that bubbled up in my throat. Everything was too hot, too cold, the contrasting power of my fear and worry warring in my chest.

My head fell back, my entire body coiling as more power continued to awaken and flow through my veins. My thoughts clouded, my emotions roiled, making my stomach hurt as I wished I could be anywhere but right here.

"Faye." A soft voice was speaking, more words, not just my name, but I couldn't focus on that. "Let me in, witchling."

"I need him…"

"You don't. You got yourself into this mess. You're going to get yourself out." Kharon. Of course it was Kharon, his smooth voice slithering into my mind as I fought the magic that desperately wished to be set free.

"I can't."

"Oh yes, you can. You carry my soul, Faye, which means you must be equally powerful and stubborn. And you must be both of those things at once." Cool hands brushed my face, curling around my hands and pulling them down.

"No," I whimpered. I needed them, that shield against the reality of what I was capable of.

"Yes," Khan said, his own fingers blessedly gentle against my jaw. "You have to be stubborn enough to be in charge of the power. Once it owns you, it will own all of you."

"But I can't. I don't know how, not on my own."

"But you can. You have been."

I shook my head, hating the hot tears that dripped down my cheeks. "No, I can't. He usually helps. He takes it from me so that I can…"

Kharon growled, so loud that it actually made me open my eyes. He was so close, I could see the way that his eyes, which glowed a bright green, were nearly gold in the center, the light so bright. "He is nothing compared to you, to us. If he claimed that he took it, it was just another lie. Only you have the power to give your magic, just like you are the only one who can rein it in. You gave; he did not take. You must be in charge."

I stared at him, my heart rate slowing a breath. The ground under us calmed, but the plates around us continued to hover.

Kharon's lips quivered, but his eyes did not cease glowing. "If my soul was chosen for you, it was not only because of your own power, but because of your ability to do what is right."

I stared at him, confusion softening my panic.

"It's not something to be feared, Faye. It is merely a part of you."

I swallowed, reaching into the center of myself where the magic tumbled like a waterfall. "I don't want it."

Kharon's face softened. "Which is probably why you must be the one who has it." He straightened from where he'd kneeled in front of my chair, careful not to bump the still-floating table. "Call it back."

Blinking, I mentally thought of that power, roiling and wild in my center. I wanted it to calm, to quiet.

"Not to calm down, Faye. Your power is not meant to be calm. Merely call it back to its master."

The Drude? I hated that I almost said that out loud. Biting my tongue, I curled my hands into fists.

"You are the master of your own powers," Kharon said gently, stepping away from me, "and many of mine."

"Come back," I whispered aloud, shocked by the immediate crash of the plates around us. Kharon's head moved a fraction, and nearly all the rest of the furniture and items stilled then slowly retreated back to where they had started.

I stared down at the plate, one of them broken. I picked up the piece, staring at the glass. A minor casualty compared to the devastation I had wreaked when I had last lost control without the Drude around.

"I'm so sorry," I finally got out, my voice raspy.

Kharon's hands rested on my shoulders, making me gasp as I looked up at him. His eyes slowly lost their glow until they were back to the ice-blue color they usually were. "Why are you sorry? That was very well done."

"I broke your plate."

Kharon looked down at the plate, picked it up carefully, and then, with a shrug of his shoulders, chucked it over his shoulder. It crashed to the floor, shattering into dozens of pieces now. My hand had flown to cover my mouth, but now I lowered it, staring at him.

"Why did you do that?" This male was quite literally insane.

Kharon sighed dramatically, a broad smile curling his mouth as he looked down at me. "I hated that setting; I needed an excuse to get rid of it anyway. I really should be thanking you."

I snapped my jaw shut. "You're insane."

"And you did quite well." Kharon moved a hand, and the shards of glass whisked across the room to settle in a large wastebasket along one wall. "When I lost control last, I accidentally turned Elon into a hermit crab."

I squeaked, "Your brother?"

Kharon nodded, face solemn. "Father was furious, but my mother thought it was a riot. She spent nearly a week trying to turn him back before realizing that the magic simply had to wear off."

I stared at him in shock, for the first time considering that this male before her, a demon prince, had once been a magical child just like her. No wonder Nicola had been so unphased by Faye's failures. She had already raised five gifted males here. "And in the meantime, she made him up the prettiest tank and shells."

I couldn't stop the laugh then, the humor of seeing Nicola and her temporarily crustaceous son. "You have to be kidding."

"I'm not." His face fell a little. "You can ask him sometime. He might deny it, but I think my mother secretly loved it. My power isn't always the most battle-forward, so my brothers often used their own abilities to drive us all mad. She tried to educate us on all aspects of our abilities, but it was hard when the abilities to throw fire and read minds came in so much handier the rest of the time."

My heart rate continued to slow, feeling returning to my extremities as I considered his words. Did he know Nicola had been my teacher? He'd been to see his father. Surely Justine or Nephesh had already told him.

I wasn't sure why it was so hard to say something, to tell him that it was his mother who had trained me, dragged me from the pit that I'd been forced into before the Drude grew in power.

But while that was only my secret, and a small one at that, the greatest secret rested with Nicola herself. And what would it mean if they attempted to find her? She was gone for a reason. Even I understood that she was safe now. The Drude had said so, and I had to believe him. Otherwise it compromised everything.

To doubt was death.

"It is Nephesh who can throw fire, right?" I asked Kharon, noticing that he'd gone quiet while I thought, perhaps trapped up in his own memories.

Kharon nodded. "And Kadmiel can read minds, though he now chooses not to. He got a very lukewarm welcome home when he accidentally read our father's mind once and tends to use it only when forced to."

I huffed, reaching out with a shaking hand for my glass, which miraculously remained half-full of water. "I'm sure that was a shock."

Kharon shot me a smirking grin. "He didn't speak for weeks, which is a big deal for Kadmiel. And I don't think he could look our parents in the eyes for months. That said, you'll find that he recovered just fine, only to grow into the most pompous of us all."

The water was heaven on my tongue, washing away some of the bitterness as the magic in my chest continued to press at me, begging for another taste of freedom.

"Faye, focus on me." Kharon said.

I nodded, taking another sip. "Nephesh is the asshole; Kadmiel is pompous. What does that leave for the rest of you?"

"Arafel is overbearing. Elon is, in all reality, still part hermit crab, and me..." He shrugged. "Well, I'm perfect."

That time I did laugh, water threatening to come back out my nose as I glared up at him. "You're kidding, right? That's what you think your greatest flaw is?"

Kharon moved around the table and set the dishes there to the right. "No, you didn't clarify, I was just sharing personality traits with you. If you want to know my flaws, witch, I can make it easy for you."

I waited, my heart pounding for a whole other reason. "Tell me."

That mouth curled again. I was helpless to do anything but watch it. That nearly constant warmth in my belly flared high.

"My biggest flaw? It appears that while I have the key to winning a world-altering battle sitting right in front of me, the only thing I can think about is how you might taste when I kiss you."

"Kharon…"

Kharon's eyelids were drooping, the blue of his eyes growing dark. "You are potentially my greatest enemy and yet my greatest temptation, witchling. And every moment I spend in your presence is like…" Kharon's jaw flexed. "Like a test that I'm failing, but I have never been more intrigued by disappointing my family as I am when you look up at me.

The moment grew between us, heavy and hot against my belly. I breathed in, goose bumps rising on my arms as I stared up at him. "I…" I stopped, wondering what the heck I was even going to say. Was I tempted by him? Oh God, I was. I wanted him to taste, wanted to know what it felt like, that freedom to have a male like him. To break every rule. Would it be worth it? It couldn't be, but there was something deep inside that longed to find out.

I breathed out, my entire body tingling. But then, just as quickly as he'd spoken, he stepped away, effectively snapping the tension between us.

"Which is why our first order of business today is not necessarily negotiation. It will be these." Kharon held up his wrist, the nearly invisible chains clanking eerily as he did.

I wetted my lips, attempting to be casual as I felt the resounding clink of the magicked metal on my own wrists. "Does that mean we are going to Tartarus?" I stood, moving automatically to help Kharon reset bowls and miscellaneous items around the room. He paused, a solid wall of warmth at my side.

"Not at all." Kharon's voice was gentle, so soft that I looked up to make sure he was talking to me. "I would never take you there, Faye."

My brows furrowed.

Kharon leaned down, again the scent of sandalwood washing over us. "It doesn't take a genius to recognize that was what frightened you earlier. I may be a demon, Faye, but I'm not a monster. Especially not where you are concerned."

"Oh." I blinked rapidly, looking down at the vase I was holding. "Thank you."

What was this male getting at? I didn't understand any of this. His motives continued to confuse me at every turn. Temptation, I understood. But this kindness… It didn't fit into the picture that I'd carved out for Kharon in my mind.

"The reapers said that he is out at Elysium today. We will meet him there after you are ready."

I nodded, hope blooming in my chest. Elysium was one of the areas that the Drude feared the most. He forbade his Corrupted from going that far into Hell, afraid of what the souls there would do when faced with those who betrayed them.

Master believed that those in Elysium would remain loyal to their current overseers. Why would they want to overthrow Lucifer and his powerful family? They were living the ideal of the Underworld.

Kharon followed closely, a product of the manacles again, as I slipped into his bedroom. A dress, nearly identical to the one I'd worn at the compound in Nebraska, was laid out. While I loved leggings and jeans as much as the next girl, I'd always loved dresses. Had he known that? Or was this a lucky guess? Somewhat awkwardly, I started to try to get the dress on.

"Wait, how do I..." But apparently the soul chains were smarter than we thought and allowed me to slip the dress over my head without snagging. It appeared they only acted like a real chain when they were separated from the other cuff.

Good to know. If we were trapped in these another night, I wouldn't need to hang my arm off the bed again. But hopefully Elon would know what to do and these would be off in a matter of hours.

Dressed, with my hair pulled back from my face in a stubby ponytail, I tapped Kharon to let him know he could turn around. He'd already exchanged his clothes for a new set, the white collar of his shirt contrasting vividly with the tense blue muscles.

Kharon's gaze darted over me, and I could see—or maybe I was feeling—the instant approval. A warm blush spread up my cheeks as he stepped back into the hall, letting me join him in the space. I had the sneaking suspicion he was putting distance between us on purpose.

His casual and bright-sounding, "Ready to go?" left me swallowing the nerves that lurked. "We're going to ferry our way down to Elon's realm."

I jerked my face up to his, but he was already speaking. "Don't panic, witch. It's the only way to get into Elon's realm without raising any alarms."

"Who are we hiding from?"

Kharon took a long breath. "For now? The rest of my brothers. You deserve to be treated like an equal, and because of my—" he gestured at where the manacles' gentle weight rested on my wrist "—idea, I refuse to negotiate the handling of my soul while you appear to be my prisoner. Also, I'm not sure you are ready to meet them all. Subtlety isn't in our genetics."

I thought back to Nephesh, to the massive beast that he'd turned into. Definitely not subtle.

"But the Punisher? Him I can meet?"

Kharon's face softened. "Elon is so much more than the Punisher. Besides, he is probably the smartest male down here, outside of present company."

I huffed but let Kharon lead me out of his house. "What is this place called?"

"The Pier of Kalos," he answered, barely looking back at me as he led me down towards the River Styx. The sound of his bare feet then mine against the dock's wooden slats was strangely soothing. This was real, the sound of our feet, the splashing of the water under us. And if I didn't look too hard, I would think this was just another river.

While my stomach clenched a little at the proximity to water, I didn't feel the overwhelming crash of anxiety like I had when

Paul had dragged me out onto the Drude's vessel. "Did you name it?"

I stepped onto the small boat that waited along one edge of the dock.

Kharon gave a short laugh, his hand on mine as he guided me to a seated position before stepping in behind me. "Has anyone ever told you that you ask a lot of questions when you're nervous?"

I shook my head. "No one has ever gotten to know me well enough to know that." Realizing what I'd said, I turned my head, making the boat rock gently side to side. "Oh, I didn't mean it like that."

Kharon was standing, looking down at me as I felt a red-hot blush crawl up my neck. This male, he was constantly making me second-guess myself. "It's fine, Faye. I knew what you meant. But yes, as someone who is currently chained to you, I can fully attest to your talkative nature."

The boat moved into the current, which was gentle today. I gripped the edge of the boat, gritting my teeth.

"And don't hold back, witchling. If you need to talk to feel better, then talk."

"You can't mean that." The Drude had once told me his Corrupted took turns on my shifts so they would hear me talking less.

"I, for one, can attest to the wonders of chattering while nervous." He curled his lips. "You do remember me carrying you down that mountain, right?"

"You were nervous?"

Kharon laughed up at the Underworld sky. "I was carrying a witch on my back—a beautiful one, sure, but still a witch. I wasn't sure whether I was more afraid you were going to freeze my balls off or make me fall in love, but I was absolutely nervous."

I found myself smiling at him, warmth glowing at the center of my chest.

"And witchling?"

"Yes?"

"I don't say things I don't mean." With that, Kharon turned back to the river, his entire being seemingly relaxed as he steered us towards Elysium and the demon prince that waited for us there.

We hit a small wave. Opening my mouth, I started talking.

8

Kharon

I'd exaggerated when I said she chattered, but I could see it. The way she began to speak when she was nervous then often trailed off or cut herself off mid-question. She was curious, but clearly someone had stomped all over her ability to ask questions.

The Drude had to be at least a part of it. And while I longed to ask her, I needed the time right now to soak up her words and her soft observations while my head tried to make sense of all the emotions that continued to grow at the center of me.

That place that I once believed was where my missing soul was, I assumed there was nothing there, just a gap, a hole, something frozen in time—no longer needed.

So why was everything about her somehow falling straight into that space? Filing it up with her sweet curiosity and soft smiles. The ones that she didn't want me to know she had. But I saw them, the beautiful way they transformed her face from that worried, faraway look, to the stunning, dangerous creature that hid within her core.

I needed to hate her.

I needed to use her.

I needed my soul back, and then I needed to send her straight to Elon to jail. Or better yet, have Kadmiel wipe her mind and set her up somewhere nice in the living world, where she could have a real future. But as I steered us around the bridge, my eyes briefly casting over the Courthouse, where my eldest brother must be holed up, I couldn't bring myself to consider that.

Yet.

I had other options to extend. But I wasn't about to take this poor, brainwashed creature and force her into negotiations while she was chained to me like some criminal. From what I knew, the only bad thing she'd ever done was be associated with the Drude. That was nothing compared to the bloodstains in my past.

"Are we close?"

"Not quite." I pointed across the river where it broadened into a loop. Unlike rivers in the living world, my river carried souls down the River Styx to judgment, and then the newly sorted souls were driven into a fork in the river. One side curled towards the Wastelands and the mountains of Tartarus, where the souls who had been judged as lacking would go. The left side angled the other direction, towards the rolling hills, where the incubus and succubus tribes made their homes and you could see the edges of Elysium. That is where the souls who passed judgement went until the time came for them to return to the living world once again.

"Do you see that?" I pointed to the just visible line of an island splitting the river in two.

Faye straightened, following my pointed finger. "What is that?"

"That island is Elon's home, and just beyond is my brother Kadmiel's headquarters."

"And Elysium…" Faye looked to one side then the other. "Which way is it?"

The boat shifted, and I saw her stiffen. Leaning forward, I pressed a hand against the nape of her neck, both holding her in place and satisfying an urge that I couldn't describe to stay close to her when she was afraid.

"Just beyond those hills. The ground levels, and my brothers have established quite the city there."

"A city?"

"Yes, of course. Elysium isn't just a waiting room. These people are healing, recovering in many cases, from their life. And while they do that, they join our little society."

Faye turned back towards the river. "I'm not sure I understand that. You are good your entire existence, only to come here and find a way to fit in once again?"

I smiled to myself, suddenly eager to show her what my world was really like. I leaned down, brushing my fingers into the river. The souls below us had been quiet, following the current placidly. But at my touch, they gathered, hungry for the soothing that my presence always did for them.

I glanced at Faye to see if she had noticed. Arafel hadn't been kidding. Just having my soul closer to whole was already making my power more stable, letting it grow in strength even as I extended my ability into the souls approaching.

These souls had already been judged by Nephesh. They were approaching the banks, where they would be guided out by a huge contingent of the Brotherhood, who led them to Elysium, where they would stay until they were ready.

I glanced back to see her glancing back and forth from me and then into the water, the water now frothy in appearance as soul after soul brushed by me, hoping for a touch of my magic.

I watched them, their bottomless eyes unblinking as they rubbed against the boat like cats, begging for attention. "It hurts, doesn't it? When they take from you?"

"No, it doesn't, not really."

"How can it not, though? They pull something from you, don't they?"

I considered her words, the fear they thinly veiled. "Only what they need. Everyone needs something, Faye. These souls, they need guidance, healing. There's nothing wrong with taking what you need."

"And what do you need?"

The truth fell from my lips before I could stop it. "To live up to her expectations."

Her head tilted, a single curl escaping her ponytail and falling across her cheek. My hand twitched with the desire to brush it away from her skin.

"Your mother?"

I nodded. "She believed in me when no one else did."

Something flashed across Faye's face, and then she was looking away, towards the shoreline, where I could see the souls rising from the water, their shadowy legs carrying them up the incline to join the white and gold–clad Brotherhood warriors who meandered up and down, creating a funnel directing souls towards the city.

Faye was silent, but I could feel her gaze on me as I directed the boat towards the line of souls, letting it run up on the shore, the sandy ground giving way as the prow pushed onto the dry land. It was a bit over the top, but I didn't want Faye to have to get back into the water until she was ready.

The Brotherhood warrior that was closest to me slowed his hand movements, turning to bow low to me. "Lord Kharon, what can we do for you?"

I stepped out then reached back to grip Faye's hand and guide her onto the shore beside me. I wasn't sure whether it was the soft footing or the sight of so many warriors suddenly staring our way, but Faye's legs buckled a bit, making her step into me. I righted her, my free hand sweeping around her low back to support her as she pressed into my side.

The Brotherhood didn't dare ask, but I could feel their eyes on her. Something rose in me, different than before, a thick sort

of anger burning in my blood. Behind me, I heard the current of
the river move, shift, growing louder.

"Kharon?"

I raised our connected hands as far as hers could reach. "This
is my soul bound. She is under my protection and will not be
touched or approached without her expressed permission."
Fates, why was that last part so hard to say? I wanted to end the
statement earlier, knowing that no one would dare get close
enough to her, but she needed to know that she was in control
here. I had already robbed her of what little she had by taking
her here and then incidentally shackling us together. But this,
this tiny thing, I could give her.

Faye's face turned to mine when I looked back at her.
Something was gathering in her eyes, and my skin shifted,
tensed as I wondered what she saw on my face that made her
look so shocked.

"Understood, sire," the Brotherhood warrior said, his name
unknown to me. "One of us will take you up to Elysium. Lord
Elon is assisting the builders today."

I nodded, watching as a warrior farther down the line
stepped out. He wore the same uniform, but there was only one
gold band around his wrists, a sign that he had not served the
Underworld for as long as the one before, whose wrist bore at
least four.

Gesturing after the warrior, I guided Faye forward. While
she gave the talkative warrior a wide berth, she did not shake

when we passed down the tunnel of white uniforms. "Are these… Are these the Bane?"

"You know about the Bane? I'm impressed," I shook my head, a small smile on my face. "But no, the Bane is my father's personal army. They look…" I glanced at the warriors around us, all very human-looking. "They look more like what you'd like a hellion would look like."

"But these warriors, they are Other, right? They look so normal."

I huffed a short laugh. "You are too. Did you expect to turn into a stooping crone the first time your power appeared? Or perhaps grow some warts and a hooked nose?"

Faye's jaw dropped, and for a moment I wasn't sure if she was going to hit me or burst into tears. When she did neither, she simply closed her mouth and looked back towards the city. "What are they, then? Some kind of Hellish bouncers?"

"Not quite. They are souls who have volunteered their service after coming to the Underworld. Many, like this one we are following, were soldiers in the living world and were not ready to give that aspect up. They are rewarded with a new physical body, powers enough to befit their station, and a home here in Elysium. Those with special talents or preferences tend to end up serving one of my brothers or their realms."

Her nose scrunched up. "Why don't you have any?"

I shrugged. "My territory is more complicated than my brothers'. The reapers are more effective, as they do not often come into any conflict. They are retrievers, highly effective but have no other drive other than that."

Faye swallowed, nodding. But I felt the way that she stepped closer to me, especially as the immense wooden gates of Elysium opened before us.

"It's… It's a real city," Faye said, awe in her voice as she stared at the stone wall that bracketed either side of the door. I saw her eyes rest on the sigil of Hell, the five-pointed star, each peak adorned with one of the realm symbols.

"The moon for Arafel and the dream realm. The scale for Nephesh and his courthouse. The waves, for yours truly. The shield for Kadmiel and his guardians. And of course, the gavel for Elon."

She stepped away from me, and I immediately missed her warmth, the ability to comfort her as we walked. Her fingers reached for the symbols, coming to rest on each before brushing a hand over the bloom of fire at the center. "Hellfire."

"Indeed. My father's symbol."

"Seems fitting," Faye said. "Fire and death together."

I stepped up beside her, covering her hand with my own and pressing it against the metal symbol. "Fire brings new life, witchling."

Faye tugged her hand free, making something in my chest cool. Still, I forced a smile to my lips as I watched her jaw drop. "Welcome, soul bound, to the city of Elysium."

Souls began to appear, passing through the gate, their steps silent. There must've been hundreds of them visibly milling around as if going about their daily business. "I had no idea. I didn't understand—couldn't even comprehend… I thought… " She pointed at a pot against the sod building in front of us. "That's a flower—a real flower."

"It is. Elon's ideas for the Underworld were revolutionary during the early days. Instead of having to expand the city and the Underworld to accept more souls, they live on top of each other within an altered timeline. Multiple souls, living in the same spaces, all on top of each other, but unaware of large groups of the others."

Faye's eyes were wide. "How come we can see them all?"

My brows lowered. "I'm not sure how he does it. I always fell asleep when he and Mother talked about that magic. And honestly, seeing them all isn't helpful today. We just need to see which timeline Elon is on. Hold on."

Clearing my throat, I reached for the connection to my brother that always hummed along my veins—or in Elon's case, skittered. *"Elon? Brother? Can I have a moment?"*

For a long moment, Faye and I stood still, waiting. Then a begrudging moan sounded in my ear.

"Must we do this now?"

I rolled my eyes. *"Always the hospitable host."*

Elon grunted then, a moment later, appeared in front of us. He was roughly my height, a few inches over six feet, but in the comfortable weather of the Underworld, he was dressed in far more clothing, a heavy dark cloak thrown over a thick black shirt buttoned to the collar. Stiff, black trousers were tucked into boots. With his hood up and his arms crossed across his chest, he was the picture of brotherly love as he stared at us.

"What?" Elon's voice was a familiar rasp. Even with his face hidden, I knew he was scowling.

"Oh, hello there, brother. I missed you."

Elon sighed, crossing his arms. "Who is this?"

"My soul bound. Faye, this is Elon, my baby brother. He's the one I once turned into a—"

"Enough," Elon said, his words slicing through the air.

Several souls nearby scrambled away, blank eyes pointed towards their overseer. I could see Faye observing him carefully, her clever eyes on the bandage-wrapped hands that his pose had exposed.

"Why is she here?"

"We're in a bit of a situation. You know, just a little pickle." I held up my wrist, making sure to shake the joint so that he could hear the rattle of the soul chains.

"Are those reaper chains?" Elon said, his voice giving away his interest as he bent slightly at the waist as if examining them. I still couldn't see his face, so I couldn't be sure. I could be sure that he was frowning, because, well, he was still Elon. My littlest brother hadn't so much as offered a laugh since the day he had to fight off the Drude in Tartarus. The very fires that Elon used to protect his realm, our home, had been the same to scar and disfigure his face and body.

I would never forget those screams. And my inability to heal my own sibling, even when he had pleaded for me to do something. Anything.

But I had failed. Now he lived life wrapped in bandages, damned to a life of pain and hiding. My smirk was faltering and sweat rose to my skin as I forced down those painful thoughts and memories. I would find a way to heal him. But first, I needed my power. All of it.

"What if I told you they were? Would that help or hurt?"

"Nothing will help. Reaper chains are designed to stay on until the soul is delivered to the Styx."

I blinked. "I thought they only lasted a day."

"They will last a day in the living world, where the magic is weakest. To be removed here, they must be soaked in the Styx for a long period of time."

I could feel Faye stiffen at my side. Without thinking, my hand reached for her. "How long?"

Elon's hooded head tilted like a giant bird, watching her. "I have not had to try it before." He turned, looking pointedly at me now. "Why am I the only one who knows this kind of stuff? I know you were there when Mother made most of these archaic magical devices."

I leaned into Faye, whispering loudly, "Insufferable know-it-all."

"Condescending attention whore," Elon retorted.

"Ohhh!" I plastered a hand to my chest. "You've cut me real deep. Ouch. Okay, now, tell us what to do again. In detail."

Elon shook his head, turning away with a sweep of his cloak. "Go swimming, Kharon. I would've thought at least you would've tried that by now."

Without another word, he continued back towards the myriad of souls that were milling about. Faye was silent as his dark form vanished into their midst. But as soon as he disappeared, she turned, her eyes full of tears of…laughter.

"Are you laughing?"

"You…he… A condescending attention whore?" Faye pressed a hand over her mouth, but a stray giggle slipped free. "I'm sorry, but I like him so much."

My smile fell, and for a long second, I considered dashing off into the crowd and dragging Elon out here for another discussion, just so she could see how much of a jerk he could be too. Something in my chest struck deep and twisted as I stared at my soul bound.

It was… Fuck, I was jealous. "Of course you like him. He's all dark and mysterious. The hood is really a whole mood."

"I liked him," Faye interrupted, "because he gave us the solution to our pickle, as you so aptly called it."

"That he did. But the method, that's what I'm worried about."

Faye's face fell, and instantly I wished I hadn't brought it up. I should've let her enjoy the moment of peace and humor a second longer. "We can take our time, and I'll make sure you're in the shallows the whole time. The river won't hurt you. Alright?"

She nodded, but I could see the fear lurking. Without thinking twice, I pulled her against me, wrapping my arms around her. Her hands, still by her face, were pinned between her body and my belly, and I could feel the way she pulled in a rattling sigh before releasing it and letting her form sag against mine.

"We'll figure this out. No more chains for you, Faye."

Her sharp intake of breath was the only evidence I needed to know what I was doing was the right thing. Giving into temptation, I let my face drop, pressing my nose briefly against her hair. She smelled like my shampoo, and the thought filled that place deep in my chest with more of that soft warmth.

When she finally drew back, I released her unwillingly, brushing that rogue curl back from her cheekbone as I turned to survey the cityscape. "I don't think we have time for a tour today…"

"Maybe another time," Faye said before her eyes went sideways. "I mean—I just mean… Sorry, that was just what automatically came to mind."

A chill raced down my body. She served the creature who wanted to overthrow my family, to turn souls against each other. To drag the dead back to the living world.

Elysium would never survive that.

She should know that. But I saw it now, the avoidance in her gaze as she wrapped her arms around her middle, looking away from me. We were on two different sides of the same war. And as soon as we could be separated and she could give me my soul, the better.

She could go back to her master.

And I could be the lord my family had always needed me to be.

"Let's go home."

Faye nodded but still didn't look at me. I didn't bother with the boat this time. I didn't want more of her nervous chatter. I didn't want to look at her, suddenly terrified that I wanted more from this witch than the soul she carried for me.

My power rose to the surface, eager and strong with her here. I gathered it up, and utilizing the water in the air, I opened a portal to the Pier. Without saying another word, I gripped Faye's arm and stepped through.

When the ground solidified under our feet, I immediately released her. When she stumbled, I forced myself not to react. Throat tight, I watched her catch herself against a pillar then straighten with an embarrassed look in my direction.

I kept my eyes up, my feet steady moving towards home. My enemy would be in my house.

But I was not letting her into my fucking heart.

***

We had only been gone a matter of hours. So why did it feel like an eternity had passed? I sat on one of the benches that were built into the extensive docking that surrounded Kharon's home at the Pier of Kalos. The sun—or in this case, the strange lack of it—what time it was. Mid-day perhaps? That seemed logical based on how long I'd been awake, but then, I had been wrong about so much today, I wasn't sure what to think.

"Are you alright?"

I turned, watching as Chris, the soul who appeared to haunt Kharon's house, sat down on the bench beside me. Impressive, considering I was still a little confused about the edge of where his body started and ended. Nevertheless, his eyes were more alive than any of the souls from earlier, and when they turned on me, they appeared sympathetic.

The soul chains clinked as I moved over to give Chris more space. My eyes flickered to Kharon who was laying sideways a short distance from us, surrounded in a shimmering arc of his magic, fingers dangling into the river.

He was healing he said warning me with a quirked brow that while he would be in a sort of dreamlike state, he'd sense me leaving.

He hadn't needed to say that. I wasn't running again.

"Rough day?"

I nodded, afraid to speak.

"Do you want me to leave?"

I was shaking my head before he even finished speaking. For a long moment, we sat, staring out over the Styx. Far off in the distance, I could see just the edge of something, a structure. I felt compelled to question him. I needed to focus on learning something. Anything to forget the way Kharon had held me. How it had felt…

I cleared my throat, "What's that?"

Chris glanced towards the horizon. "The Court of Hell."

I nodded as if I knew what that meant. After a moment, Chris continued, "That's where Lucifer resides, where the lords were all raised."

"Oh, right, of course." I stared at the structure. It was tiny from here, but I suddenly pictured a massive castle, swept up in a mix of Gothic architecture and French Regency opulence.

Silence fell between us, my heart aching as I scrambled for questions to ask him. What did you ask a soul that didn't seem horribly stupid? I was tired of embarrassing myself. I was tired of being wrong. But Kharon's words haunted me.

I had done the work.

I was right.

My Master was right.

He had to be. But being here, God it was messing everything up. My head ached from it all.

I licked my lips. "Can I tell you a secret?"

"Of course." Chris leaned in, bumping my shoulder. And by that, I meant it was a smooth, gentle pull of cold air against me as he brushed through my shoulder.

I gasped but tried to ignore the oddness of the situation.

"Wait… First, is he really asleep?" I asked, gesturing at the demon still dozing on the dock as far away from me as possible.

Chris looked over at Kharon, rolling his eyes. "Yes, as close as he gets while healing."

"Okay, uh, good."

"What is it?" Chris asked, his expression worried.

"I knew… I know Kharon's mother. The first witch." I wiped at my nose, which kept running at the most unhelpful times. "She was my teacher."

Chris's pearlescent face didn't react, but his shoulders went stiff.

"I didn't know who she was for years. Only that the Drude had acquired her to teach me. And I need to tell Kharon, but then, what good would it be? She has been gone for years; hidden away somewhere even I can't find her."

I sniffled, ignoring the tear that burned its way down my cheek. "And you know the worst part? I'm so mad at her."

"Why?"

"Because why didn't she tell me? She never explained any of this." I jerked a finger at the river, at the Underworld just beyond. "This was her home, and she let me learn to hate it, and now I don't know what to do."

Chris let me cry silently for several minutes before saying gently, "I'm sorry."

My laughter was broken by a short sob. "Why are you sorry for me? I'm the one who caused his mother to be taken."

"Because you aren't the reason she was taken, at least that I know of." Chris stared at me. "She's been gone far longer than you've been alive."

I wiped at my tears angrily, wishing that made me feel better, but it didn't. I was still so confused, my reality and the consequences of all of this pressing so hard against my chest I could barely breathe.

"Aaand," Chris said dramatically, drawing the word out until I looked at him, his figure even more blurred through my tear-filled eyes, "because she was obviously very important to you too. Having her lie to you may not be the same as not telling you the truth, but it hurts the same."

He surprised me so much that I actually stopped crying, turning to face him as he sat beside me.

He shrugged. "What? The undead can be observant."

I laughed, just once, but something in me felt lighter. "Thank you, Chris."

"You're welcome, Miss Faye."

I swiped a hand across my face one last time, my eyes finding the Court of Hell again on the hilltop. I felt the breeze of movement as Chris left. And for the first time in years, I consider what it might mean if I failed this task. If I didn't give Kharon to my Master, it would change everything. But…only if I went back.

I didn't know what was right, but I knew what had to happen next.

After gathering my wits and every bit of courage I had left, I walked down the dock until I could sit beside Kharon.

And then I waited. An hour—or hell, maybe five—later, he shifted, his eyelashes fluttering open to reveal those beautiful, ice-blue eyes. They focused on me immediately, and I didn't miss the way his hand moved to brush over my crossed legs. "Faye, are you alright? Was I out too long?"

"No." I shook my head. "Kharon, I want you to do something for me."

He rose to an elbow, watching me closely.

"I want to learn how to swim."

Kharon continued to watch me, his eyes taking in every inch of me time and time again until he must've been sure that I hadn't been coerced into this. "You're sure about this."

"I am. I've always wanted to…" I swallowed, preparing for this confession. "The Drude must've known whose soul I carried. He never wanted me to be around the water. I got scared of it. He never let me learn and…"

Why was my throat tight, my words so hard to get out?

Kharon was suddenly sitting, wrapping me up until my body was half on his lap as he held me. It felt so good, so right, that I didn't stop myself from relaxing into his hold. "I'd love to teach you."

"Really?" I said, my voice watery.

"Absolutely. We'll start tonight."

I smiled, feeling the burgeoning joy at asking for something and the simple response of pleasure from him. "Okay."

Kharon's mouth opened, when my stomach suddenly growled, loudly, between us. He blinked quickly, and as if it occurred to him what might be making that noise, he suddenly looked horrified. "After we feed you."

I laughed and started to get up. To my surprise, Kharon didn't release me but rather curled an arm around me and rose swiftly to his feet. Then, and only then, did he let me slide down his front until my feet were safely back on the dock slats.

My heart thundered in my ears as my hands moved down his torso until they were plastered flat to his naked belly. The muscles under my hands leaped.

I swallowed, my nails digging in. I wasn't even sure why I did it, but the surprise that ghosted across his features, just before his ice-blue eyes turned to midnight, was enough to send a bolt of pleasure straight through my core.

"Sorry," I whispered, beginning to pull away. But Kharon's hand snapped forward, pressing over my fingers.

"Don't be," he said. "I can handle whatever you throw at me, Faye. I promise."

Only after I nodded did he release my hands.

I led the way back to his house, feeling the heat in his gaze on my back every step of the way.

And, hell help me, it feel wonderful.

9

"Are you sure?"

"Completely."

"But really?"

"Faye, I literally make the river flow. I won't let you drown."

I danced around the edge of the dock, staring down at where Kharon stood in the waist-deep water. "But…"

"Witchling, we can do this two ways."

My eyes snapped to his, briefly distracted by the expanse of smooth blue skin on display across his body. He'd taken his shirt off, and seeing all of him like this, even after our shower, was a temptation. Maybe I needed this dip in the cold water for more than one reason. "Okay…"

"One, you can walk to the end of that ladder that I just made for you…with my own two hands, mind you."

I swiveled my head to look at the ladder he had indeed made.

"Or," Kharon continued, "I will be forced to get out of this river and come get you."

Unlike his threat from yesterday morning when I tried to run away, there was something darker and graveled in his voice when he said this.

I swallowed then moved closer to the ladder. "I get it, okay. Can you turn around or something?"

"You're completely dressed…"

"I'm going to take my dress off," I huffed, folding my arms.

Kharon's brows rose fast, and I could tell I had surprised him. There was a rather distinctive bob of his Adam's apple, and then, with deliberate steps, he turned to show me his back.

I yanked my dress over my head, tossing it onto the dock and, before I could second-guess myself, climbed down the ladder until the water lapped at my hips. It wasn't warm, but neither was it cold, slowly brushing over my body as I felt the current's tug.

Something touched me, something cool and gentle. I squealed, turning to see a soul, set a little apart from the others who had brushed against my legs. "Oh my God, what do I do about them? Did I hurt her?"

Kharon must've turned when he heard me squeal, because very large hands were at my ribs now, guiding me the last step into the current and holding me there as if he were worried I was about to run for it. Or climb him.

And honestly, he wasn't wrong. The ladder was too far away now though. Climbing him might work. My hands curled around his forearms, holding tight as the soul meandered her way back over to where the bulk of them flowed down the river.

"You didn't hurt her. She probably just felt your power and came to see. They are drawn to me, and therefore you." Kharon's thumbs moved, gentle strokes against my ribs as he held me against his heat. When I looked back to him, I was struck by how close we were. And how good it felt to be this close.

Blinking, I tried not to stare at his mouth. "What do I do if they come back?"

Kharon's jaw tightened. "Push them on, guide them forward."

"I don't know how to do that."

His smile was small, strained, "You will."

Suddenly I felt the sand under my feet and felt his grip lessening. In response, I curled my hands tighter, dragging myself back up against him. "No, wait, don't let go. I thought you were going to teach me."

Kharon cocked his head, a smirk on his handsome face. "I'm going to teach you to swim, witchling, not to stand."

I sputtered but didn't protest this time as he released me and moved back a few steps. The water tugged at me, but it felt almost playful as I stood in the shallows. "It feels nice…"

Kharon nodded, but I saw the gleam in his eye as he shuffled forward. "Good. Are you ready to try deeper? This is about the same depth as the bathtubs at the Court of Hell."

He offered his hand, but I swatted it away. "A bathtub?"

Kharon grinned at me. "We're all tall. You have to have the tubs big, or else none of the good parts get clean." His brow rose and danced a little at his insinuation.

"You are horrible," I said, but the words lacked any kind of real aggression. This time, I let him take my hands, towing me a little farther into the water. But when the water brushed against my bra, I stopped again. Something about the water levels rising close to my neck made me pause.

"Kharon?"

He glanced back. The water was still low on his body, so he probably hadn't noticed. "Ah, yes, sorry. I keep forgetting how little you are."

I snorted, attempting to put my hands on my hips, but the water did nothing to help me, and a moment later I gave up and just stepped away, back towards the shoreline.

"Wait, wait, little witch, it's alright." He stepped forward, stopping me with one warm hand around my hip. I froze, my skin burning at the gentle touch. "Wait. I'm sorry. I shouldn't have made fun. Let's start with the basics."

Glaring, I let him turn me back. "Okay, so what now?"

"I'm assuming you know how to keep yourself afloat."

"You presume too much," I said, my cheeks already feeling hot. "I know nothing."

To my surprise, it wasn't disappointment that crossed his face, just a careful look of determination. "Let's start there."

He started to pull me deeper again, and I dug my heels into the sandy river bed. "Kharon, what are you doing?"

He stopped in an instant, smirk vanishing. "I'm sorry, I need to touch you. May I?"

I looked from his face to the river and back again. Finally, I nodded.

Kharon was on me in a moment. Sweeping me up into his arms, he carried me bridal-style towards the deeper water. "Fates, your nails are sharp. I've got ahold of you. You can relax."

I nodded, nervously twining my fingers around the muscles in his forearm as he moved us to deep enough water that it was lapping against my back, even as he held me. If I were to swing my legs down and try to touch, it would be too deep. I would have to bob to keep my face above water.

I tensed, panic seeping in. My power immediately responded, and I could feel my fingertips get ice cold.

"Easy," Kharon said, tightening his hands on me. "Don't you feel me? Do you feel that I'm right here?"

I nodded, still pushing up against his grip, trying to get closer to his neck, away from the water.

"You're still in control, Faye. I'm only a vessel."

My nails must have been digging into his body, but he didn't complain as he stilled, hovering me over the water.

"Are you ready?"

"No."

"Alright, let me know when you are."

I sat there, rigid and confused and waiting…because why wasn't anything happening? He had said that, but then, was he just going to stand there holding me?

Awkwardness invaded. And I could feel how thick my tongue was when I turned away from him. "I'm sorry. This is so…"

"This is normal, Faye. You are protecting yourself. It's alright. I'm happy to stand here as long as you need me to."

"I'm not heavy?"

Kharon remained quiet so long that I tilted my head up to see his face. He was watching me, his gaze intense. "No, witchling, not at all. You are not a burden. I will happily carry you until you are ready to try on your own."

His words were a trigger. Power raced down my spine until I could feel it coiling and rolling around itself at my core as I turned my gaze back down to my hands. A few minutes later, I felt it. The gentle confidence, the swelling of determination.

I gritted my teeth; my mind was set. "What do I do?"

Kharon answered as if he'd been waiting for me all this time. Which I supposed he had. "Stretch out, your arms to the sides, legs straight, and push your belly to the sky. You are built to float. Let the water carry you."

I immediately jerked to look up at him, "What? Just do nothing?"

"I will be here, but the water, it will hold you."

I nodded, letting my legs slowly straighten. I began to arch back when something occurred to me. "Don't stare at my boobs."

Kharon's voice was comically flat. "Never."

I glared at him a moment before giving up on the pretense of being mad at him. Trying to focus, I let my head fall back, my curls meeting the cool water. Feeling it lap over my ears was stressful, but I could still feel Kharon's hands at my lower back and under my knees. He wasn't going to let me get pulled under or away. I could tell that.

"Am I doing it?" I felt like my spine was completely arched, my legs quivering in the water as I attempted to make them as straight as possible.

"Almost," Kharon's voice said, the sound of it calming me just a fraction. "You have to relax just a little bit. Let it carry you."

"Water doesn't carry; it drags," I said before I could stop myself.

Kharon shifted me, lifting me and making my head rise out of the water in an instant.

I gasped, throwing my arms around his neck. "What? Did I do it wrong?"

Kharon's dark brows furrowed. "There's no *wrong*, Faye. But you are…resisting it. You're not a log that is bumping along down the river." I watched as his hand reached out, swirling across the surface. "The moment you stepped into the water, you were a part of it. Just like them." He pointed to the souls moving through the waves. "Just like me."

"But…"

"Until you accept that, you will be able to swim, but you won't be a part of the river." Kharon's face suddenly grew serious. "Not that you have to be. But your magic is based on water, isn't it?"

I nodded. "She thought so."

"She?"

"My teacher." The truth burned my tongue, waiting on the tip, begging to be freed.

But Kharon didn't seem to want to push it further. "Good, then let's try again."

The rest of the evening, we alternated between Kharon holding me while I attempted to float, and him showing me basic maneuvers for treading water. Both I was able to do, but there was a level of uncomfortableness with the movement of the water around me that I still hadn't shaken. And when the sky above us grew dark and Kharon started to walk me back towards the shore, panic suddenly settled in. I'd been so caught up in our lessons, I hadn't remembered something very key.

"Wait, where are we going?"

"I'm hungry," Kharon said, blue head shining dark in the dim light. "I figured you might be as well."

"No, we have to stay here, until…" I held up my wrist. Still invisible, the manacles were still very present on my wrist.

Kharon's shoulders dropped, as if he'd forgotten the reason to be in the water in the first place. "Oh, yes, right." He held up his own wrist, looking at it in the way that I knew he still felt the tie between us. "Apparently it needs more time."

"Apparently," I whispered, afraid of making my words short as he carried me up to the shore and placed me back on my feet. It didn't matter how gentle he was. I felt the distance between us like a wrecking ball to the chest. More fear filtered in all those empty spaces. "Do any of you know what you're doing? This is insane."

I turned towards the pier and the log-slatted house on the docks before it. I needed to get away. I needed space. God, I needed space. How could I have been so lonely with the Drude and yet suddenly need space so badly I could barely breathe?

I needed this chain off. Even now, as I stormed away, I felt the gentle tug as Kharon hurried to follow me.

"Faye, where are you going?"

"I… I just need a moment."

"Faye, you can't just—"

I whirled, my magic coming into my hands like silk, filling my palms with a spill of water that raced out, curling around me, tunneling around me until I was standing in the middle of a translucent wall of water that filtered and moved and danced around me. Outside of it, I could see the Kharon's shadow, the sound of his voice against the water. He was worried, but he wasn't upset, and finally, there was peace.

I didn't stop when my knees demanded to be bent, when my behind hit the dock slats…and finally, I dropped my head into my hands and wept.

I wept for myself, trapped in a world I didn't understand.

I wept for Justine and Nephesh, who I had both befriended yet attacked.

I wept for Nicola and my inability to understand her teachings.

I wept for the Drude and the pain I felt from him each day.

But most of all, I wept because my life, as I had envisioned it, would never come to fruition. Because even in my darkest, angriest moment, I knew now I could never hand Kharon over to the Drude. I knew what my master wanted, and I could not surrender this demon to it. No matter how crazy he made me.

I would betray my master, the cause, everything. All because of this blue-skinned male who held me like I was made of gold.

And that, more than anything else, was turning my mind to a mess of confusion.

Where did that leave me now? I looked up, watching the water—my water—dance around me. And dance it did. It wasn't angry. It wasn't frosty and covered in ice. It was water, smooth and cool, the remaining light from outside filtering through in a myriad of colors as I finally wiped the tears from my face.

Come to me, I asked, opening my palms once again. Unlike before, the water dissipated, most of it leaping for my palms.

The remaining sank back into the ground under me, revealing a dark-faced Kharon.

His gaze raced over me. "Faye? Are you alright?"

"I called it back, my magic, and…and it came to me."

To my surprise, his face immediately filled with joy. A moment later, his hands were under my arms, hauling me up towards the sky as he spun me around, spun both us around, cawing to the last of the Underworld light in victory.

I laughed, letting my hair fall back, the fears on my face sinking into my skin without another thought. And as Kharon lowered me back to the ground, it was me, not him, who reached out and slid my hand into his.

When those beautiful blue eyes found mine, I smiled. "Thank you."

He brought our combined hand up to his lips. "Tomorrow, we will get these off."

"Tomorrow," I echoed, my heart thudding in my chest as he led me towards his house.

***

Kharon

I had fluffed this pillow roughly ten times now. But there was something about it that just needed more fluffing. I stared down at the offensive bedding, narrowing my eyes. Maybe I needed better pillows. I wanted her to be comfortable. I wanted her to sleep like she was sleeping on a fucking cloud. Because at the end of the day, I'd still failed to remove the chain from her wrist. And she was spending another night in my room as my prisoner.

Fuck.

I hadn't paid attention to timing, but it had to have been hours under the water today. Elon hadn't known the entire timeline, but we had to be getting close. And once her cuff was off, then there would be nothing stopping the two of us from working out how to get my soul out of her and into me.

I knew what she might ask when we did, but…suddenly that didn't seem as important.

"Kharon, you're destroying that pillow."

I looked down, realizing my nails were the sharpened claws that so easily could slip free from my magical hold. I held up my claws, staring at them. When had they come out?

"Sorry about that." I nervously plucked at a feather now sticking out of one of several holes. "Let me grab you a new one." I moved to the hallway, selecting a new one from the stack there, being careful to hold my cuffed arm close to the doors to not drag Faye out of the hall with me.

When I stepped back in, Faye just happened to turn her back on me, dropping the blanket that she'd slung over her shoulders after dinner.

It pooled at her feet, a pile of fabric that captivated me, but only for a moment. Only until I let my eyes travel up her ankles, over smooth calves, long legs, to the slender thighs that my shirt's tail only covered partially. And then of course, the shirt itself was a shoddy attempt to hide the gentle curve of her hips.

"I, uh… I brought you another one," I said, holding the pillow out.

Faye turned, gripping the pillow and taking it from me, but not before I caught a glance at the way her nipples were beaded, pressing against the thin fabric. The resounding throb of need in my groin nearly shocked me to silence.

"Are you alright?" Faye was leaning in, her hand outstretched.

Oh Hades, father below, if she touched me now, I wasn't sure what I would do. My fangs burned; my blood throbbed like fire raced through it. All that time today in the river had done nothing but stoke the demand in my blood to hold my soul bound. To drag her closer. To taste her.

"Yes." I stared down at her so long that she reached out to touch my arm.

"Kharon? You're acting weird. Even for you."

"Sorry." I jerked away from her touch, my mind reeling. "There. Now you should be comfortable."

I watched Faye's expressive face as she observed me. "I was fine last night, you know. No need to worry."

"Ah, yes, of course."

Faye nodded, but I saw something else enter her eyes. Determination. For what, I wasn't sure.

"You know…" She shifted, settling on the edge of the mattress. "You could just sleep up here."

"What?" Why did my voice come out so rough? I cleared my throat, pressing a hand against my chest. "What did you say?"

"I just meant that the bed is plenty big, and I don't take up too much room."

"Oh." I swallowed, suddenly visualizing what it might mean to crawl into bed beside her. I had worked so hard to maintain my senses, to not let my instincts drive me. But this might push me over the edge. "No, I'm sorry. I can't."

"Oh." Faye blinked, looking both surprised and confused the instant before she turned away to pull the blankets back. "No problem. If you change your mind, you know where to find me."

"Yeah. I mean, yes, of course." I tried to lie down on my pallet in a convincing manner, hoping that she bought my nonchalance about the fact that she had offered to sleep beside me. She had trusted me, even that small bit. It bloomed in my chest, a bright, shimmering beacon of hope right where the second half of my soul would go.

I could nearly feel it.

As I curled onto my side, I let my mind wander, but only for a moment, because as soon as my head hit my pillow, shredded as it was, sleep claimed me.

***

Sitting in a chair at a long wooden table, behind which a flickering fire cracked, Arafel stared at me. The entire scene looked like something out of the Court of Hell. "Finally. I wasn't sure how long it would take you to get here."

I glanced down, seeing that I was sitting in a similar chair of my own. "What do you mean?" I groaned. "Fuck, are you dream walking again? I'm trying to sleep."

The Lord of Dreams didn't even blink. "We needed to talk.

"We?" I stared pointedly at the empty chair across from us. "Who's sitting there?"

"Me," a deep voice said, making my gills flutter in irritation as Nephesh suddenly swept in out of the mist that surrounded our scene. Arafel hadn't spent much time on the illusion, and therefore the lines were fuzzy, fogged by the edges of the dream.

Groaning, I forced a smile to my lips. "Great. Lovely to see you, big brother."

"Stop the act, Kharon, and sit down. We need to talk," Nephesh said, sitting down and tossing his shoulder-length silver hair over his shoulders.

I eyed him. He appeared…calm. Relaxed, almost.

I drummed my fingers on the back of the chair closest to me. "Where is your little mate?"

"Home," they echoed simultaneously before looking at each other. They stared and then, almost in tandem, gave goofy, very un-demon-like smiles. I rolled my eyes at just how far gone these two were for their humans.

"Allow me to clarify. I meant the one I haven't met yet—Justine, is it?"

To my surprise, Nephesh, who had never relaxed a single day in his millennia of existence, seemed to sag into his chair. "She's back at the courthouse, meeting with Atlas."

I recognized the name of the Brotherhood warrior who remained lead at the courthouse. Nodding, I pushed on, my jaw clenching and unclenching as I did. The words were difficult, even if I found the sentiment true. "I'm happy for you, brother."

Nephesh blinked at me, obviously surprised. "What did you say?"

"You found your soul and convinced its carrier to stay and be your mate. That is quite an accomplishment..." I couldn't stop myself, "For an enormous asshole."

But instead of rising to the bait, Nephesh ducked his chin. "Yes, I'm a lucky male."

I huffed, indignant, as I looked at Arafel. "Did you hear him? A lucky male." I pretended to shout over my shoulder. "Lucifer, come get your heir. Something is wrong with him."

"Kharon..." Arafel's voice was gentle. And when I looked back, my dream magicked brother was watching me with sad eyes. "We came here to apologize."

I huffed, first sitting and then kicking back my chair, buying time until my eyes stopped burning at his statement. "For what? Being dicks and invading my dream?"

Arafel and Nephesh shared another long look, Arafel spoke first. "Yes, among other things. We were not there for you when you needed us in the living world."

"You mean when my own soul bound trapped me, with my own magic, and threatened to turn me over to the Drude?" I swatted at the air. "No big deal. We handled it."

We, like Faye and I were a team. I wasn't sure why but expressing this seemed more important than the shared shower, the meals, the swimming lesson combined.

"We heard, quite dramatically I might add," Nephesh said, deep voice shockingly gentle, "but we know what it must have been like, to call for us and get no answer."

I had nearly forgotten. Those first moments on board the ship with Faye and the Corrupted seemed like a lifetime ago. Had I called for them? I must have. "It's fine. This doesn't need to be a conversation. I was just acting on instinct and called out. I'm sure you two were off saving the world But I'm back now. Don't worry, I will keep the water running."

"Kharon…" Arafel started, dark head tilting as he looked at me.

"Enough, brother. Enough. I don't want to talk about this anymore." I pushed back, preparing to stand. But Nephesh stopped me with a phase so powerful, I nearly hit the ground.

"I'm sorry, Kharon," he said, his throat moving. "I'm so very sorry." Nephesh kept looking at me, his golden eyes quiet for the first time in decades.

"For what?" I croaked out, frozen in place by my eldest brother's gaze.

Nephesh rolled his shoulders. "For blaming you. When my soul bound died, I thought that all of my hopes died with Anna.

My blaming you, it was stupid, but I was just so desperate. I was scared and took it out on you."

I stared over at him, trying to see him as my brother instead of the figure of fury and wrath that he'd been so often around me.

You're a waste of power and bloodlines.

That's what he'd said.

"Just because you found a mate and haven't scared her away yet doesn't mean that you've changed Nephesh." I settled back in my chair, crossed arms on the table, "You say you're sorry? Sure. I'll believe it when I see it."

The tension in the room bracketed up, but Nephesh only nodded. "That's fair."

I huffed, my eyes burning with a strange pinching pain. "Are we done here?"

"No," Arafel said, gesturing back to the chair I was attempting to vacate. "Sit. Please," he corrected as I glared at him.

I crossed my legs, watching them both. "What else?" I flashed a smile, including my fangs, "I don't think we're to the hug-it-out stage."

"We think there's a pattern with our soul bounds," Nephesh said. "My Justine, she met Faye in the compound. They're both witches, and Justine claimed that Faye is far more powerful than she is, even now, installed here as a princess of Hell."

He'd made her his princess? That made sense, but still the reality of it kicked low in my gut.

"And Lucia, while her powers remain similar to mine, is more powerful than I had pictured a human being. I have some mahrs looking into it, but she has to have strains of other witches inside her bloodlines."

I stared between them both. "Are you saying Mother put our souls into witches…on purpose?"

Nephesh nodded, while Arafel spoke. "We do."

"And why does that matter?" I rocked back in my chair, making the front legs rise off the floor as I stared at them. "It doesn't affect us. Witch, demon, we are all Other but different."

"It may help illuminate who has Kadmiel's and Elon's souls."

Understanding dawned, and I clucked my tongue. "That's fair, but what does it have to do with me?"

"We need to know more about your soul bound. Since she's been with the Drude, she's virtually impossible to track. No family. No history. Hellfire, we can't even figure out which bloodlines she might have come from. Kadmiel can find nothing."

A rumbling growl began, the sound rolling from my chest at his words. "You asked Kadmiel to look into her." The fire of my temper rose higher.

"I asked Kadmiel to hurry the fucking system up," Nephesh bit back, showing his sharp white smile before taking a long, loud breath in and out. When he spoke again, the tone was level once more. "Father is barely holding on to the wards of this world. Any more pressure, and we will begin to fold. Starting in the dream realm, perhaps, but our world is made up of souls and power. One cannot survive without the other. No souls, no power. Even the power from the visiting souls who sleep serve their purpose, even more so now that Arafel's soul resides in the Underworld."

"Your point, big brother?" I gritted out.

"Find out everything about Faye's family. We need it."

I snarled, low in my throat. Nephesh met it, his eyes flashing red. "I don't make the rules, Kharon, but we are each forced to live by them. She could be the key to finding the remaining souls and stopping this stupid war. Don't let your hatred of me stop you from helping your family. And possibly hers."

I stood, a dark cloak flowing over my shoulders. "I never have, Nephesh."

Arafel stood as well, following me to the edge of the mist. "Kharon, wait. We should talk about this."

"No." I stood, braced at the edge of my dream. "It's clear what you need from me. I will deliver, just as I always do.'

And then I stepped into the mist and into wakefulness.

10

Kharon

I jerked awake, my body arching for a moment off the floor in my bedroom. But my arm wouldn't move. It was stuck, trapped, frozen. I looked over, shocked to find Faye's head resting on my shoulder. Her face was smooth in sleep, hands pressed to my chest as she lay plastered up against me.

"Oh," I said out loud before clamping my lips shut.

When had she come down here, and how had I slept through it? Glancing at the window, I could tell it was time to wake up. How long had she been here?

I relaxed, letting the encounter with my brothers fade to the background as her soft, sweet presence against me calmed my racing heart.

One beat, two beats, four, five, six. I counted the beats of her heart against mine, letting the reality of her living self press into me, grounding me in a way that left only a sense of peace and calm in its wake.

My eyes relaxed, my breathing slowed, and for a long moment, I thought perhaps I might fall back asleep. This time without the arrogant, interfering siblings visiting.

But then I felt it.

Something cold.

Sharp.

Close by.

I jerked up, unable to stop from upsetting her this time. I held her close, making sure her head didn't bump against the edge of the bed or anything else as I sat up. When I reached a hand to the door, it burst open. Chris, who must've been close by, pressed inside.

"How many?" I asked, making sure Faye was sitting up by herself before rising and stretching my legs.

Chris threw me an exasperated look. "Only one, but it's a nasty one. If the reapers are correct, she will be close any moment."

"What's happening?" Faye rubbed her eyes but stood quickly, her fingers tugging the shirt back into place down her legs.

"A soul has broken free, likely in an attempt to avoid judgment at the Courthouse."

Her face didn't change. "What do you need?"

"From you?"

I stared at her up and down but growled when Chris did the same. I hated another male's eyes on her, even if it was only my friend. "I need you to stay safe."

Silently, Faye held up the wrist holding the soul chains.

I cursed, putting my hands on my hips as I stared at her. I could let the reapers take the loose soul, but if any were lost, I wasn't sure how much power I could extend to heal and make a new one.

"Okay, new plan." I gave her a long, hard look. "You're coming with me."

She blinked, color leaching from her face. "To chase souls?"

I stepped up against her, admiring the way she narrowed her eyes at me. I bit my tongue to hold back the smile. "Don't you know? That is what you are made for."

Before she could utter another word, I reached down, slinging her arm around my shoulder so that her body followed in a smooth arc until she landed on my back. Panic and surprise were on my side, as she latched her arms and legs around my body.

"Kharon!"

"Which way," I asked Chris, ducking as I passed through my bedroom door and out into the living room. From there I could see the crowd of reapers waiting. My blood pumped hot and thick in my veins at the thought of a chase. After that discussion with my brothers, I was itching for a fight, a fuck, or…well, I'd take this chase as a gift from the fates. I was fastest on water but fast on the ground as well. We would run this soul to the floor. My lips curled. And I would do it carrying my enemy on my back.

"Kharon, I don't have pants on," Faye said it as if I may not have realized.

"I can't see anything."

"But everyone else can!"

I huffed, dropping my shoulders to pass into the front of my house, the docks creaking under our weight as I stared at the reapers, letting their image-based memories filter into my mind. The solution immediately came to me. "Do you see them?"

Faye's chin bumped my shoulder as she looked around. "Of course." Her legs tightened reflexively around my waist.

"Well, they don't see you. Not in the way that you'd think." Pressing my hand against her thigh, I dropped the barriers around my mind, ushering her in and letting her see the strange, black-and-white imagery, nearly topographic, that the reapers sent to me.

"They…" She hesitated, her fingers gripping my shoulders tightly. "They don't have eyes."

"No, they see through a series of magical pulses, much like echolocation. It's how they recognize friend from foe…but they won't care at all whether or not they catch a glimpse of your underwear."

She shifted, nervous still.

"Trust me, witchling, if I thought a single other person might come across us, see you like this, then we would be claiming more than one soul tonight."

Her sharp inhale steadied the primal part in my chest, the part that wanted to keep ahold of those thighs, the satin skin just under my fingers. It would be so easy, to swivel her around, to banish the reapers to the distance. To let my mouth finally touch all those sweet parts of her I'd only glimpsed.

To press up my shirt and find out just how soft she was.

"My lord?" Chris's voice was an ice bath thrown over my head.

I widened my legs, preparing to put her down.

I lowered my voice so only she could hear. "Do you still need to change, Faye, or do you believe me?"

"I believe you," Faye said immediately, her voice also a little rushed.

Nodding, I sent the reapers off in the direction the soul had last been seen. It wasn't until I started running did I wonder if those thoughts, the feel of her skin under mine, had been in *my* head or in hers.

Heat infused my body as I broke into a run, following the snakelike path of the river towards the Courthouse. Questions like that would have to wait.

At least for now.

Once these chains were off, all bets were also.

It took only a short run to catch up with the soul. We whirled past trees and small clearings, crossing into the smooth hills that lined the edge of Nephesh's realm. The reapers grew more frantic, more excitable as we went, darting back and forth across my running path. I wanted to correct them, but my own mind was too consumed with the thrill of the chase to act. It was still foggy, the outline misted by the distance between us and the magic that surrounded the reapers.

"If I have to put you down, stay at my back," I whispered to Faye.

Her fingers tightened from where they held my shoulders. "Kharon, I can help."

"With what? You work for the Drude. Pardon me if I don't think that's a good idea."

My own words surprised me. This was the same woman I'd just held against me, glorying in the idea of having her in my bed. And now… Fuck, I was messing this all up now. My hand slipped back to squeeze her thigh, my mind desperately searching for an apology.

Faye was quiet for only a moment until she leaned higher on my back, looking ahead. "Since when is any of this a good idea?"

I laughed, the sound ringing out around us as I sent my reapers to the sides, wrapping the soul in a smooth arc. I could feel her now, the soft presence of the soul coupled with the bitter, disorientating scent of the newly Corrupted.

The soul paused, the outline clear now as she slowly spun in a circle, observing each of us. She was younger than many in the Styx, maybe in their twenties, the mass of long hair hanging down her back as she snarled at us from a gaping black mouth. I could feel Faye recoil but not retreat. Good. She had to see. She should see what happened to the Corrupted.

This soul, until they had been Corrupted, would've had a chance to be at peace. To be healed. But now…now they were this. Any sign of their former deeds, good or bad, evil or saintly… None of that mattered. They were only Corrupted now. And the duty to keep them from using the Drude's connection and entering the living world fell to my shoulders.

"I have failed you, soul," I told the Corrupted, watching the frantic movements as the female soul considered her chance at fleeing once more.

"Let me go to my master," the soul said, her voice lightly accented. "I have been chosen to live again."

"No," I said as gently as I could. "You have already lived your life, soul. It is time to decide what comes next."

"I have already decided," she screeched, suddenly throwing herself towards Faye and me. My magic reared up, flowing out of me in a spray of mist that sent the soul stumbling back to the center of the space.

I knew what had to be done, but it wasn't pretty. And it wasn't easy. Especially now that my powers continued to waver. I could only hope that Faye's presence here would allow me to do this on my own. Otherwise, I would need to call one of my brothers or, God help me, my father to lend me the strength.

"Let me heal you. Let me take away this corruption."

She skittered away. "No way. I am too young. I don't deserve to die." Her voice was higher with every word, those dark, wide eyes now searching desperately for an escape.

I paused, letting her quiet for a moment before stepping forward. "The cities of the Underworld are full of those who did not deserve to die. But you, you can choose to go to your next chapter with your head held high, or you can choose to fight those who would give you a chance at something new. Something free of all flaws and pain."

Her bottomless eyes blinked, her hands lowering. As we watched, her slender shoulders dropped. "No more pain?"

I shook my head. "No more pain." My heart squeezed as this young soul slowly sagged before us.

The Corrupted soul shook her head slightly, the lines of her form blurring. "But he said…"

"The Drude cannot replace what was taken from you so early. You will live a half-life, a torn life. And when you die again, and I know you will, there are no more chances to join us here."

She shook before us, and I heard Faye's rapid breath at my side. "I hurt for so long. I don't want to hurt anymore."

It was easy now, the magic rising eagerly to my palms. "You are safe here. There will be no more pain. However, no one but you can make the choice about whether or not you surrender to this world. Only then can it heal you."

For a long breath, the soul looked at us, the center of them a churning black void, eating away at the pearlesque coloring. The reapers moved restlessly, and based on the way her body shook, I knew the Corrupted soul noticed. We were running out of time. The need to find her master, her new master, would only get worse from this moment on.

"No," she whispered, shaking her nearly invisible locks. The darkness at her center, the Drude's magical tether, swelled.

I could feel Faye stiffen at my back, small hands bracing on my back. "Why does she look like that?"

I could only spare a brief look behind me. "Like what?"

"She's so dark. She's…different inside."

I raised my voice, hoping the soul could hear my words. "When she served the Drude in the living world, that magic followed her here, corrupting her soul. If she returns to him, she will be either placed in his team, in another human's body, or he will put her to work here, destroying the Underworld from the inside."

"No," the soul screamed now, their voice changing tone mid-shout to something dark and wrong. Even her face changed for a moment. She paused, her hand going to her throat before staring at us again. "That's not what he said. He told me I only have one task, and then I will be given another chance. Then I can go back to my family."

Sadness was gone, fury replacing it quickly.

"He is lying. He is lying to you."

"He told me. He promised me!" the soul screamed again, and then letting loose a strangled cry, she turned and leaped at me.

This time, it wasn't the reapers that moved fastest. It was Faye. She slipped in front of me, the chain on my wrist tickling as she moved. A moment later, she held up a hand, a long sheath of ice shooting from Faye's palm across the space until it could spear the woman's pearl-toned chest. The soul stopped, her voice dropping off as her cry lost power.

Her hands groped for the ice as everyone in the clearing stared at the ice that shimmered between us.

"Stay back," Faye said. Her arm shook, but each word came out clearly.

"Faye," I whispered, putting my hands on the witch's shoulders. "Faye, can I have her?"

"Why? You saw it yourself—she was going to go back to him."

I could feel the vibration, the desperate confusion, rising in my soul, mimicking the half still contained within Faye. Closing my eyes, I placed my hands on her shoulders and let a bit of my magic seep into her. As it had before, it flooded her in an instant, as if she were another branch of my own form.

Leaning in, I pressed my mouth to her hair. "I know you're scared, but you're safe now. She's safe."

Faye shook her head, the silken strand brushing my chin. "She… She's just like me."

"No," I said roughly, watching the reapers as they crept closer. I nodded to the closest one. "She is nothing like you."

"He gave me a job too. A task." Faye practically spat the words as she watched the woman struggle to grip the ice that held her still and impaled. "I'm nothing. Just another pawn."

I growled, deep in my throat. "You are everything, Faye. Let me show you how."

Faye shook her head. "We are the same. This is what I will become."

"Stop saying that." I tightened my grip on her shoulders. "Watch. Look at what you can do."

Opening up the magic to her, I let more of it filter through her body, pushing it down her shaking arms to where the frozen magic split from her hands.

While the ice was beautiful and deadly, it was still water. And I understood water. Water spoke to me, to us. Even now, I recognized just how much alike we were. How uniquely crafted she had been made, my soul bound. My witch.

"Let it pass," I whispered to her. A breath later, her magic allowed mine in. "You can trust me, Faye. Let me in."

She braced herself, her magic resisting it, tight and harsh. At the other end of her ice, the Corrupted soul whimpered, pulling more desperately.

"I'm a weapon. I just hurt people," Faye whispered, "I can't… Oh God, look what I did to her."

"You may have been his weapon, but that's not who you are. Not to me."

Her hands shook, and I felt her turn. I was helpless to do anything but gaze down into those beautiful, tear-filled eyes.

"Show me." Then in a flash, her boundaries dropped. My magic surged in, driving down the ice, making it light up a vivid glowing green and blue. She gasped but held on, letting me use her as a funnel, pouring my magic into her until the healing reached the soul, filling the hollow black center of her with bright glowing magic.

My muscles twitched, my magic desperate now as it came back to me, sliding up Faye's ice with a sluggish crawl before slowly making its way back into me. I tried to pretend it wasn't hard and it didn't hurt, but it had.

I had extended myself too far.

Fuck.

I wavered on the spot, but only for a moment. Faye's hand reached for mine, brushing over my hand with delicate fingers. "Kharon. I… I don't understand."

A swirl of black moved forward, and instinctively I slid my hand lower across her middle and yanked her against me. The reapers were not careful, nor did they have emotions. I didn't want them to mistake her for anyone available for capture.

"Wait, witchling, and watch." My heart was a slow, thudding noise in my ears as I held her. I didn't move my hand, even as hers slowly found my forearm where it curled across her middle, straight between her breasts to where it rested against her belly.

The reapers finally stepped back, a glowing soul chain now on the soul who stood before us. She was so different, her outline clear, glowing a soft frosted tone as she looked from one faceless reaper to the next. When her face settled on us, she ducked her chin.

A bow.

I raised my chin, my body tight. I was still lord here, and now she knew it.

One of Faye's hands left my arm to press over her mouth as I nodded to the reapers. They moved the formerly corrupted soul forward, pressing her back towards the Styx, where she would be carried to safety.

To judgment.

To the end that she deserved.

"You healed her," Faye whispered into the quiet. "That's what you do, isn't it?" She turned in my arms, urgent eyes finding mine. "You heal all of them."

"I am only here to give them the best chance at this chapter in their existence. It is not my job to judge, nor is it my job to punish." I shrugged, my free hand running over my smooth head. "Why not take away their pain?"

Her eyes were searching my face as I spoke, her movements nearly frantic. "I…" She wetted her lips. "I…"

And then she was up on her tiptoes, one small hand on my belly, the other reaching for the back of my neck as she towed me down. For a moment, I knew only bliss, the sweetness and relief of her touch, and then our lips met.

It changed everything.

The moment her mouth met mine, all other thoughts vanished. My panic over the reapers coming towards her. The pain of my magic struggling to rebuild. The anger at the Drude over doing this.

It was all gone. And all that remained was her.

And fuck, she was perfectly sweet. Her lips were soft, warm, parted against mine as she pressed up against me. Her hand flexed on my stomach, the short nails digging in as I growled against her mouth. She jerked back, her mouth already opening to apologize, when I stepped into her again, this time bending at the knees and using my grip on her back to lift her up my body.

This time both her hands went to my head, cupping the back of my skull as my mouth crashed back to hers. My hands moved around the curve of her ass, my cock aching at the perfection of her body in my hands. But it wasn't enough. Not yet. I tightened my grip, lifting her until she understood, wrapping her legs around me as I dragged her purposefully over the length of me that was dying for the heat of her against it.

She gasped, her head falling back for a moment. I took full advantage, my mouth kissing a path down her jaw until I could tilt my head, sucking against that fluttering pulse of her throat.

"Kharon," she whispered, her thighs quivering around my hips.

I relaxed my hold, pressing my face into her neck as I prepared for her to push me away. To come back to her senses.

One of us should, and I didn't really want it to be me.

"Don't let go," Faye suddenly whispered, her throat moving against my mouth.

My heart leaped in my chest, feeling dangerously fragile, as my hands tightened against her, and I forced her up to where she was against my mouth again.

This time, her mouth was parted in a soft gasp, and I used the moment to sweep in, to let my tongue taste her, brushing over the slick heat of her mouth as her body rolled in my hold, bringing every fantasy of what a mate could feel like to light.

I hadn't wanted to know. Because I was not like my brothers.

I did not have a life outside of the Underworld. I was a part of it. A living, breathing element within the process. My mother may have taken my soul, but she knew better than to give me something like this. Like her.

But still, right now. Oh fates… I wanted to forget all of that. I had always told them I was a selfish prick. Now I was living that reality. Because she was the enemy.

She had something I needed.

But I didn't care, because right now, she was the only thing I wanted.

Her magic rose up against mine again, slithering up my arms to mingle at my chest, where the pounding of my heart nearly distracted me so much that I didn't hear the crackling of sticks underfoot.

But I did.

Ever so far away.

The overwhelming desire to hide her away, to curl around her, to turn my back on whomever approached and flee so that we could continue this moment for eternity nearly overwhelmed me.

But I was too weak to take us back through the mist.

I would've had to run.

And I did not run. No matter how weak. And so, slowly, I pulled away, my hand leaving one thigh to brush her curls back from her face.

She looked confused, and I wasn't sure if it was because of the kiss or the fact that I was pulling away now. There was no chance she couldn't feel me against her, the throbbing length of me pressed where it desired most to be.

"Kharon?"

I smiled at her, carefully setting her on her feet in front of me. I raised my voice. "My, my, my… Look what the dog dragged in."

A low snarl filled the air. Faye turned, still in my shadow as she faced the sound.

"Faye," I said with my hand on the small of her back, "we have guests."

11

Faye

I was moving before I even realized it. All it had taken was the flash of red hair that stepped up beside the enormous white-haired male.

"Justine!"

She must've met me halfway, our bodies impacting with a soft noise and a lot of giggling that sounded maybe a bit like cries for me. She was here, in the Underworld, alive, and… Oh God.

I reared back, my magic gathering to me like a fountain as I stared up at Nephesh. The last time I'd seen him, he'd been escaping from the Drude's compound after I had attacked him. After I had hurt them both.

Magic curled around me, darting between Justine and myself as I stood there, waiting.

Nephesh looked different, he felt different, the power thrumming in his veins a darker, thicker mass now. And the first thought I had was that if he were to attack me, there was no way I could fight off a power like that.

"Calm down, girly. He's not going to hurt you." Justine's voice was soft, swinging with the usual lilt of her words. "Right, babe?" She looked back over her shoulder, and to my surprise, Nephesh rolled his golden-brown eyes.

"I'm not going to hurt you, Faye." His eyes moved over me to something just beyond. "Hello, little brother."

Kharon's snarl lit up my insides, as did the protective heat that suddenly stepped up at my back. "Big brother."

"I'm glad you're back. We've been waiting to stop by…uh…in person." Nephesh stepped forward, now even with Justine. Close enough I could see the softened features, the way his hair was neat, clean. Even his odd-colored eyes appeared relaxed.

"You…what?" Kharon was obviously making the same observations I was.

Justine's hand moved, intertwining with Nephesh's as the big demon continued to speak. "We wanted to come by. Father said that you got caught in the time lapse too, but it seemed like you had been missing for weeks. Even before I was pulled into the living world."

"I—yes, I was gone for a short time." Kharon's voice was still laced with suspicion.

"Did the reapers tell you that we had come by?"

That comment had Kharon shaking his head. "They translated only that they received help, not from whom specifically."

Justine elbowed Nephesh. "I told you they wouldn't tell him. But yes, that was us. It was a great way to get to know the Underworld."

"Wait, wait, wait, wait…" I held up my hands, feeling overwhelmed. "How did you get here?"

"After we had that little fight at the Drude's compound, my magic kind of exploded, and we ended up falling through a portal."

My cheeks were burning as she spoke so casually of the time I'd helped to hold them captive.

"I'm guessing Lucifer helped, but he won't say. And then, well, I decided to stay. With Nephesh." Justine looked up at the taller male, her eyes nearly glowing with affection. "He's mine."

Nephesh grunted, but I could see the way his lips lifted on one side.

"And now you just live here?"

She nodded.

My mind was reeling. "How does that work?"

"We haven't figured it out completely. Lucifer and Kadmiel both have theories. But we believe that somehow, since we were chosen to carry their souls, we are, for lack of better words, made of stronger stuff. Lucia—that's Arafel's mate—still has half his soul and doesn't seem to be suffering any of the usual effects from the Underworld. And I've only been here a short time, but I feel like I'm only getting more powerful."

"That can't be true," Kharon said, his brows lowered in confusion.

Justine only shrugged. "Kadmiel thinks it is a fail-safe built into the spell from your mom. But Lucifer disagrees. He thinks it's just the repeated exposure to the souls that we had for so long that's keeping us safe." She leaned in conspiratorially. "I think Lucifer is having a hard time imagining all the things his wife never told them about her magic."

Nephesh huffed, echoed by Kharon making a very similar noise. Both paused and looked at each other before pointedly looking away.

Nephesh spoke first. "We came to make sure you were alright. But also to tell you that the soul exchange does not appear to be a death sentence. Not in the way we once believed."

Kharon was so silent, so still at my side, I could actually feel the tension radiating off him.

Finally, I gave in and I looked at him, knowing exactly what he was thinking. They knew of a way to give him his soul back. No more hiding. No more waiting for answers.

"Just to be clear," Nephesh said, pointing between us. "A moment ago, I thought you were—"

"Busy," Justine said, slapping his hand out of the air. She gave him a pointed look that made my chin drop and my cheeks warm. Had they seen us kissing? Fudge, I had no idea what to do with that information. A few weeks ago, I had told this woman that I hated demons and that I was going to resist all of it, to serve the Drude loyally until my last breath. Then at the first showing of affection and kindness from Kharon, I'd basically thrown myself at the only one I had any power over.

As if sensing the maelstrom of confusion in my mind, Kharon's hand gently touched my elbow. The smallest touch, but it was a cue, a question, an ask. Without saying anything, I agreed, leaning into him.

"Faye and I were on our way back to the Pier. If you'd like to join us, I'd be happy to put you up, but we still have a few things to sort out."

Nephesh was nodding. "The soul chains."

I could hear the rumble of concealed laughter in Kharon's voice as his head bobbed above my shoulder. "Yes, that's something."

"Did you…" Nephesh paused, gaze darting quickly between Justine and Kharon. He swallowed.

Kharon crossed his arms. "Yes, Nephesh?"

The older demon looked curious. "Did you actually go down and ask Elon?"

Kharon's shoulder moved, a shrug, it must've been, but I didn't take my eyes off Nephesh. It was Justine who spoke first. "That's not fair. I wanted to go to Elysium, and you said no."

"No, thief, I said that the souls don't always like me and might opt for torches and pitchforks." He looked at me, his pale cheeks just a fraction darker. "I used to be…aggressive in my judgments, both good and bad. I fear it has created a bit of a divide between the souls of the past and myself."

"Aww." Justine reached up, pressing a hand against his cheek. "Old habits die hard, don't they?"

Nephesh rolled his eyes, but the way his head moved into the simple caress told me everything. He liked her teasing. He liked her touch. And them together… How had I ever wondered how a demon and a human worked? They were clearly one half of the other. A match made in Hell.

I snorted at my little joke, and they all looked at me.

Kharon saved me once again. "Must be some water in her nose. I'm teaching her to swim."

Justine's face lit up. "That's amazing, Faye. Good for you. You'll fit right in here."

"I'm not staying," I blurted out, suddenly feeling hot as all eyes turned to me. I don't miss the strange expression that flies across Kharon's face at my words.

"Riiight." Justine dragged the word out, her brows lowering in a way that said she was desperate to ask more questions.

Unable to stand those bright eyes on mine, I turned mine away, back to my feet. They were bare and dirty.

"Thanks for the offer, but we're going to head home. Long day, and after all this time, I'm still adjusting to sleeping in my own home." Nephesh was refreshingly transparent, and when I looked slowly up at Kharon, I could see his face was creased.

"Yeah, of course, brother. Whatever you need."

"We'll see you soon, though, right?" Justine was obviously less willing to go.

Nephesh intertwined his fingers with hers and raised their combined hands to his lips.

My throat hurt watching them, torment pulling at my insides. But I still managed to nod. "Kharon will bring me," I promised her, the lie bitter on my tongue.

Justine nodded, but I could see the shadow of worry flash across her pretty face before Nephesh tucked her in close. "It was nice to meet you Kharon," Justine said automatically, oddly polite in the awkwardness of the moment.

"Of course, Justine," Kharon answered, and he pressed me to his side as he bowed towards her. "Until next time."

Enormous white wings bloomed from Nephesh's back, every bit as beautiful and powerful as they had been the first time I'd seen them. The heir to Hell's golden gaze found mine, his magic a booming pulse around us. And then he nodded, sweeping his mate off her feet and propelling them forward into the horizon. The breeze from his wingbeats blew my curls back, and I blinked as they disappeared from view.

Kharon's hand was warm on my lower back. "Witchling, are you alright?"

I nodded. "Just surprised, I guess."

Kharon narrowed his eyes. "Why?"

"We were enemies." I pressed a hand against my forehead, the thoughts inside a maelstrom of emotions. "We *are* enemies. Just like you and me. We're not supposed to be friends. We're not supposed to be anything."

Kharon stepped up, and I jerked my hands up. I had to keep him away. To keep him firmly at a distance. Because when he got close, oh God, I couldn't think straight. But that didn't stop him.

Smirking, Kharon continued forward until my palms were flat on his chest. "You and I are not enemies, Faye. We never have been. Not really. Not even when I wanted you to be."

With a whine, I dropped my arms by my side, leaning forward to press my forehead against his chest in defeat.

"I kissed you," I whispered to him, feeling his arms rise to wrap around me. He was warmth and comfort and an unspeakable need. I wondered briefly if he could feel me shake against him.

"You did." His voice was velvet.

"I liked it."

Kharon snorted. "Of course you did."

I groaned, poking him in the side. "What is happening to me?"

His hand rose, stroking over my curls with a caress that made my heart skip a beat. "I don't know. But I promise I'll help you figure it out."

I had to tilt my head back into that soft touch. "Why are you so nice?"

"I'm not. Your standards are just supremely low."

I laughed for real now, slapping my hands against his middle as I sniffled against him. "Get away from me."

He threw me a wide smirk, his white fangs flashing. "Wish I could, witchling, but you and me, we're stuck together."

Sighing, I looked down at my wrist again. "Good point."

12

I never took much notice of what I did during the day. Perhaps because before the Drude came into power and Corrupted began to pop up, my days were fairly relaxed. I floated from one space in the river to another, letting the souls that needed me most call to me and pull me towards them. But now, having Faye at my side as we coasted down the river on my ferry, I was incredibly aware of how boring this all seemed.

To her credit, Faye had remained mostly quiet since we got on the ferry after our little interaction with Nephesh and Justine.

And honestly, I didn't know what to say to her.

Mostly because I was afraid if I opened my big mouth, then I would simply beg her to come over here, to sit across my lap and let me kiss her again.

My eyes shuttered as I thought back to it. How surprising it had been, for my sweet, eternally shocked little human to suddenly become liquid fire in my arms. It had been a very long time since I'd kissed anyone, but with her, it felt as natural as breathing.

And fuck, I wanted to do it again. Forgot this river, forget my needy family. I wanted to curl around her, bask in my selfishness, and let my needs come first once again.

I was not a warrior. I was not even a very good demon.

I was a hungry male, and I wanted this female. Even if she had no idea what that meant. I sighed, maybe more so because of it. I wanted to be the one to show her what it meant to belong to a demon. It made sense now, the way my mother had split us apart, the way she had put us in a match that seemed so perfectly suited to our needs.

Nephesh was fury with fire. Justine was his fuel and his finesse.

Arafel was a dreamer with a human heart. Lucia was logical with a sharp edge.

I was mercurial and cynical. Faye was… Well, Faye was deeply loyal and powerful.

I knew now that this match meant something greater than just the two of us, and I had an unsettling feeling that I wasn't going to like what it was going to prompt me to do. But the bottom line was that our priority was still getting my soul out of her and back inside of me. If I was forced into this fucking war, then I needed to do it with all my faculties. I was not about to embarrass myself. Especially not when my father was watching me so closely. And not when I might have someone worth fighting for.

"What are you thinking so hard about?"

I glanced back at Faye. She was curled up at the edge of the ferry, her fingers tracing lines into the floorboards. "My father."

"The devil."

I grimaced. "Yes, but please don't call him that. He likes it far too much."

She tilted her head, obviously trying to decide if I was kidding or not.

"No, I'm not kidding. I would start with King of Hell or just plain Lucifer. That is his name, after all, when he was…" I trailed off, realizing that was one story we did not have time to get into. I looked back after a breath. "Just before. In all honesty, though, you can call him whatever you want. Fuck if I care."

"I just… I didn't think I'd be here long enough to meet him."

"Good point," I sighed, pressing my oar forward towards the heavier current. "He may not even show his face. But I have a feeling he's been watching us."

Faye jerked. "What?"

"Well, not in his form so much as one of his people."

"Oh, like the Bane."

I shook my head. "They are all too pompous to do anything like that—but wait! You never told me how you know about the Bane. You've mentioned them before, but they haven't been in the living world since the last world war."

Faye's demeanor changed instantly. "The Drude knows them."

I stared at her curls covering her face, hiding her from me as the reality of the situation rose in my chest. "He wants them. He wants to Corrupt them. Doesn't he?"

The silence grew heavy, and then finally, she gave the smallest nod.

I sighed. "Well, he's going to exhaust himself trying. They are all tied directly to my father. They serve no one else, not because they are that local, but because they cannot. They would cease to exist should they leave his side."

She looked out over the river. "There is so much here that he doesn't know about. But there are things, things he knows. Even I don't understand how."

I lowered my brow. "What do you mean?"

"He described each of you so well, like he knew you. He knew so much about the dev—Lucifer's palace. He even knew things about Nephesh, even before we were able to capture him."

Dread filled me. We had always been confused by the same thing. For years, my father suspected spies working against us. Even here, deep in the Underworld. But we'd never been able to prove any of it. But this woman, she knew him better than anyone. "Witchling—Faye, I have to ask. Do you know who he is? Who he really is?"

But she was already shaking her head. "I don't. I wish I did. I've been with him since I was a child, so nearly twenty years now. And in all those years, the only thing that I've been able to garner is that he is far, far older than all the rest of us."

"Why do you think so?"

She looked uncomfortable, one hand clenched against the edge of the boat. "I guess I assumed, but it's because he is no longer aging."

"What?"

"In all the years that I have been with him, he has aged in reverse, it seems. His power makes him young. His age is nothing but an illusion that he wears like a mask."

"What does he really look like?"

She was shaking her head now, her curls flopping around, and I could taste fear in the air, bitter and harsh. "I can't."

But I didn't stop. I needed to know. "You can. This creature, he is hurting my family. He is hurting so many families. Look around, Faye. Look at this world. What is it doing? This is a world of healing. A world of peace and growth and, yes, punishment. But it must stay this way. We must keep it this way. The power of it means nothing to us, other than to give us the ability to continue to govern it. And he wants to take it all for himself."

She shook her head, her voice thick with tears. "No, no, he doesn't. He can't."

"Then explain to me, make me understand why he wants to drain our power, our ability to help people. You can't believe that rubbish he's telling you after this? After you've seen what we do?"

"Stop, Kharon, please." I knew she was crying now, but I couldn't stop.

"No, I won't." Before I could second-guess myself, I was kneeling in front of her, pulling her until our knees met on the ferry floor. "Look at me, witchling. Tell me you think I'm the monster he's made me out to be."

She was struggling, deliberately looking away from me as we kneeled there, the river gently pushing us along. "I don't know," she gritted out finally, still not looking at me.

"You do. You know what's right and what's wrong. You know that you've come here and seen the real Underworld. The real me. Now tell me that you can't serve that creature anymore. Because I'm not the only one who feels this connection between us. And it's more than magic. More than a chance."

The words fell, rushing from my mouth. "This is fate, Faye. I know you know that now. The Drude, he will destroy us, Faye. He is winning this war, unless you give me my soul back. And unless we find my brothers' souls. We will lose not just the war, but this entire world. An entire world destroyed in an instant. Do you understand that?"

"No!" she shouted, her fists landing on my chest, once, twice, pounding there as she finally looked up at me. Her eyes were filled with tears, her mouth open on a cry as she threw herself at me. I caught her easily, holding her against me as she beat her hands against my chest.

"Don't you get it? It doesn't matter what I believe or what I think. He has me, Kharon. He controls me completely."

"But why? How? You are so much more powerful than—" I said, but she cut me off.

"He has my family."

"What?" Her skin was clammy under my hands. Slowly, her fists lowered, and we sat there, my eyes transfixed on the tear slipping down her cheek. "What did you say?"

"I'm the only witch from my family," Faye said, the words sounded sluggish on her lips. "And they may be terrified of me, but I…I love them. If I don't do what he says, then he will hurt them."

"Your family…"

Faye nodded. "Everyone thinks they are dead or something, but after I left, they just went back to their normal lives. They never looked for me or even wanted me back. They were always scared of me and what I can do. But I don't care. It's the least I can do, protect them from him." Her eyes lifted to mine. "You have to know that he kills everyone, Kharon. He doesn't care. I knew even as a child that my deal with him meant that they were only as safe as I could get them. And I haven't been able to find a way out of any of this. But you…" She swallowed. "If I give him you."

Understanding darkens around us. "You can make him stay away."

"Freedom," Faye whispered. "Or the closest to it I will ever hope to have."

"Witchling, why didn't you tell me?" And nothing on Hell or Earth could stop me from sitting back on my heels, gathering her close as I did. Together, we curled up on the floorboard. "I would not have judged you."

Her head fit perfectly under my chin. "What good would it have done?"

"I understand," I whispered into her hair, the silken curls brushing against my nose. "I do."

"I will always be his."

I smiled to myself. She was wrong there. She had always been mine, but I knew my place. And in this case, I was a bargaining piece. The one she needed more than anything else. The knowledge was somehow soothing, as if the pieces of her were suddenly fitting together. And there was a kind of power in being so important to her, even in this way.

Maybe because I'd never been so necessary, so desperately needed by anyone. And as her hands opened, uncurling from fists and sinking into the cloak that I'd thrown over my back, I actually let myself relax, sink into this truth. Because in a world where nothing made sense, she finally did.

"And now, God, I've messed it up so much, Kharon."

"You haven't messed anything up." I smoothed a hand up and down her spine, feeling the soft, slender curve of her body. "We will find a way."

"What?" She pulled back, tear-splotched cheeks turned up to my face. "How?"

"I'm not sure yet, but between you and me, my brothers might be assholes, but they are powerful ones. We won't let anything bad happen to you or your family. Alright?"

She hesitated, eyes searching mine. I held completely still, letting her observe me, letting her check me for lies.

"Do you trust me?"

She nodded slowly.

"Then let's get back to the Pier. We have a plan to make." I started to release her, to move away, when her fingers dug in harder.

"Kharon..." Her voice was a soft caress in the darkening light. And then she was pushing up against me, her grip on my chest barely noticeable. "Thank you," she whispered. Then her mouth was on mine, the kiss so gentle, so careful, so unbelievably precious that it made my heart burn and throb in response.

So sweet.

So gentle.

Fucking fates. What had my mother been thinking with this setup?

I couldn't be trusted with a soul like hers. My own had to be corrupting her with every breath in her chest. I was all wrong for her, and yet like this, with her fingers quivering against me, I couldn't help but think of how good it felt to be needed and wanted. To be vital to someone, even if it was just because of what I could do for her.

She pulled away, hot-pink color bright on her cheeks as she settled back on her heels and watched me.

Instead of saying something and betraying the thoughts that still churned inside of my chest, I dropped my fingers into the water and simply set my magic curling around us, turning up to go against the current.

The magic rushed to my fingertips in a rush, making my heart pump fast in my chest. I glanced to Faye to see if she'd noticed any difference, but she was looking away, watching a reaper patrol the shoreline of the Styx.

But I knew the difference. I felt it. She had my soul, and having her this close, having her touch me…God, it was sending shocks through my system. Reawakening my abilities. Reawakening so much more.

We remained silent, sitting side by side on the ferry until we made it back to the Pier. As I stood, there was a gentle tugging on my arm, a shiver of foreign magic slithering over me as I looked back at Faye. Her face held the same shock, but instead of looking at me, she was staring at her wrist.

The soul chains were gone. Off our wrists, they shone a soft shade of silver at the bottom of the boat. Faye reached for them,

"Leave them," I said immediately. I didn't want them against her skin again.

She jumped, looking up at me guiltily. "Sorry."

"Don't be. I just don't trust those things."

To my surprise, she laughed. "I guess we can shower alone tonight."

"Thank the devil below."

She raised a brow, and I grinned at her. "Old habits."

13

I knew we were avoiding the topic now. Actually, we were avoiding several topics. Starting with that kiss…and ending with the fact that there was no longer anything forcing us together. But now, two days in the Underworld, I found myself struggling to make a plan to leave.

Maybe that was because even manacled, I had been given more freedom and more allowances than ever before.

Maybe it was because of my magic. It loved it here. I could feel it, the way that it settled deeper and deeper into my chest, like some kind of curled-up cat purring there as I watched Kharon make us a simple dinner. I still found myself drawn to stay close to him, as if the manacles had somehow made me more aware of how close I could be.

I rubbed my face as he handed me a fork. I needed to get a grip.

I had to get him back to the Drude.

I would do anything. As long as they were safe. They may not want me, but I wanted them to be safe. I could live out my days as the Drude's witch knowing that my magic had finally done something good. But right now, standing in the kitchen, swirling pasta around my fork, I was having a hard time doing anything other than watching him.

He really was beautiful, the blue skin stretched over all that muscle. That permanently smirking mouth that I knew exactly how it tasted. My throat was so dry, and I swallowed hard, trying to focus on anything else.

Because why did I want to kiss him so much again?

"Is it alright?" Kharon's face went serious, brows lowering.

I nodded, nearly choking on my bite. "Yes, sorry, just distracted."

Kharon nodded, taking his own bite. I cocked my head, watching him long enough that he scowled at me. "Stop staring at me. Even you must know there's no dignified way to eat noodles."

"I was actually just wandering if you ate real food. Don't you just…I don't know."

"Suck the land free of happiness and feast on unicorns and rainbows?"

I blushed, looking down. "Yeah, I guess."

"They're horrible for my cholesterol. Only one unicorn a week."

Rolling my eyes, I gave him my back as I took another bite. He chuckled then leaned into me, bumping my back with his shoulder. "I don't need to eat, not like you do. But I do enjoy it,

especially when there's someone to eat with. There is a quality
to a shared meal that transcends physical needs."

I looked back over my shoulder at him. "Wow. That was,
well, that was actually really beautiful."

Kharon grinned. "I have my moments."

My nose wrinkled, but my throat itched with the need to
laugh. "Can you take anything seriously?"

"Oh, I take everything seriously, witchling."

I took another bite, chewing as I considered his words. I
didn't sense any lies in these words—in fact, it felt honest. More
honest than he had in a long time, I guessed. Perhaps he was
like me, hiding parts of himself by masquerading as this
smirking, carefree male, but in all reality, he was an observer. A
healer. A guide.

My throat grew tight as I considered this truth.

Because every moment I spent here, I got closer and closer to
this male. And it definitely wasn't the soul inside of me calling
for him. It was genuine enjoyment. And that scared me even
more.

I needed to get out of here before my head and heart decided
on different things.

"Kharon?"

"Yes, Faye," he chirped, his voice light as he took a bite of his
own meal.

We still hadn't sat down but were leaning against the counter
in his kitchen. It made it easier to avoid his eyes as I spoke
again.

"I have a deal to make with you."

I heard the sound of his fork hitting the edge of his bowl. Then the soft noise his throat made as he swallowed. "Interesting choice of words there. You know that a deal with me will be unlike any you've made. Even with the Drude."

I nodded. "I do."

"Wonderful, then please delight me with your thoughts. I am on the edge of my chair, figuratively of course."

Fear made my stomach clench, and suddenly that pasta didn't sound as good anymore. I reached over to put my bowl down before I dropped it. "I will give you your soul. But…" Why were the words so hard to get out? "I need you to go with me. To the Drude."

To his credit, Kharon didn't even blink. He simply took another bite, chewing the pasta painfully slow as I watched him. I felt like an idiot, asking a demon prince to sacrifice themselves for the soul they need so much, but I needed to say something. I need to protect my family. Myself. My future.

It all hung in the balance. And maybe, with his soul, he would have a chance to fight back. The Drude couldn't possibly affect a demon like Kharon anyway. Especially since he had his soul back.

"You want me to hand myself over to my family's greatest enemy, and in return you will give me my own soul back. The soul that is required to save an entire world. The very same world you are currently resting in."

My nails bit into my palms as I forced myself not to back down. I pictured Mom and Dad, my brother Alec, all of them safe and untouched by this world they could never survive in.

I could do this. I would do it for them.

And as soon as I had this soul out of my chest, I wouldn't be so caught up in Kharon's story. This connection would dull, nothing compared to the family I longed to protect.

"I know it sounds crazy, and it is. But I cannot give you what you want until I get what I want. And what I want is to—"

"Hand me over to your boss to be made into fish food."

"Kharon…"

"I'm not saying no, just making sure I'm keeping up."

I rubbed my palms over my eyes, regret and fear and self-hate stirring up inside of me in such a flurry that I actually felt my powers beginning to rise up. *Control*, I thought to myself. *I have to get back under control.* Emotion and attachment had never gotten me anywhere but in debt. I couldn't do that anymore.

"Faye…" Kharon's voice had softened once more.

Clearing my throat, I gathered the overeager magic, coiling it tight inside my chest. "I know. I just need a moment. I'm sorry. I just—"

"Faye, I need you to get behind me."

My head dropped, eyes wide open. "What?"

Kharon had gone unearthly still beside me, one long-fingered blue hand now on my side, pushing me, guiding me until I was behind his bulk. My heart thudded in my chest. Now that I wasn't panicking, I felt it too. A presence. Something so much darker than I'd ever felt, and while it wasn't heavy like that of Elon's, pressure filled the air around us.

I looked up, again tucked behind Kharon, surprised to be once again the defended, not the defender.

Words in a language that I couldn't understand poured from Kharon's mouth. A second later, he pressed his arm back to brush his fingers over my forearm. The moment we connected, the language became clear. Understandable. A gift for him to me at this moment that left the hairs on my arms standing straight up.

"I don't care what he said. You aren't allowed to come here. Never here. This was my mother's place before mine, and you sully her magic by even daring to walk into it."

"Excuse me, my lord, but it could not be avoided." The voice was high-pitched, whiny.

"I somehow doubt that very much." Kharon shifted, spreading his legs, as his magic swirled into the air around us. The air chilled, the room dimmed, and I could nearly feel my magic lift from my chest, begging to help him. I clamped down on my control, begging my body to stay in control.

I must've triggered the attention of the other voice now, because there was a ragged inhale. "Oh, did we interrupt? Your father will be delighted that we found both of you at once. You're needed in Hell."

"Leave her out of this. We are perfectly content here."

Muffled clicking sounds filled the room as something dragged across the wooden floors. "Is she so scared of us that she hides behind you? A healer? Clearly, she doesn't understand our ways."

My temper flared, warring with my self-preservation as I considered what might be standing there, at the edge of the suddenly too small room. A demon? Another one? Maybe Kharon's other brother? Or, oh my god, could it be Lucifer?

I gathered my courage, intent on stepping out, when Kharon's voice suddenly rang out, thick with laughter. "You are the one who is confused, Alecto. I'm standing here to protect you, not her."

With a sweeping grand gesture, Kharon released my arm and stepped to the side. "Commander Alecto, please, meet the Drude's witch, and my soul bound, Faye Sullivan."

My magic leaped to my hands before I could stop it, the freeing pulse of power and pleasure warring at the pride in Kharon's voice as he stepped to the side. There, standing in a half-hunched pose, was what I could only describe as a monster. Skin red as blood, with dark shadows ringing their eyes, and dark heavy horns curling away from sunken temples. He must've stood nearly seven feet tall if he bothered to straighten up.

But as it was, he remained hunched, his ebony armor hanging from a muscular but malnourished-looking form. As if he had grown too big for his skin and the muscles had only just barely kept the entire form together. And the eyes that blinked slowly down at me were black as night, appraising me in a moment with intelligence that left my throat dry. When he moved, I saw gold chains shimmer across his chest.

"You are the Drude's witchling?"

My magic flared, understanding the threat in his stance. Kharon moved to my shoulder, cocking a hip with a casualty that I couldn't have pulled off in my entire life.

"I hate that nickname." My heart raced, but I managed to keep my voice steady. "My name is Faye. Just like Kharon said."

The demon—he had to be a demon—watched the undulating crystals of my magic as they swirled in my open palm. "Faye. I'll be sure to convey your wishes to His Majesty."

"See that you do," Kharon said, his tone a bit haughty. "And since we are doing introductions, Faye, this is my father's favorite killing machine, when one of his sons is too busy to do it for him."

"I prefer Commander Alecto, the leader of the Bane." The demon grinned at him, fangs chipped and ragged. "And I love my nickname."

"Gross," Kharon said, bumping me lightly. "Faye, darling, if you wish, you can eliminate him now. He will eventually regrow and limp home to Daddy. And he technically deserves it. He isn't allowed in the Pier. None of them are."

My magic leaped, and I wasn't sure for a moment whether it was me or Kharon calling on it like that. Either way, I felt another surge of pride and gratitude with Kharon's blind trust in my abilities.

Blue light bloomed from my palms before swirling around my fists in a flash that made my eyes burn temporarily. Power, more than I'd ever held before, danced around, tiny droplets scattering, some dropping to the floor, where they hissed and smoked.

The demon's face was surprised, and I saw his clawed feet take a half-step back. "Kharon…"

"Go ahead, Faye. This is your home right now; you are allowed to defend it."

The demon snarled, "You invite the enemy witch into your home?" His teeth were rotting, the smell enough to turn my stomach. "Just because you want her in your bed doesn't mean you should trust her in your home. Fuck her elsewhere—"

Fury laced my blood in a moment, and the power moved, as if acting on its own, streaking between us to strike the center of the demon's chest.

He blinked, a clawed fist pressing against where the blue light had vanished into. After a moment, he looked back at us, obviously confused. Then a slow, ugly smirk curled his mouth. "No wonder he's been hiding you. Your power is pitiful…."

His words trailed off, the hand on his chest curling into a fist as I stepped towards him. The spells, the memories, the natural instincts flowed through me with so much joy that I could feel my mind buzzing with them. But yet, the magic remained happily contained in my grasp.

"Pitiful?" I said softly, stepping towards him.

The demon's black eyes widened, but he didn't move. He couldn't. Not anymore.

"That's not very polite of you, you know. Coming into this house, spewing your hate."

I was so close now I could see the way his body was filling, bristling with my power as it spread through his veins. A poison. A parasite.

Power. *My* power.

I looked back over my shoulder. Kharon was watching, his face full of—oh God, it was full of pride.

My chest might have burst as I turned back to the demon.

"Next time, knock."

And then I threw my fist forward. It was only a soft punch, but it wouldn't take much. Not with what my magic had done. And around my hand, I felt it as his entire form shattered and crumbled to the floor in a shower of ice and unholy snow.

Kharon made a noise of surprise, but when I turned back, he was grinning, his hands on his knees as he stared down at the fine dust of the demon male.

For a breath, I worried I had done something wrong. "Kharon…I—"

But then he stepped forward, gripping my face between his warm hands. "You are absolutely brilliant."

I stared up at him, my magic already curling around me, happiness and pleasure warring at my center. "He will regenerate, though?"

Kharon rolled his eyes, flicking a bout of his own magic towards the dust that carried it outside the Pier doors. "Eventually, yes."

"And then your father will want to see you."

"Us," Kharon said, his eyes on mine. "Yes."

I swallowed, feeling more certain than anything in my entire life. "How long?"

His brows lowered. "Maybe a day."

"Okay," I said, and then I pressed in, letting my body collide with his as his hands dropped to my back. "I don't want to waste it."

And then I kissed him.

Every indecision, every question—hell, every thought I might've had vanished the moment my lips brushed his. He didn't kiss me back. *He devoured me.* His arms tightened around my waist, pulling me up until my toes barely skimmed the floor. His mouth, his lips, his tongue—they tasted me, savored me, teasing and gentle one moment then harsh and demanding the next. My entire body throbbed with the shock of it, the need and want battling away any lingering questions about what this male was.

Because he was mine.

Sure, that was super complicated, and I had no idea what it meant after today. But today, tonight, he was mine.

Tomorrow, we would go back to our assigned war zones.

But for now, right now, I needed to know what it would've been like in another world. Or another life. One where I wasn't ten times the monster he ever would be.

I sank into him, letting him lead me, show me what I liked. And when I chased his slick tongue with a tentative lick and press of my own, I actually felt the shudder race across his flesh.

***

Kharon

"Witchling…" I kept my voice soft, low against her mouth as she pressed her lips to mine. She tasted divine, the scent of her making my eyes nearly roll back in my head as she ground herself on my leg. Sweet, dangerous little thing as she was, this movement, the mimicked need that burned between us, made me ache.

"I'm warning you," I whispered, dragging my lips across her cheekbone, loving the way she panted.

"Warning me? Against what?"

I smiled, reaching her ear and snagging the softness of her lobe between my teeth. "That you can only push me so far, Faye, before you see just how much demon I have in me."

I released her ear with a soft pop, my mouth finding a satin-skinned pulse thrumming just below. Faye whimpered, but just for a moment. The sound cut off as she cleared her throat, her hands moving to my chest.

I thought she might push me away. But not her. "What would a demon do? In this situation?"

"This situation?" I huffed a short laugh against her throat then pulled back so I could look at her face. Her hips still moved against me, ceaseless in their pursuit of release. "The one where you are seconds from having my cock so far inside of you that you'll be dripping me for days."

Faye's head fell back, and my hand snapped up to grip it. The blue of my skin contrasted against the line of her throat. "That situation?"

"Yes, oh God." Faye was blinking fast, the muscles in her thighs leaping. "Yes, that one."

Leaning in, I breathed in huge gulps. She always smelled good, but like this, soaking her panties against me, she was immaculate. I needed more. Needed to taste her. But first, my little soul bound had asked me a question. I tightened my grip on her throat, feeling her body tense.

"If I were to let my demon side out to play..." I pressed my nose against her hair. "This little outfit you have on? I would shred it. Why hide what is mine? I want to be able to see just how wet and slick you are for me."

The hand not on her throat slipped down to cup her ass, urging her higher against me. "And if you tried to escape... Fates, I hope you run for me. I hope you run and tease me with this beautiful, tight cunt. There is nothing I would like better than to take you down, into the dirt, to press your back low, your ass high. So that when I fuck myself into you, nothing can stop me from getting deep, from locking myself inside all that heat."

Faye gasped, her eyes falling shut.

I clucked my tongue at her. "Eyes open, witchling. I want to be sure you're paying attention. Because if you ever want all demon, you will have him. But be aware of what you are bringing onto yourself. Because once you have me like that, with my true nature exposed, there will be no going back. Not when I fuck you. Not when your body milks the cum from my cock. Not ever. So, before you beg for the demon, make sure that is what you want."

She stilled, her movements slowing as her gaze bored into mine. "Kharon…"

Of course she wasn't ready. To be with me and my more primal features was something you built up to. And I was alright with that, for now. My witch was a complicated woman, and while I was intent on untangling her, we would not be starting with a chase through the Underworld. No matter how much my cock wanted it.

Soon, I chanted to myself. *Soon.*

I leaned down, pressing my nose to hers. "But for today, for right now, I want only one thing from you."

Faye's eyes were blown dark, her lips parted as she panted up into my mouth. "Anything."

I hummed a soft laugh. With a quick movement, I lifted her entirely, setting her on the edge of the counter behind us. Faye blinked but settled in as I stepped back and away from her.

"Where are you going?" Her voice was breathy, and it went straight to my cock.

I palmed my erection, loving the way that her eyes immediately dropped to where I soothed myself.

"Not far, witchling." I leaned against the other side of the countertop, just out of arm's reach. "But far enough."

Faye swallowed. "Did I do something wrong?"

My heart leaped to my throat. "Absolutely not."

"Then why am I on the counter?"

I couldn't stop the smirk that slipped over my face. "It *is* where I like to eat…"

Faye's jaw dropped, her cheeks darkening as she glanced down at her still-spread knees.

I interrupted her thoughts. "But there's something else I want you to do."

Her eyes flickered up to mine, waiting. The control of the moment only made me harder. "I want you to show me how you touched yourself. All those nights, stuck in that compound, I know that you've played. Show me, Faye. Show me what your pretty cunt likes."

***

Faye

My heart was pounding in my ears. And I knew Kharon's words should be shocking me. Affecting me, God yes. But shocking? No. Maybe deep down I had always pictured him like this, all that smirking arrogance backed up by a dominant, powerful male.

And yet, I was not the only one breathing hard. I could see his chest rising and falling. The harsh sound of his rumbling growl still rang in my ears.

Show me what your pretty cunt likes.

Eyelids fluttering, I leaned back, one palm on the counter, the other moving to the hem of my dress. I wanted to show him. I wanted him to see. But I also wanted to maintain this power over him, or maybe it was power strung between us, each of us giving and receiving as need filled my core.

"You want to know what I like?"

Kharon's hand was still over his cock, fist rocking gently as I raised my hem farther up my thighs.

"You want to see?"

"Fuck. Yes."

Power. Need. Perhaps they were the same with us. I was drunk on both as I raised myself up, freeing my bottom to rest directly on the counter now. He told me he ate here, the innuendo clear. He wanted to eat me.

My cheeks heated, but not in embarrassment—in awareness of just how ready I had been for him to dive into me. I tried to steady my heart and hand as I let the skirt of my dress rise ever so slightly higher. Kharon shifted, his eyes unblinking. And I knew at that moment, he could see my panties.

I wondered briefly if he could see how wet they were. A breath later, though, I realized it didn't matter. Because I was sure he could smell me. "Good girl," his voice rasped. "Keep going."

I didn't need any more encouragement than that. My fingers slipped up my thigh, moving to the crotch of my panties. And with a quick jerk, I pulled them to one side. Across from me, Kharon jumped too, cursing under his breath when I dragged a finger up and down, over myself.

Moaning, I lingered near my clit, watching as Kharon's body actually shook.

"Is it good there, witchling? Do you like that?"

I nodded, my finger tracing a slow circle, my core pulsing at the nearly painful ache. He had been right. I hadn't exactly been able to date with the Drude around. But this pleasure, I knew how to give that. My body was familiar, the clench of my muscles as I teased my entrance exactly what I knew I needed.

But what I needed versus what I wanted were two different things tonight. My eyes ate up Kharon's beautiful face, the way his chest and shoulders heaved as he stared at me. I wanted him. Maybe I wasn't ready to be chased down. But still, at my center, where the fire of desperate desire lurked, he was who I chose.

My pleasure spiked as Kharon stroked a hand down his cock. "I want to see you."

His jaw ticked. "I'm not sure that's a good idea."

"Why not?" My finger teased my core, the slick sound growing as I stared at the demon.

"Because these pants are the only thing keeping me from being inside you."

I hummed, letting a single finger slip inside. "And that's a problem?"

Kharon's growl was deep. "You push too far."

I lazily fucked my finger in and out of my body, my muscles twitching. "I push exactly the right amount. I want you, Kharon. I want you now."

His snarl was half feral and half pained as he took a step towards me. "I might hurt you. I want you too badly."

"You won't," I assured him easily, moving my finger back to my clit. If he could play dirty, so could I. "We both know I'm powerful enough to stop you."

He still hesitated, fists curled at his side.

"Kharon," I whispered. "I'm getting close. And when I come, I want it to be around you."

"Oh fuck…" The words fell from his mouth, the surprise obvious on his face as I spoke my truth. And while I'd never spoken to anyone like this before, that heady thread of need told me it was exactly what he needed to hear.

And then he was there, his hands on my ass, yanking me to the end of the counter. A moment later, my dress was pushed to my hips and his mouth was on my thigh, then right at my center, licking and sucking as I writhed against him.

"Oh God," I chanted, my hands gripping his head, my thighs rising up to clamp around his shoulders. It was everything I never knew I needed. Kharon's thick tongue danced over my clit, tracing circles there as his fingers pushed their way between my thighs.

"Fuck, witchling, you taste even better than you smell. I would gladly live the rest of my life here." His hand relaxed, tracing where my own arm moved to hold on to his head. He pressed my hand harder against his head. "Push all you want, love. I can hold my breath for a very, very long time."

Moaning, I watched as he lowered his head again, that talented tongue making my breath come short in my lungs as I pushed and pulled him, letting his fingers and mouth torture me to the edge of bliss.

"Kharon, oh God, I'm so close. I…" My words were slurred, my mind a fog within the pleasure.

His mouth pulled away, just for a moment, just long enough to look up at me. "Come for me, witchling, so I can taste how much you need me on my tongue."

And then he slid that perfect tongue over me again, swirling my clit as two fingers thrust deep, curling inside me. My muscles snapped tight, the pleasure coming over me in sharp, barely manageable waves as I came hard against his mouth.

Kharon moaned too, the vibrations flowing over me as I rode each and every clutching wave. At last, I sagged, my hands cramping from holding on to him and the countertop so hard.

He pulled away, his smirk firmly in place as he pressed wet lips to my quivering inner thigh. "Fates below, we should have done that days ago."

I laughed weakly, watching as Kharon straightened up, his body a rock-solid form between my knees. "We can always make up time now."

Kharon's lids lowered, his face softening. "We don't have to do anything. I don't expect—"

I cut him off with my hand over his mouth, "Don't even say it. You promised to…" I was briefly distracted by his thumbs as they stroked my hips. "You promised to fuck me." I lowered my hand.

"If you insist." Kharon smirked down at me, his hands going to his belt.

I swatted his hands out of the way, his soft laugh making my heart dance as I jerked open the lacings of his pants and reached in for him. Arousal and top-tier orgasms did a lot for my typical shy nature, and when my fingers slipped around him, I actually gasped.

But so did Kharon, his head falling back. "Fuck, Faye. We should move—to a bed, to a couch, to…"

I guided his cock out of his pants, my fingers sweeping across the weeping head as I traced my fingers around him. He was perfect. Thick, his skin there a few shades darker than the rest of his skin tone, and God, it was burning hot in my hands.

I wanted him inside me.

"No beds. No couches." I shifted closer, pushing my hips closer to him, "Well, maybe later, but right now, I want you like this. Exactly as you are. Exactly as *we* are."

Kharon's eyes found mine, watching me closely for a long moment, and while I wasn't sure what he was looking for, he must've found it. Because a moment later, his hands curled me closer. One hand under my ass, the other slipping between us to guide the thick head of his cock to my…what did he call it…my cunt.

Even thinking the word made a shiver slip down my spine. But nothing compared to the moment that he leaned in, his mouth on my shoulder, against the slope of my neck. "Be a good girl now and take it all, yeah?"

I moaned, nodding enthusiastically as his hands moved, his hips jerking forward. Thick and hot, he was stretching me with quick pushes. I knew I was mumbling, but I wasn't what I was saying until Kharon's hand moved, covering my mouth.

"The mouth on you, witchling. Stop talking, or else I'm going to come before I get all the way in." He clamped his teeth on my neck for a moment then released. "And we don't want that, do we?"

I shook my head and gasped again as Kharon started thrusting in earnest. Now he was getting deeper, stretching me around him, the thick base of him rubbing against my clit every time our skin came together.

"Perfect," Kharon said. "Just perfect."

I moaned, wrapping my arms around his shoulders and surrendering to the growing heat in my belly. I could feel him growing tighter, bigger, and I knew that this time, I wanted to come with him. "Come inside me," I whispered to him. I wanted to experience all of him.

His smooth thrusts jolted. "Oh fuck, yes. Did you like what I said earlier? About dripping with me?"

I nodded, moaning against his shoulder.

Kharon's movements were fast now, growing harder as one of his hands slipped low, brushing over my clit. "Good. Because there is nothing I want more. You're going to feel me for days. Right here, right in this perfect pussy. Now come, Faye. Come for me."

I was helpless to resist that command. His cock was deep inside, throbbing as I let my head fall back with a cry. This time when I came, I felt him join me, his teeth sharp against my shoulder as he thrust deep and held, heat jerking inside me.

It was everything.

We were everything.

And as I finally relaxed, I felt Kharon's hand on the back of my head, cradling me against his chest. I laughed deliriously into his shirt. It had been perfect, even if we hadn't managed to remove any of our clothes.

"I'm not sure laughter is the reaction I was looking for," Kharon said softly.

"We didn't even undress," I said casually, turning my head with a sigh to look up at him.

His face was relaxed. He looked…happy. It made my heart skip a beat.

He tucked a curl behind my ear, leaning in to press a kiss to my forehead, then my nose, and finally my lips. I sighed.

"Next time, no clothes," Kharon said seriously when he pulled away. "Understood."

With a soft grunt, he turned, lifting me as he went.

I squealed, wrapping my arms around his waist as he began to walk from the kitchen. "Kharon!"

"What the witch wants, the witch gets," Kharon said simply, aiming for his bedroom. "Help me out, darling. You can start with my shirt, while I—" we tumbled into the softness of his bed, his still-hard cock making sparks race down my body once more "—start here."

14

Faye

Hell, or rather the Court of Hell, was not what I'd pictured.

We had approached the enormous Gothic-style castle, surrounded by its armored and guarded walls with extreme caution. But unlike what I'd expected, the gates swung open wide at our arrival. And the multitude of creatures, the demons, that lurked inside the walls kept a respectable distance as we moved towards the large central entry. They were immense, at least three stories tall, the heavy wooden doors wide open. Just inside, I could see an intricately stoned interior. The circular foyer was dominated by a crackling fireplace burning just inside. On either side of the entry, I could just catch a glimpse of a spiraling staircase crawling into the darkness above.

When we passed through the doorway, a demon, this one more gnarled and bent, approached Kharon with a confidence the others had not dared to.

"Lord Kharon," he said, his voice a whispering rasp. "Welcome."

Kharon stopped, his hand moving to my back, and sighed loudly. "You act like this is a surprise. Your games are getting old."

The demon's shrewd gaze was bold, flickering over me with quick, sure movements. Slowly, his mouth curled, revealing razor-sharp teeth. "Is it not?"

Something like a growl slipped from Kharon's mouth. "You sent your dogs to get us, Hiriam."

Hiriam. That meant he was Lucifer's right-hand man. He might act like an underpaid butler, but Kharon had told me that this ancient king turned demon was the backbone of operations in the Court of Hell.

I eyed Hiriam as he moved closer, deeply aware of the way his nostrils flared and moved. A predator, scenting me. That's what he was. I could tell. Even with his weathered body, his soul, the part of him that I could almost feel around him, was dark.

"I did no such thing. You know. Alecto. They do what they want."

Kharon huffed darkly, his hand pulling me closer to his body. I wasn't sure if he was nervous or if he had felt my own anxiety, but either way, I appreciated the gesture.

"Where is he, then?"

My eyes moved past Hiriam's gnarled form and to the walls of the foyer. There was a portrait there, or rather the remnants of one. The canvas torn and tattered, the gilded frame tilted ever so slightly off square. My magic hummed under my skin as my gaze followed what little I could see of the painting. The human-looking hands, folded demurely. The deep ruby–toned background around one edge. The rest was destroyed, hanging in shreds from the frame.

I breathed out, suddenly wishing I could ask about this painting. At why it remained, a destroyed icon among the opulence of its surrounding pieces.

"His Majesty is in the throne room."

"Oh Father below, of course he is," Kharon cursed, rolling his eyes skyward. "Should we have brought gifts to lay at his feet?"

Hiriam hummed, thin lips covering the horror of his smile. "I think you did, Lord Kharon. I think you did."

And then he was walking away, his limp an audible reminder of his body's crooked nature as we moved down the hall under a grand, gold, molded arch set into the dark stone of the castle walls. This room was much brighter than the entry, with windows bringing in soft light from the outside, but with the tint of them, this space was cast in a dull, red light.

I shivered at the power that emanated from every corner. My attention was rapt on the doors ahead of us. I knew two things without a single doubt.

Lucifer himself lay behind that door.

And secondly, living souls weren't welcome here.

Even my magic quivered in my chest as I followed Kharon and Hiriam. "Kharon," I whispered, and he turned his head in my direction. Seeing my concern, his lips curled up, making my heart leap even now. "What…what do I do?"

His hand tightened on mine. "You carry a soul born from Lucifer. You have as much right to be here as anyone."

"Except I'm…"

Kharon was there then, crowding me, pushing my hands down, until his own hands found my cheeks and pulled me in close. Hiriam was forgotten in a moment, only memories from the night before, the feel of his body against mine. That was all I could see, all I could feel as he stood there, holding me.

He dragged in a long, deep breath. "Remember, you are mine," he growled, his breath hot on my mouth. "And I will drown this world in their own tears before I let him hurt you. Do you understand me?"

Hiriam's clawed feet clicked away, the sound of his exit echoing off the walls.

I nodded, equal parts afraid and in shock over his words. Because I was still the enemy. No matter what we were, I knew how they would see me. How they would hate me.

Kharon's forehead bumped mine, his smooth, cool skin in such contrast to my own flushed complexion that I could actually feel the burning in my bloodstream slow. I took a long, deep breath in, letting the scent of him calm me. I felt it washing over me, driving everything else out of the way.

No one could change how this felt.

No one else could understand us.

"I knew it!" A screeching voice sliced through our peace as both Kharon and I leaped at the noise. A second later, a bright-red flash of something nearly tackled me to the ground. Kharon staggered in surprise but managed to keep both of us, and the iron-banded arms around us, standing.

"I knew it," the stock of red hair said as they clung to my middle.

"Justine?" My voice was a rushed whisper.

The girl, who was comically half-bent over so she could wrap herself around me, looked up, a wide smile in place. "Of course it's me. Who were you expecting?"

"You…" I swallowed, blinking as Justine released me and rocked back onto her heels, grinning still. "You're here." *And you still don't hate me*, I said internally, or at least she didn't seem to.

Justine raised her hands wide, spreading them as she walked in a small circle. "I am. Home away from home." Her nose wrinkled. "Well, technically this is Court, but it's close to home."

Home. She said it so easily.

To the side, I could see the lurking shadow of her mate appear. Nephesh went to his brother's side, extending one forearm, which Kharon gripped with his own. "I'm glad you came, brother," Nephesh said, his voice soft.

His eyes moved over Kharon's shoulder to meet mine. To my surprise, it wasn't anger I saw, but some kind of mutual respect.

A breath later, the big demon, the heir to Hell, bobbed his head to me.

A curt greeting, but still a greeting.

My throat ached. I had tried to kill him mere days ago. And not just that, I had hated myself when I had failed.

And yet, somehow we stood here, on his home ground, and I was unafraid.

"Who am I?" I whispered, unable to stop myself.

Kharon and Nephesh glanced my way, their demonic hearing giving me no chance to explain before they both glanced at each other and then back to me. Nephesh approached, cutting between Kharon and me, and I could almost feel Kharon's frustration at that. Wait. I *did* feel Kharon's frustration. It seeped into my mind like a drug, making my fists curl. But still, I didn't move. I didn't back down, even when he contacted me and told me that this male, this demon, would destroy me.

"Nice to see you again, Nephesh," I got out, feeling the warmth of Justine at my back. My tongue felt thick, awkward. "I, uh, I wanted to—"

The doors behind us suddenly swung wide open, revealing a long, slender aisle between two crowds of people.

And at the very end, there was an enormous throne, the dark onyx of it a swirl of darkness in shadow. Everything inside me begged to stay away. This was the core of the Underworld. The heart of this land.

The place that the Drude wished more than anything else to find.

To infiltrate.

To destroy.

I had to get out of here. I had to. Everything in me screamed to run away, to keep myself as far from the male at the other end of that aisle. My instincts, my training, and my heart all aligned as one thought.

I could not be here.

"Oh God, Kharon, I can't." My nails were digging into the skin of his forearms, but I didn't care anymore. If only he understood—that this was a bad idea, the worst idea. If I knew any more about this and the Drude made me tell him, I—Oh God, I would destroy everything. That's what I did.

I whimpered in my throat as Kharon's palm warmed my back. "It's okay. I'm right here."

No, no, no. This male, he didn't understand. He didn't see the danger I was putting him in. The danger I was at my core. I could not be trusted. "No, there's something else. I can feel it. I can't be here."

Kharon's lips brushed over my hair as I plastered myself against his side. The comfort was nearly painful as my body and mind warred with the need to be as close to and as far away from him at the same time. I knew he could feel me shake. But he didn't understand, he never would, that everything I knew, everything I was, was owed to their enemy. And he could take it all back, take me back in an instant.

"Shh, witchling, I have you. And I know you're nervous, but trust me, this is the first step in getting you and your family safe." Kharon's body curled around mine, blocking me from seeing the throne. "It's just you and me in this."

My shaking lessened, but I still couldn't bring myself to move. Because yes, he was right. But there was more I needed to explain. To help him to understand. God, I hated this. I hated it so much.

"Kharon," a thunderous voice boomed through my head, and my entire being seemed to freeze. As for Kharon, he simply sighed.

"Let's go, soul bound," Kharon whispered.

"Kharon, wait—"

"It's alright, Faye. He can't hurt you," Kharon said, turning us back to the aisle, his expression stony. "I won't let him."

Him hurting me was the last thing on my mind.

I walked down the center aisle, feeling the dark eyes of the various creatures, magical and mystical alike, that stared back at me. All I could do was stare forward at the throne, now graced by a tall, muscular form that was dressed all in black. A shining crown upon ebony locks.

The Drude's ultimate enemy.

The male I was meant to destroy.

My teacher's mate.

Lucifer.

Kharon's hand on my arm felt like fire and ice as I stopped before the King of the Underworld. Lucifer's eyes, chips of opal and granite, met my own. A hand at his side raised. Black flames danced across his skin, the magic not a showing of power, but more of a casual reminder. He was a master here.

I was nothing but a bug he intended to squash.

But instead of raging back, my magic banked, lurking low and cold in my gut as I stepped in front of the devil himself.

"The Ferryman's soul returns," Lucifer said softly. His face, it would've been handsome in another place, another person maybe. The high cheekbones, the sharp cut of his clean-shaven jaw. Even the black suit he wore like tailored armor screamed authority. He was king here. The only king.

The one king.

The one that I was meant to destroy.

Lucifer rose, and briefly I considered running. I would explain to Kharon someday, maybe, if I ever had the chance to. He would understand then. Maybe he would even forgive me.

Kharon stepped between us, his body a living shield. "Father, this is—"

"I know who this is." Lucifer stepped down before us, his magic receding into his flesh as he moved to stand in front of Kharon. To my surprise, Lucifer turned to me, and his face…it softened. Just a fraction, but I could almost feel it in the way the entire world around me relaxed.

"You were Nicola's student," Lucifer said softly, only for Kharon's and my ears. He had known? How could he have known? Kharon stiffened at my side, the connection in my chest chilled as the two males waited for my response.

Heart thudding loudly, I nodded.

Lucifer huffed, his chin dropping. "Come here, daughter," he said, stepping forward and wrapping me in a hug.

Daughter? What was happening? I held my breath, shocked as Lucifer's immense form bent to wrap his arms around me. His touch was gentle, his hands barely brushing my clothing as he leaned over me. When he straightened a moment later, Lucifer sent a sharp look at both Kharon and Nephesh. "We have much to discuss. Are you both staying?"

Nephesh wrapped an arm around Justine, the former thief's face serious as she observed our interaction. Those sharp eyes missed nothing, and I knew I was due to explain more to her at some point. But…not right now.

"All of us are," Nephesh responded, his tone dry. The demon's resting bitch face was in full force as he waited for his father to respond.

But Lucifer only sighed. Reaching out, Lucifer brushed a hand over Kharon's shoulder. "Grab your brother."

Kharon pressed a hand against Nephesh's shoulder, and in a blink, we were in a different room. Lucifer dropped his hands from our bodies as soon as we entered the large room, a fire burning in a hearth large enough to park a full-size car in.

Justine seemed comfortable here and immediately moved over to make herself a drink from the cart by the door. I almost followed her, but I'd not had a lot of chances to drink in the living world and wasn't sure if Hell was the right place to begin breaking in my drinking habits. In fact, I knew it wasn't.

"What is this? Something you can't say in front of your fans?" Kharon said, his voice rough, but I could feel the residual worry lurking.

Unsure of what to do, I toddled over to the fireplace, content to look at the dancing flames while I tried to compose myself.

"There are many things I can't say in front of the creatures of Hell, Kharon, but I did this for our own good. We need to talk."

Kharon seethed, "We know. You sent your dogs to the Pier."

To my surprise, the devil snarled, the sound so sinister that the little hairs on my arms actually rose. In my periphery, I saw Justine freeze, her drink halfway to her lips. "Alecto went to the Pier?"

Kharon's brow furrowed. "Yes, but..." He paused, the silence growing around us. "It's handled. Faye and I spoke with them."

Lucifer growled, "And then?"

"Faye turned them to ash."

Lucifer's growl cut off with a surprised noise. "What?"

I swallowed hard, feeling the eyes from the entire room and unsure how I felt about that. Finally pulling my eyes from the flames, I faced Kharon's family, cheeks warm, nerves rattling.

"He didn't knock," I finally squeaked out, my mind supplying the only fact it was capable of remembering now.

Lucifer looked at me, then to Kharon and then to Nephesh, as if confirming something. Then the King of Hell moved to stand before me.

"You turned my demon to dust?"

I nodded jerkily. There was no denying it.

There was a soft hiss, and a deep voice cut through the tension in the air. "She dusted Alecto. Well, shit, now I like her even better."

"Hello Arafel," Kharon said begrudgingly, turning from me to look at the immense figure that had walked out of a shadow that I was quite sure hadn't had a demon in it a few moments ago. But I didn't dare move. Or breathe. Lucifer still stared at me like he could see straight to my soul. Maybe he could. The thought sent a fresh wave of anxiety rushing through my veins.

Was I dark inside? Like the Corrupted?

But as the dark, winged male approached, a wide smile on his handsome face, I couldn't take my eyes away from the devil before me for more than a moment.

There was hugging happening, I thought, not all of it consensual, as Arafel dragged Kharon into something that was a blend of a hug and a tackle all at once. In all the ways that Kharon had described his brothers, he had not described them as huggers. I was more than a little confused. But as I caught a glimpse of Kharon's face, I recognized the look of surprise in his features too.

When the brothers all separated, I shivered despite the fire at my back. The panic, the shame—residual, I was sure, from the Drude's teaching washed over me.

I felt wobbly, reaching out to press my hand to the mantle as I took a deep breath in. The moment my fingers brushed the mantle, my mind cleared, and a familiar scent, a familiar feeling, one I hadn't felt in years, filled my chest. It was tight, making my breath tumble out of my mouth as my fingers curled against the stone.

"You feel her."

I gasped, pushing away from the fireplace as I opened my eyes. Lucifer was there, his dark eyes eagerly taking in every inch of my face. "What?"

"I do too." He reached up, pressing his palm against the carved stone. "This land, this place, it was built with our magic. It was inevitable that our memories, traces of us are everywhere."

Swallowing, I leaned back from him, but my feet wouldn't move.

"You see, Nicola and I are the Underworld's foundation, the skeleton." Lucifer glanced back at Kharon, Nephesh, and Arafel. "Arafel is the brain, Nephesh is the heart, Elon is the voice, Kadmiel the eyes."

My throat was desperately dry. I was shocked the words even made it past my lips. "And Kharon…"

Lucifer leaned in, his lips curling, "I think you already know the answer to that. I know that the Drude does. Why else would he choose you to bring my son's soul to him?"

I should be running, fleeing this male, but instead I was fascinated. "Choose me?"

Lucifer huffed out a short breath. "You are indeed more powerful than most witches we have seen in generations, but your bloodline, that is what makes you important. It's why he has kept you alive all these years, especially when the others last mere weeks."

The others, I wondered, my heart skipping a beat. What others? My mind raced to countless answers. But one kept emerging, the simple conclusions that Lucifer believed that Drude had other witches. I knew of none, other than Justine, and when Nicola had been with us. But that was, oh God, years ago. There was no one else. I was sure of it.

My chin rose. "He kept me alive because he needs my power. We have an understanding."

The devil nodded, stepping back, a hand rubbing his jaw. Black fired danced up and down his fingers. Was he even aware of his magic anymore? I craved that control, that casual use more than my next breath.

A dark chuckle slipped from the devil. "He does need your power. But he also knows exactly who you are to him."

I shake my head, my curls brushing my cheeks as I dispel Lucifer's theory. "No, he didn't, not until Nephesh and Justine. Then he must've realized how important the soul bond was."

"Did you not find it odd that he also wanted to capture Justine?" Lucifer looked over at Arafel. "He also pursued Lucia, Arafel's soul bound, now mate, which forced him to bring her here. I've been told he cares for you, as much as a creature like him can. And I'm glad that your bloodlines kept you safe, but you must understand that you were a bargaining chip. One of several options I'm sure he was maintaining. You are quite lucky to have been the one with my son's soul."

My head was throbbing, but I went on shaking it. I was his weapon, yes, but a bargaining chip? No. I had been chosen because of my power, my abilities. "No."

"Yes, Faye Sullivan, daughter of Tanya and Silas. Granddaughter of Alina, great-granddaughter of Thomas. great-great-granddaughter of Helene."

Nausea bloomed in my gut. Those names, they felt right. They felt familiar. But it had been such a long time since I left my family. I'd wanted to look into my bloodlines. Nicola had supported me, since understanding bloodlines often helped understand what skills and magics would be most aligned with my magic. But the Drude…

Oh God… I swallowed hard. The Drude had stopped my research, telling me that he was my family now. That I had hurt him by looking.

"Stop, stop, stop. Why do I know that?" Justine said, suddenly appearing at my side. Her fingers found mine, cool and soft.

"Because, witches…" Lucifer strode away, finding a highbacked char and folding his form into it with a loud sigh. "I may have been a fool to lose track of the most powerful lines, and I'm intent on remediating that."

"Lines? Bloodlines? Does that mean we are related?" Justine pointed between herself and me.

"Not necessarily," Lucifer spoke again, his fingers steepled. "But it means that while we are getting closer to finding the two remaining missing souls, or at least the lines who should carry them, the Drude has been looking for far longer."

My mouth was dry. Too dry.

"But that's not why I brought you here today." Lucifer smiled, crossing one long leg over at the ankle. "I brought you here to broker the deal that we all know is coming."

Dread was a living thing inside me. "What?"

"My son. While the Drude may plan to use you as a bargaining chip—" he smiled slowly, cool eyes moving to rest on Kharon "—I have my own cards to play. Beginning with what happens if I give your master my son."

15

I stared at my father. "What did you just say?"

I felt Arafel's bulk settle in at my back. And to my surprise, Nephesh shifted away from our father, more towards me. Were they… Were they stepping up for me? My mind couldn't linger on that now, so I focused on my father's face once more. His eyes, cold as ice in this lighting, rested on me. And when he spoke again, the words were slow, spoken with such exact care that I couldn't misunderstand him again.

"Tell me, Faye Sullivan, what would the Drude do, should I choose to hand him over my son?"

Nephesh's rumbling growl made the hair on the back of my neck rise. But for the first time in my memory, it appeared that he was growling *because* of me, not *at* me. My magic unfurled in my chest, slipping down my veins in a cool caress.

Whatever my father was up to, it could not be good. Faye's eyes were wide, frightened, as she looked between my father and me.

"What are you talking about?" Arafel asked, his voice a dark hiss. "You cannot be serious."

Lucifer sighed, his hand flipping over on the arm of the sofa, a crystal glass, half-full of amber liquid appearing there. He slowly raised it to his mouth, taking a quiet sip. "I'm deadly serious."

The room was silent, and I could see the fear shining out of Faye's petite form. I wished she weren't so far away. But she remained on one side of the room, with my father's form at the other. As if sensing my train of thought, Arafel's hand went to my arm, holding me in place.

I didn't fight his grip. Not until I knew what was going on. And there was something so comforting about my older brother's hold. Together, he stood with me as we watched our father, waiting for him to explain himself.

My father tugged on the cuff of his shirt, his movements short, sharp. "Do you know what will happen if the Drude captures the remaining soul bounds?"

Silence. I could feel Faye's heartbeat, or maybe that was mine. Since yesterday they had become muddled in my mind. Not one, not even two really, just the sound of us beating loudly in my chest.

Undeterred by the growl from Nephesh, Lucifer continued, "He will find a way in, and he will move across this place, corrupting everything we have made. He will release Tartarus into the living world. He will, in a way, eliminate death. The circle will break—life, death, it will lose all meaning. And us, our family, any good we have ever done or ever could do, will be undone. And it will happen in an instant. The Drude is not just powerful. He is aided by those who are wield their own abilities. Like your witch here."

Now I was certain, it was my heartbeat that raced in my chest. We each knew what the Drude intended to do, but hearing it, the words falling from my father's mouth, something like a blade slid against my ribs, making my breath come short in my lungs.

Lucifer stood. "If I could sacrifice myself, I would. But sadly, that will not work. Even if I wanted to transfer my power to you all, I cannot do it without your mother." There was a heaviness in his words now.

"So, you will sacrifice one of us instead?" Nephesh's words were clipped. His mate, the redhead, acted like she might move towards him but was conflicted about leaving Faye. In the end, she simply widened her stance at Faye's side.

"Not one of you," my father said to my older siblings, moving towards the three of us. A panther stalking its prey. "Him."

I sighed. Of course he was pointing at me. Of course he wanted to sacrifice me. I was the unwinged, unextraordinary middle child. Losing me, losing my healing, would affect almost no other aspect of the Underworld. Souls did not need healing to be judged. What I did was an act of hospitality that no one else would even consider.

I did not change minds. I did not judge souls.

I drove the fucking boat.

My head lolled back, feeling the smooth, slick mask that I was so much more comfortable in slipping back into place. Everything Faye had said to me last night, it didn't matter. She would be gone soon, and apparently, she was taking me back to serve as a proverbial sacrificial lamb.

"Ah," I crooned. "Of course it's me. They requested the most attractive sacrifice, eh?"

Faye took a step towards me, but I stopped her with a laugh. "My head will be the prettiest trophy on his wall." I swept my hand back at my brothers. "It's not like you can send them. This one is too busy being your assassin, and the other one is too obsessed with making tiny baby demons… I don't have any real purpose here. It makes sense that I go."

"Kharon…" Arafel's voice was low.

I shook free of his hold. "When do I leave?"

Father stared down at me, his face unreadable. "I'm not sure."

Hiriam knocked on the door, appearing at my father's side the next moment. "Dinner is ready, sire."

"This family is insane," Justine said, and I barked out a short laugh.

"You're just now noticing?" I swung my arm around to pat Arafel's shoulder, hard. The black leather of his armor was cold against my palm, and the male underneath stiff as a stone. "Let's go, everyone. Let's eat and discuss handing me over to our greatest enemy. Hurrah."

Faye

"That was…not what I expected."

Kharon sighed, coming to lean against the door jamb between his room and the washroom, eyeing me with shining blue eyes. I had slipped out of my dress and stood in just my panties and bra, but the way he stared at me, it heated my blood, made the blood rush to my cheeks.

"What were you expecting?" Kharon said, moving into the room, his eyes still locked on me as I watched him appear in the mirror behind me. Slowly, his head bowed, his mouth pressing a kiss at the base of my neck and shoulder. I shivered at the contact; his mouth was utterly distracting. Even now.

"I don't know." I rolled my head away from his touch, feeling the heat of his hand as his arms slipped around me, pressing an open palm against my belly and pulling me back against hot, hard male. My mouth opened, but I'd forgotten what I was saying. I reached back, finding the smooth skin of his cheek then up over the back of his neck, loving the way his kiss against my neck deepened, sharpened as his teeth grazed me there.

I would have a mark. The thought made me arch my body against him. His free hand stroked down the side of my body, petting me, letting me arch into his touch with a soft pant.

"You're trying to distract me," I whispered, my voice breathy and soft.

"Is it working?"

I smiled, and then my mouth was open again as his free hand rose up, smoothing over my ribs then rising higher to cup my breast. My hips moved against him, wishing I could get more friction as he held me in place. "Yes," I confessed softly, wishing that he'd roll his hips against me like I remembered. I wanted to feel the smooth movement of his muscles under that blue skin.

My magic hummed, the borrowed soul tightening around my heart as my belly turned molten. I knew I was begging him with everything in my voice. But what had just happened… Lucifer's declaration, followed by the silence of that meal. We needed to talk about this.

"We need to talk."

Kharon hummed then pulled his mouth away, eyes glowing green looking down at the mark on my shoulder for a long moment before he met my gaze in the mirror. One side of his mouth rose in that trademark smirk, and his head tilted.

"I know we do, witchling. But right now, right here, all I can think about is the way you feel wrapped around me." His hands tightened on my skin, the graze of his claws a delightful reminder of who and what we were.

"Kharon," I whimpered now, watching my chest rising and falling ever more quickly as his eyes skimmed down my form in the mirror.

"Shh." His breath brushed by my ears as he ran his nose against my shoulder. "I don't know what is coming for us, for me. But let me pretend, just for a time, that I'm everything in your world. That I'm the beginning and end. And that I would be lucky enough to have you every day for eternity. That I would deserve it."

"Kharon—"

"No." His hand swiftly moved from my breast to grip my throat, holding it firmly in his palm. "No more talking. I don't want apologies or explanations. I want you to come on my fingers, my name on your lips… I want you to watch every second of it, knowing that it is the peak of my existence to share this moment with you."

His hand tightened, his face pressing against my still-pinned curls. "Nod, witchling. Nod, and I am yours."

I was already nodding, my head bobbing as Kharon's body suddenly crowded mine against the sink's marble vanity. The hot length of him pressed against my ass as his hand left me. A moment later, my curls were tumbling free, brushing my cheeks as I watched Kharon bury his nose in them.

"The way you smell…" His lips turned up for a moment, a true smile, before sinking into that smirk once more. "It makes me hungry." His eyes found mine in the mirror. One long, black-clawed finger found the front of my bra, where the lace was delicate, stretched between my breasts. "Don't you dare look away, witchling."

I shook my head, and the hand on my throat disappeared. The other danced across my collarbone, the sharp claw dragging, hovering just above my flesh as he watched his hands in the mirror. Transfixed.

And then his claws ripped down the center of my bra, setting my breasts free in the bright light of the bathroom.

I gasped, and my hands lurched upwards, cupping the small mounds and holding them as I squealed. I opened my mouth, intent on scolding Kharon for ruining my bra, but those long fingers turned my face to his, and he leaned over me, his immense form curling around me so that he could kiss me. His lips were fierce, demanding, and after a moment, I gave up on hiding from him, my hands dropping as I reached back. I needed to hold on to him. To make sure he was really there, that he was really real. That any of this was.

His skin was hot against my fingertips, his shirt magicked away somewhere that I couldn't see. I sighed as his tongue licked into my mouth. He was as confident and bold as ever, and I was instantly drunk on the taste of him.

When he pulled away, I followed him, my mouth still searching for his as I did.

"Kha—"

My words died on my tongue as fingers found my now exposed breast, his thumb brushing over the peaked nipple. "You never hide from me, Faye." His words were a dark rasp behind me.

I watched him in the mirror, at the reverence on his face as his other hand entangled with my arms, making room to slip down my belly, and under the elastic of my panties. There he paused, watching me, his eyes flaring so bright and brilliant that it made my heart lurch.

Beautiful. Patient, even in his desperation.

"I don't want to hide anymore," I finally whispered, and he rewarded me by pushing his fingers under the satin.

"Good girl," Kharon whispered, his nose pressing into my hair as he slipped low, those strong, thick fingers brushing over my clit with a light pressure I would've never guessed him capable of. "Such a good fucking girl for me." His shoulders were moving, his breath coming faster as he breathed me in.

Between my thighs, his fingers were bold, stroking, teasing the slick line of me, brushing over my clit before pulling back and making my hips writhe and jerk against his hold. And I knew he was fucking enjoying this torture. But secretly, I was too, loving the way that he held me in my wildest moments, when my magic churned in my blood, my frustration and arousal burned together like gasoline and an open flame, wishing that I could revel in it.

In him.

Just before I almost gave in and begged, before I pleaded with him for more, he broke, two thick fingers pushing deep inside, making my body clench and spasm as he invaded me completely.

My eyes fluttered.

"No, little witch, you look at me. You watch what we are together."

My eyes snapped up to the mirror, lazily watching as his wrist moved slowly, dragging long fingers from inside me and then pushing them deep again. I gasped, my body pushing back, begging for more. My hips were completely at odds with my mind as I stared at him, watching the way his forearms bunched and tightened, the pale blue of his skin twitching as his muscles worked.

"Do you see," Kharon purred in my ear, his hand still working inside me, "that you may carry my soul, but you have ownership over the male too. That I would gladly step aside, let you bring this world to its knees, and still, beg you to let me do this one more time."

I was a panting mess, his words making my thighs shake as his fingers thrust deep, holding, testing, and brushing across the slick heat of my body just as his hips bucked against me from behind.

"Do you see?" Kharon asked again, his eyes devouring me in the mirror, his thumb brushing over my clit once, twice, his grip on me the only thing keeping me standing.

"I see you," I cried out, my orgasm crashing over me with the power of a hurricane, making my body shake. I went limp in his arms as wave after wave of pleasure was wrung out of me. His fingers still moved, curling and rubbing, dragging every bit of pleasure from me as our eyes held in the mirror.

"I see you, Kharon." I realized I was saying it again, my hips still rising up and back against him. And it's as if my words broke him too. His free hand was fumbling, his movements jerky and rushed now.

"I can't… I thought I could, but I can't. Fuck, Faye, let me in. I need to feel you like this. I need to know…"

And I was nodding, pushing my still-quivering body back against him. Searching for that fullness I now needed more than my next breath.

"I just need to feel you, only for a moment. Fucking perfect, Faye. Oh shit…" His words died off as he pulled his fingers from me, yanking my panties to one side, and then he was feeding his length into me, tunneling deep as my body stretched and quivered against him.

"Oh, oh!" I was shaking against his invasion, my body suddenly ratcheting up against the vanity, the heat in my belly expanding as Kharon seated himself hard and deep inside me. "Kharon!" It was too much. I was going to lose control again.

His hands were guiding me, slowing me down until my belly leaned against the vanity, and his hips ground against me. And his mouth, God, he was praising me. His words were falling like rain over us, telling me how good I was. How perfect I felt.

And I absorbed it all, feeling the way my body was primed to fall apart all over again. But this time, I wanted him with me. I watched him in the mirror, his beautiful body, the way his pants were still high on his hips, only the thick length of him freed to fuck me.

He was pumping into me, cursing in another language, his hands moving to my hips, both holding me back and dragging me closer. He was watching me, his eyes glued to where he moved inside me, but I couldn't stop watching him.

I waited until his attention was back on me, his thick body twitching deep inside me. Then my mouth finally found the words I'd been holding on to for so many years. Never dreaming that they meant anything more than the words to a song.

The fantasies and dreams of a child who would always be alone. But I wasn't alone anymore.

Softly, I sang, the words, the magic curling around us.

Deep in the heart, behind the dreams of a witch, lies the hope of the one who will make your soul whole. They'll be loving and kind and always be faithful. The one who makes my heart beat ever on.

I groaned, tightening my body as the magic settled into us with a cool brush down my spine. "Now, you're mine."

Kharon's head fell back as he let out a roar of pure primal pleasure, his hips stuttering to a halt deep inside me, pressing as far as he could go. Heat bloomed and my orgasm followed, my body clenching around him, milking him of everything.

My eyes finally closed, and I fell forward onto my arms, my lungs dragging air in as I felt gentle hands smooth down my sides.

"Now?" Kharon let out a soft chuckle. "I have always been yours."

I smiled. Perhaps he was right, but now the truth was inked onto our very souls.

And I wouldn't let anything bad happen to him.

Not now.

Not ever.

16

My knees shook. "I don't think I can do this."

Kharon's grip on my hand never wavered. In fact, it probably tightened, the smooth, strong muscles there entangling with mine like we were two pieces of the same puzzle. Like we were more than two bloodlines tied together by magic.

We were designed to find each other. Destined to change everything.

But this part, this surrender. It felt horrible—wrong in every way. Everything in me screamed to push him away, to beg him to stay safe. To go hide in the Underworld, far away from me. In another life I would stay, risk the wrath of the fates and the Underworld. If it was the payment for more time with Kharon, then I would gladly pay it. I would rather spend weeks here, at his side, than years in my old life. But my family, they didn't have a choice. Because of me, they would always be in danger.

But this would change it all. It would give me my power back. The leverage I'd always craved.

"You can and you will, witchling," Kharon said, his voice calm, serene. "Because you have to."

"No." I stepped back, towards the Pier, where I knew Chris and a small flock of reapers would be watching. "This isn't right. I can feel it. This isn't how the story is supposed to go."

Kharon tugged me back, his grip steady as he ducked his head to press his forehead against mine. "What did we decide?"

My lips were quivering, and I felt the hot press of tears along my eyelids. "That the Drude won't hurt you, not until he finds the other souls."

"Right, good girl. And?"

"And by then we will have a better plan, and we can bring you home," I finished in a rush. Arafel and Nephesh were with us. We'd already established a plan to speak in our dreams with Arafel. I knew they were just as upset as I was with this plan. Kadmiel and Elon had both been occupied and unable to speak, but Arafel assured me that family always came when needed.

"And?" Kharon said, his lips curling as his eyes slid shut.

"And…um…" I bit into my bottom lip. "I'm not sure… What did I miss?"

"And…we decided that you, Faye Sullivan, are the best thing that will never be mine. And that you will live your life as only a demon might, without preamble or apology."

My lips quivered. "I don't think we decided that yet." Because it felt like he was saying I would be doing it without him.

Kharon hummed. "I'm fairly sure we did. In fact, I'm a hundred percent sure we did."

"Liar." My arms slipped around his neck at the same time a tear slipped down my cheek.

"Never," he whispered. "Say it back to me, Faye. Promise me." Hearing my name on his lips, in this moment so far devoid from the passion-filled sounds from the night before, it was eerie. A realization that our night together might be the last time we would have that opportunity.

"Kharon—"

"Say it back to me." His fingers were warm against my sides. "Please."

I pressed harder, feeling my heart pull, the muscle overextended. "I-I—" I was going to say can't. But instead, the words fell between us, shattering my heart in one swoop. "I promise to live my life without preamble or apology."

"Good girl," Kharon whispered then pulled away to press a kiss to my forehead. "Now, there's just one last thing."

I tightened my hold on him, waiting, dreading the passage of time before we would be back in the living world. And all of this would be gone from me forever. His hand raised our intertwined fingers and released me, opening my fingers wide until I was pressing my hand to the center of his core.

"What are you doing?" I asked him, my gaze rising to meet his intense glowing green eyes. His features were calm, the mouth I loved kissing so much pulled tight.

"You are going to take my soul, Faye."

"What? No way. To live without a soul," I gasped, trying to jerk free of his hold, "is worse than death. You will wither, Kharon. Wither. I can't bear the thought."

"I have survived worse. And while I know that some demons and witches can see souls, it doesn't appear that the Drude can. My soul is safest with you. With the other half."

But I was still shaking my head as the power under my hand pulsed. "I can't do that."

"You can, soul bound." His hand pressed against the back of mine. "Let me help you."

His hand glowed softly, the pressure increasing as his magic slowly seeped into my flesh, and then beyond, into the core of his being, where the soft, glowing center of his soul waited.

I clamped my eyes shut, suddenly unwilling to see this male gift the most vital part of himself to me.

Kharon hummed, his chest rising and falling in a deep breath, and then his soul was there, filling my hand with a heat and power that left me speechless. I pulled my hand away, eyes fluttering open. The golden globe balanced in my palm, Kharon's hand carefully holding mine underneath.

I stared at it, at the way it moved, shimmering and flowing in my hand like a dancing drop of liquid fire. "It's beautiful."

Kharon let out another breath. I looked up, into his now-dimmed eyes. "You are beautiful, witchling."

"What happens now?"

His gaze was so intense on me, I couldn't look away. Kharon stepped into me, our bodies as close as our gathered hands would allow. The warmth of him, the comfort, the familiarity that had bloomed so hard and fast between us, coupled with the weight of this—this responsibility---it left me breathless. "Now we do what is best, for the people in our lives we love the most. Even when we don't like them."

My lips tried to curl, but another tear streaked down my face. With one movement, I pulled his soul into me, pressing it deep in my chest, where I always felt him, where I hoped I always would.

The soul slipped into my flesh, disappearing in an instant.

Kharon's mouth did lift then, a wide smile slowly unfurling until I couldn't help but smile back. "All this time, we couldn't find a way to take our souls back, but giving them away, that part seems so simple." He dropped his hand from me, curling his arm around my back. "Keep it safe for me. Keep *them* safe for me."

I nodded. "Of course."

And then, his magic reared up, water pulling from the river by our side and whirling around us. I had thought we would go up the river to the living world like he said he had done before. But he had been worried about leaving the theoretical door open behind us if the Drude's spies knew we were coming.

A portal it would be. Similar to how Arafel traveled, he said, we would use his magic to slip through the magical barriers that kept the Underworld safe and hidden. And just as the water began to curl in on us, I closed my eyes, trusting Kharon to once again carry us to the other side. Only this time, we were heading back to the enemy, not away from them.

When the water receded in a rush, I didn't let go of Kharon. I held on tighter, feeling the sunlight from above burning hot on my shoulders. There were voices and people and presences all around us. But I didn't open them. Not until I heard him.

The one voice I'd been so desperate to hear and, at the same time, so terrified.

"My, my, my," the Drude's voice drawled. "I had almost given up hope that you had survived your trip to the Underworld."

Kharon's hands slipped down to my forearms. He squeezed, urging me to look up at him. I did, and suddenly I felt it for the first time. Because there was something more there, something I had missed. In his stunning aquamarine eyes, there was regret.

And an apology.

"She brought me here, just as she promised," Kharon announced.

I could feel the eyes of the Drude and his Corrupted all around me, but still I couldn't look away from him. From my soul mate. I waited, watching. Fascinated by the unfamiliar expression on his face.

"As she did."

"Make the deal," he whispered to me.

I coughed, the words caught in my throat. "You promised me that if I brought you Kharon, you would leave my family alone. That you could never hurt my family ever."

The Drude's rattling sigh was somewhere behind me. "I had almost forgotten about that."

Kharon's fingers were like iron in my hands, the water that had brought us here curling around our ankles. I stared at it, unable to look at the Drude as I spoke again. "Promise me. Or else…"

"Or else what, Faye. What will you do to me?"

I nearly cowered, but I had changed. I knew my own power. And here, for the first time in our relationship, I held all the power. I had the card he wanted most. "Or else I take him to someone who will give me what I want."

The Drude snorted. "The kitten does have claws, then." He moved around, circling behind Kharon so that I could see he was draped completely in a black cloak and hood. Not a single part of him was showing.

"Fine. You give me Kharon, and I promise I will leave your family alone."

I swallowed, my pulse hammering in my ears. "Permanently."

The hooded head inclined to me. "Permanently. I swear it."

I could almost feel the promise in the air as my heart thudded. It was done. They were safe. Two goons, probably the most recent replacement for Paul's crew, stepped forward to grab Kharon. But before they could touch him, he leaned in, leaning down, his lips at my ear.

"Without apology, witchling."

And then he pushed me. And while movement was a surprise in itself, I was not prepared as the magic that had dripped around our ankles suddenly flew upwards. The water enshrined me, and a moment later, I felt the earth drop out from below me.

"Kharon!" I screamed, my entire being flying against the water walls that swirled around me. They did not give. Not until there was footing back underneath me. Then the waves fell slowly. Maybe they realized that I needed an extra moment to look around to realize that I was back in the Underworld.

That Kharon had sent me away.

That it had been me he was keeping safe one last time. My hands curled as I fell to my knees, slamming my fists into the ground. Magic skittered away from me, lighting up the dark earth that I was kneeling in.

Pain.

Grief.

Fury, but not at him. For him. That I had even asked him to do this, I should have known that he was only going along with this because of me.

I screamed, the sound so unlike me. I had never been allowed to shout; I'd never been allowed to scream. But now, the sound ripped out of me, like a wound opening in my chest, the manifestation of the pain of everything I'd endured, before Kharon, and now, after Kharon. Two bookends in a chapter of my life cut devastatingly short.

The silence that fell after I ran out of air was thick. Rocking back on my heels, I had only one solution in my mind.

There would be no *without Kharon*.

I was going to get him back. I stood up, looking around at the strange dark world that I found myself in. I was enclosed, the arched ceiling above me dark with onyx stone as stalagmites hung from the tops.

A cave.

I'd never been in one, but I could recognize it easily. The problem was, I only knew of one place that caves were even mentioned in the Underworld. And I couldn't be there.

I just couldn't.

A soft, rasping noise sounded, then another.

"Who's there?"

More of those noises. Oh God, not noises. Those were voices, speaking words. Words I couldn't understand, maybe because I wasn't supposed to. They belonged to creatures no longer living, not just dead though.

Damned.

I was in Tartarus.

And worse again, I had a sneaking suspicion that I was in Trypa. The home of the most dangerous and damaged souls. The ones even Elon could not resuscitate.

"Oh God, oh God, oh God." I dropped to a crouch and shuffled forward to the edge of an outcropping, where I leaned over, hiding. Why had Kharon dropped me here? He couldn't have meant to. But that didn't change anything.

I was here, curled up in hiding, holding the soul of Lucifer's son, while the worst souls imaginable roamed around me. My eyes clamped shut as the noises came closer. There was no way they wouldn't see me. And there was no way it was Elon making those noises. This was something else.

I hummed to myself, my mind a hurricane of thoughts as I considered my very pitifully limited options. I could stay here, hiding here, waiting to see what came around that corner. I could hope that Kharon meant to send me here for some other reason.

Or I could… I swallowed; I could fight. The soul at my center flickered, bouncing in my chest. My power throbbing there as I closed my eyes tight.

Kharon would fight his way out. He'd have a killer catchphrase and unleash himself upon whomever or whatever dared come his way. And he'd do it smirking. I was his match. His soul bound.

His soul…mate.

I would not waste this chance he gave me. I had to get back to the Pier, or maybe Lucifer's Court. I wouldn't die here, waiting to be devoured by some soul deemed unfit for return to the living world.

I was chosen. Not just for him, but by him.

"Fuck this," I whispered, the curse word foreign on my tongue. But even the wound of it brought a small smile to my lips, my magic blooming in my palms. Kharon would be so proud. I had to tell him that I'd finally branched out in my vocabulary. I thought he'd be proud of that.

Taking a long, deep breath, I tucked his soul in deep and let my magic flow. It eagerly filled my chest, flowing down from my core, filling my very soul as I stood and faced the direction of the echoing voices.

I was no demon. My eyes didn't glow. But I was a witch and, finally, maybe for the first time, damned proud of it. Because a human wouldn't have been able to save my mate. A witch was designed for war. For fighting. For defending what was ours.

Stumbling, I stood, the ground under my feet uneven. I was in the midst of a craggy rock cliff, and by standing I was able to see a soft glow of red. I moved towards it, my magic simmering with every step I took. The rocks hurt my feet, but it was a simple pain. I released my grip on my power, letting my magic heal me as I moved higher and higher within the tunneling cave. Staying as far as possible from the edge of the path and the darkness just beyond. My skin was hot, not from exertion but something else entirely. A warning.

I straightened in a flash, cringing at the light that flickered in from an opening just beyond. But there were other figures there, moving closer.

"And who, exactly, are you?" The voice was barely human—in fact, it couldn't be. It crawled across the space to my ears. I watched, heart hammering, as a dark shadow moved down the trail towards me.

Fear and fury blended as I stared at them. I did not have time for detours. Kharon was waiting. With every bit of arrogant swagger I had taken on from my mate, I called out a response. "I am busy."

"Busy," the shadow laughed, the sound grating on my ears. "What an interesting little thing you are. I wonder how you taste."

I turned, my power manifesting, blooming from my palm as I faced the voice. The magic lit the space, illuminating the male standing there. The hairs along my arms rose as I stared down at them.

They were human male. Or had been at one time. But his human form was no longer complete. Entire patches of flesh left bright red and blistered. As if they still actively burned. His shirt was charred and hung off a skeletal frame. The arm that reached towards the rock wall at his side was his only one.

The other, nothing but a scarred stump.

Horror tugged at me, my mind screaming to get away from this creature. To run far away. The pebbles under my feet bit into my heels as I backed one step away, putting more distance between the creature and me.

"Stay there." My voice shook, but not as hard as my hands did.

The soul was unphased by my command and moved forward, his eyes wide and hungry. "Carefully, pretty lady. That edge is a sharp drop. Don't want you to accidentally fall over it."

"Who are you?"

The creature tilted his head, blood dripping from his ear to his shoulder as he did. "Me? I no longer have a name. Not really. Damned. That is what I am. No need for a name here." He took a shuddering step closer.

"I said stay back." My power flickered as my emotions wavered.

His foot returned to the earth as he heeded my warning. Slowly, he shook his head. "I'm not the one you have to worry about. There are far worse here in Trypa."

Trypa. The belly of the Underworld's beast. I swallowed my fear, trying to keep my face neutral as I scrambled to think of what to do.

The creature tilted his face to the sky, as if smelling the air. "They are coming." His eyes found mine, the entire iris bleeding black. "You should already be running."

With a gasp, I turned, my feet climbing and pushing higher as footsteps sounded around me. I made it only one more level before I froze again. The creature from below was already there. But he wasn't alone.

There were two others, and God, they were so much worse. Flesh hanging off of them. Wild, blank, black eyes blinked at me as they panted raggedly.

"Don't come any closer," I whispered, magic flaring back to life as they created a soft loop around me. I could smell the burnt flesh. The rot of their skin. Vomit threatened at the back of my throat.

What would Kharon do? What *had* he done? I was his partner, the other half of his soul. I held it in its entirety. And he trusted me to get back to him. He trusted me. This was my home too.

My head jerked up. I was his partner. That meant only one thing.

Closing my eyes, I prayed. I reached inside, looking for that bond, for what it meant. It was there, still boldly glowing at the center of me, curled around the bright light of his soul. And there, right under it, veins glowed bright, spreading like bloodlines into my body.

And there, at the edge of those veins, the little spikes of power danced. I brushed my mental grip over them. Strumming the contact like the delicate strings of a violin.

Calling them.

Come to me, I asked.

But there was nothing. One of the damned creatures sounded like they were getting closer. Their smell nearly overwhelmed me, making me gag as I tried to focus in on those powerful little hooks.

I pushed again.

Come to me. This time I did not ask; I demanded.

"She smells delicious."

"I want the first taste," another dark voice said.

A rattling growl filled the air as two of the creatures faced each other. I opened my eyes, letting my magic spill out, dancing around to create a boundary between them and me.

"First to try to touch me will be the first to die."

One of the new creatures cackled, the sound like gravel. "We are already dead, river queen. You have no power here. You hold nothing over us."

And then I felt them. I felt the swell of their arrival. The joy of their hunt swept through them. I smiled, closing my fist as my magic leaped back to me. "That's where you are wrong," I whispered. "Here, I am power."

They were close, so close. The creatures stepped closer, intrigued, I thought, by my words. Smiling, I echoed their words back to them. "You should already be running."

The reapers swept into the clearing like shadows come to life, their hoods and capes flapping around them as they swept to my side, swirling around me, waiting, and confirming that powerful request. And then, without a moment of hesitation, they turned to the creatures who now stepped back, surprise on their tattered faces.

They waited for my release, and the moment one creature's mouth opened, I freed them from their tether.

As one, they swept forward, the darkness wrapping around the creatures, the clanking of chains and the quiet screams of the creatures dull to my ears as I closed my eyes, centering myself as I waited for my reapers to return to my side. One by one they did, forming a thick dark curtain of magic and might between the rest of Tartarus and me.

Kharon said that they did not feel.

But I did.

"Kharon needs us," I said simply. "Are you with me?"

Slowly, as if uncomfortable or perhaps unsure, the reapers inclined their hooded faces.

I looked around. "I need to get back to the Pier. Quickly."

The reapers straightened, and as if of one mind, they turned and began moving over the rocky ground. They kept to their circle, herding me forward as one unit up and over the edge of the cliff face. When we reached that peak, I gasped in shock.

I was looking out over a land of actual hellfire. Below me, there was a crevasse, almost like the center of a volcano, spiraling downwards layer after layer of cells and shapes, and oh God, the smells and sounds.

"What is this?"

The reapers didn't move, but they looked to one side.

"This is the home of the damned, the very pit of hell," the voice said, this one clear, crisp, familiar.

"Oh my God. Elon!" I rushed towards Kharon's youngest brother, noting how the large male stepped back to give me a long, hard look. My mouth opened, desperate to explain, but the king of punishment spoke first.

"He went to the Drude, didn't he?"

I nodded. "And he sent me back before I could stop him."

Elon looked over at the pit just beyond us. "Of course he did."

I was shaking my head. "I don't understand."

Elon took a few steps away, turning to peer down into the pit. "While we are not exactly human, not exactly demon, we feel the instincts of both." He crouched down. "Instincts to protect what we love the most. And Kharon has been waiting his whole life to love someone. It appears that lucky someone is you."

"Are you being sarcastic? Because your brother loves you, and it seems like you're just making fun of him. I don't like it."

Elon looked back at me over one shoulder. The wraps on his face covered so much of his expression, but I knew that look in his eyes.

Misery.

Sadness.

Confusion.

"He loves you," I repeated again. "Do you know how much he tortures himself over not being able to heal you?"

Elon's dark eyes blinked, surprise there, before he looked back to the pit. "That is not his job to heal me."

"But he believes it is. He wants so badly to help you."

Elon stood abruptly, his expression going dark. "Why did he send you here?" For the first time, one of my reapers approached him. "Don't even think about it, creature."

The tendril of power that connected me to the reaper pulsed as I urged them to come back towards me. The cloaked creature did, floating in that earthly way between Elon and me.

"I have no idea. I need to get back to him, but I have to get back to the river first."

Elon's shoulders dropped. "You think the ferry will work for you too?"

"I do." At least, I hoped it would. The reapers had come to me. Hopefully that meant the rest of Kharon's abilities were now my own.

Elon was nodding. "And how will you get my brother back?"

"I'm a descendent of the first witch coven, I carry a demon prince's soul, and I'm really, really pissed off. I will figure something out."

I looked at him, suddenly realizing that he could help. This could be the moment that he needed to offer his help. And as if Elon realized the same thing, his head lowered, one bandaged hand sitting on his hip.

"I don't know how far I can take you."

I swallowed, disappointment burning in my throat. "He would do—"

"I know, Faye, but he is a better brother than me. He is a better male than me. I can't leave this place. I cannot hold them back any longer. It takes every breath and every moment of concentration in order to keep them in their cells."

His shoulders dropped. "I have already made too many mistakes by leaving my realm. I have to protect Elysium. I have to protect these… For all that their souls are damned, they are still mine to protect."

I jerked my chin up and down. "What about your other brothers?"

"I will take you to the Pier. Kadmiel is already in the living world. He will be the best ally for you." Elon nodded to the reapers. "And don't forget, these creatures, they are specifically made to straddle both worlds. Call them anywhere, and they will come."

I considered his words carefully. "Thank you."

"Are you ready now?"

Blinking, I released my hold on the reapers, and they flitted away, back to patrol the river far, far, below. "I can't let him stay there a moment longer than necessary. And we know the boundaries are skewing time. Kharon has already been there too long." I swiped angrily at a tear. "I know what it's like to be a prisoner of the Drude."

Elon paused, his hands wrapped in bandages curling into fists. "I misjudged you before, and I regret it."

"Don't bother with regret." I stepped closer. "Just get me back to the river. I am focused on revenge."

Elon closed the distance between us, his enormous frame throwing me into shadow. "Hold on to me."

I nodded, fitting my arms to the thick muscle of his forearms. Elon's head fell back, his eyes closing as black smoke, thick and curling, suddenly bloomed from below us. Before I could react, enormous, skeletal wings stretched wide. The skin between was leathery, similar to a bat as he stretched the wings wide. I could see the scars there, the darkness, as the smoke curled up and around the clawed tips of the wings.

"Do me a favor," Elon said. "Don't tell Kharon I did this."

"Do I want to know why?" I whispered as Elon bent his knees, his arms stealing around my waist for a long moment.

"Because if anyone, even my brother, put his hands on my mate, I would lose my collective mind." Elon grinned at me, the white flash of teeth such a surprise that I gasped. "And I'm not in the mood to get beat down by the Ferryman."

"I—" I didn't get to respond, as suddenly the ground was falling away. Elon's magic and the beautiful, powerful wings thrust us harshly into the Underworld sky. I gasped, trying to breathe in as the air whooshed past me.

Elon maneuvered me, holding me both carefully while trying to keep me from touching as little of his body as possible. A surprised laugh rose in my chest, spilling out at the surprise and joy of this movement. It was beautiful from here. Even the ugly terror of the pits dropped away, showing off the mountain range there, as well as the silver veining of the river as it curled around an island off to one side.

"My home," Elon said quietly, banking to the side.

I pointed past it at a large structure at the curve of the river. "What is that?"

"Hell's pointe, Kadmiel's realm."

"It looks like a lighthouse."

Elon shifted me a little, his wings carrying us quickly down the mountains. "It is where souls return to the living world from."

"Oh." I stared, trying to make out more of that building and the rolling fields that surrounded it. "I didn't know."

"Many don't. It takes so much power, and we cannot risk it. But someday, this world will be the circle of power it once was."

My hair whipped in my face. "You sound so sure."

Elon flapped hard, dropping lower as we skimmed up the side of an immense grassland. "Three of my brothers have found their souls. Three new powerful sisters." Elon's eyes glowed a deep gold as he dropped even lower. "For the first time in a very long time, I have hope. Not just for the Underworld, but for myself."

My heart ached a little at that. That this bandaged, kind-hearted male was hoping that he too might be able to find a match. There was so much beauty in that hope. I could only pray that he was right.

"You deserve something good," I whispered, unsure he would even hear me. But his head dropped, his eyes finding mine, staring from under the bandages.

"That is where you are wrong, Faye, but maybe someday, I will have a chance," Before I could speak up again, he jostled me a little. "Hold on. we are going down here. I can't risk going much farther."

"Thank you," I said, shouting now against the rush of wind that surrounded us as Elon bounced me higher in his arms, dropping his legs low so that he could land on his boots in the delicate pebbled shores of the river.

Instantly, he set me on my feet and backed away. "Do you know where you are?"

I looked around, recognizing some of the surroundings. But more than that, I could feel the soft pulse of power as I knew that the ferry would come for me.

"I must return. I'm sorry I…" Elon's body sagged. "I wish I could do more."

"It's okay," I said, cutting him off and stepping back. "I'll get him back."

Elon's mouth curled again, just for a moment. "I believe you, witch."

And with that, his legs bent, leathery wings spread wide as they swung low, propelling him into the sky once more. A moment later, he was disappearing, just a dark speck against the horizon. Turning back to the river, I watched as the dark ferry slowly came into view, steering itself towards me while I watched the waves and souls move underneath it. Maybe my eyes were playing tricks, but they moved slower now, the ghostly shapes more lethargic under the current.

Worry spiked, but I focused my eyes straight ahead as I waded into the knee-deep water. It was cold today, so cold that I had to bite back my groan as I slowly pulled myself onto the ferry.

It bobbed and weaved in the water, threatening for a moment to buck me off. I flattened my hand on the side of the ferry, summoning more of those strange little tendrils that had begun to spiral from my center. I opened my eyes again, focusing on the ferry as I did. It steadied in the water.

Breathing out, I pushed onto the ferry then stood shakily. There were oars, but when Kharon had used the boat, he barely touched them. And I needed to go up the river, not down. And there was no way that I was strong enough to do that on my own.

I had to do this as he had.

Closing my eyes, I pushed my magic out, imaging it pushing me forward, thrusting me towards the Pier. Back towards Kharon. The magic burst from me, eager and wild under my palms, pushing me out to the center of the river. I had momentum, but steering, it was nearly impossible. A cold sweat broke out on my skin as I separated my palms, facing the back of the ferry as I tried to steady it in the water. I didn't have time for this. I needed to be fast.

"Let us," a voice said. No, not one voice—a chorus of voices, speaking over the tops of each other, blending so softly and wistfully until I could no longer tell one voice from the mass of them. I looked down at the souls, at their huge blank eyes and ghostlike fingers that brushed over the ferry.

The spikes that lined the ferry appeared as dark and dangerous as their fragile skin, so thin that it appeared like webbing in some place brushed over the hull.

"Careful," I burst out. "You have to be careful." The souls continued to swirl around me, more dropping their hands and drifting away as the current buffeted them.

"Let us help you. We can guide from the rear."

I stared into the river, the countless souls that stared back. "You would do that?"

"The Ferryman served us all. We need him back."

"I need him back," I whispered.

The soul tilted their head, the eerie chorus of voices speaking up again. "Where?"

Breathing hard, I stood and moved towards the front of the ferry, gripping hard. "To the Pier. Please."

The souls immediately set off as my power started, pushing the boat against the current, soft waves lapping at the ferry as we cut through the river.

We made excellent time, and while I knew I needed to keep going to push upriver and into the living world, for the first time, a sense of peace settled over me.

The souls carried me onwards, and my magic and my newly acquired demon soul hummed deep in my chest. It was time. I was going to face my past and secure my future.

17

Kharon

I wasn't sure what I thought it would be like to be in the Drude's care. I'd pictured something like a jail cell. Or perhaps an entire prison. At least handcuffs.

But sitting at the edge of a table, playing checkers with a guard who appeared only half aware was not how I pictured spending the past two weeks.

"Your turn," I said loudly, nudging the guard with my toe. He was a corrupted soul, and I just felt like something was wrong with him. Maybe the magic had been done poorly. Or perhaps he was just the sleepy sort, but it took him ages to respond to generally anything.

I'd considered killing him and making a run for it, but I knew that I couldn't do that either. It had been the first thing the Drude had said to me after I woke up in this room, Faye gone, the Drude standing in my doorway.

Just watching.

"This soul is a temporary tenant in this body. They all are. If you kill him, please know that you are killing a father of four who coaches his daughter's soccer team. Or at least he did before I popped that soul into him."

My brows rose. "You thought I would run? Don't you remember the deal?"

"I do, but I know that you and your brothers have a tendency to stretch the truth and boundaries of their deals."

I nodded. "Fair. My brothers and I are quite different. But you won't find me to be running anywhere. I go where I'm needed, and I'm needed here."

And after that, I'd essentially been sitting in this blank-white-walled room since. Food was brought to me. And I knew that magic—powerful, thick, and suffocating—flowed around me constantly. And while my magic remained strong, there was a nearly constant throbbing pain in my chest.

My soul's absence.

I'd given it to her.

My lips curled now, thinking about that moment when I'd handed it to her.

And then the smile vanished, because I also remembered pushing her back, straight back through the portal into the Underworld.

While her deal remained intact with the Drude, I knew she could not stay here. Not again. She had worked too hard, loved too deeply to be left with the Drude once more.

No, my mate was going to be my replacement. At least for the time being. The river would yield to her. The reapers, I believed they would eventually accept her. And her witch blood should allow her to stay in the Underworld for as long as she needed.

And my family would be safe.

Her family would remain untouched.

It was the best ending we could imagine. Until Elon or Kadmiel found their soul mates, my father still did not have the control in power that they needed.

Souls were being lost. I couldn't allow that. Not on my watch.

"Knight to A4."

My eyes snapped back to my guard. Or perhaps he was more of a companion. Honestly, he was my fucking guilt trip. I looked down at the board between us. "I'm not sure that's a real move in checkers."

He started again, and I sighed, leaning forward and moving his pieces around for a moment. "Next time, I choose the game."

"You won't be alive that long," the guard said, his mouth hanging dully.

I snorted. "What a livewire you are. I believe this is Friday night. Why aren't you out doing human things? I'm guessing he promised you a second chance at life, right? Why are you in here, guarding my sorry ass, instead of out partying or whatever you wanted so badly to do."

The guard's dull eyes remained unfocused, and I didn't think he was going to answer. Bored, I pushed one of my pieces around, jumping one of his pieces and collecting my winnings.

"I wish I'd stayed."

That statement got my attention. "What did you say?" It was the most he'd ever spoken to me.

"Can you send me back? To hell, I mean. I don't want…" He swallowed, the words taking a long time to form. "I don't want this. I wanted to be me. I wanted to live my life."

"Your life has ended."

"I know now." The guard's head lolled towards me, eyes blank and begging. "Help me."

My throat tightened, squeezing across my vocal chords so hard I couldn't speak, not at first. "I'm sorry. I have to stay in good standing. Faye…"

The guard's gaze sharpened; he straightened in his chair. "Is Faye coming here?"

I sighed, knowing that he must have triggered words implanted into his subconscious, and clearly Faye was one of those. "No, my friend. She's not coming here."

The guard sagged again, eyes slowly crawling down my body to rest on the checkerboard once again. "You've already won."

"What?" I looked down at the board, but he was already turning, his ungraceful movements making me cringe as he stood and made his way back to his post by the door. The game was clearly over. And while I knew he wasn't completely in control of himself, his last words intrigued and confused me.

But there was no use trying to see what he actually meant. He was already back in zombie mode. I pushed back, rising to my full height and stretching. Just as I did, there was a strange pulse at the back of my mind, flickering down until it stayed in my chest, burning, hot and painful. I pushed a hand over it, my eyes closing as I tried to locate the source of this pain.

It was different from what followed me, reminding me of the soul that I'd given away.

This was a tug, like someone pulling at one end of a rope. But who?

All around me, things were coming to life. Doors were opening and closing. My guard was stumbling into the hallways as more guards appeared—higher-trained, based on their weapons and outfits.

A moment later, guns were trained on me, a half dozen men swarming in through the door to drag me out into the halls.

I sighed, moving with them. "This isn't necessary, gentlemen"—I noticed a female on the perimeter— "and ladies. I am here on my own accord, and I will not be leaving."

"Get in there," one yelled, another two pressing hard on my shoulders as they guided me down the short hallway into a large office space. At one end there was a desk, one chair behind it, and a smattering of chairs were scattered around the front of the bookshelf-lined room.

My brows dropped. I remembered seeing this room before when I first stepped out of the portal here. But again, the familiarity hit me. It looked just like my father's office. It was missing the fireplace, but otherwise it was similar, down to the books that lay across one heavy coffee table.

"Drude," I said, as the dark-cloaked male walked into the room. His hood was down, and I didn't bother reacting to the severe cut of his features. I had seen much worse in the Underworld. As he moved and sat down at the chair behind the desk, his cloak billowed out, showcasing a dark-gray suit wrapped around his lower body. I frowned, curious where he might have gone dressed like a mortal.

"Still cosplaying as my father, Drude?" I grinned, flopping down on a chair in front of his desk. Other than a snarl, the creature who had been tearing my world apart didn't seem overly interested in me. In fact, he appeared almost frantic.

"Lose something?" I said, still trying to egg him into another argument. Or even better, a fight. But he ignored me, pressing a hand to his phone and holding it up as he continued to dig.

"Plan B. Please inform the asset of the situation. Be in my office in five."

The Drude's eyes flickered up to meet mine, his lip curling with dislike. "Make that less than five."

There was a click on the other end, and the Drude dropped it to the surface of his desk with a clatter.

I snorted. "What's up with you? Did someone forget your birthday?"

He didn't respond, merely continued digging things out of his drawer.

"I don't have a birthday. Do you want to cry about it with me?"

The Drude's head snapped up. "Will you shut the fuck up?"

"No," I said dryly, pleased at riling him up, heating my blood. Even with that obnoxious tugging. "I like this side of you, Master Drude. You seem positively human."

There was a ragged snarl, and then his arm snapped out, throwing me against the far wall, where I stayed, pinned painfully against it, his magic holding me in place.

It burned like a hot poker, but I didn't dare let him know that. My magic, held in place by my own choice, roiled at the chance to fight back. But even if I managed to fight him off, what would it matter? I knew the consequences. If I left, if I did anything, there would be deaths. Maybe even Faye's family.

I couldn't let her down.

I couldn't let my family down.

I closed my eyes, shoved my magic down low, and let the pain take me over. An hour later, maybe two, I opened my eyes to see the Drude still pacing his office. His movements were edged with mania. Something has changed.

When there was a knock at the door, the Drude looked over at it then back to me. With a shake of his head, the magic that had held me aloof released me. I slipped to the floor, stumbling about the room as I did.

"Thank you," I said loudly, straightening my shirt as I watched one of his people, dressed head to toe in black, open the door and whisper loudly to him.

"No," the Drude said, surprise evident in his voice. "Send her up."

Something like dread uncurled in my gut, making my throat dry as I watched the Drude look over at his shoulder to me. "Someone missed you."

No, I chanted internally, over and over again as I moved around the room. There was only one door, and I was violently aware that I was underprepared for whatever, or whomever was about to walk through that door.

Please, I pleaded internally. *Please don't be her.*

But no one was listening.

Not anymore.

Because as the door opened again, one of the corrupted held it awkwardly as my soul mate stepped into the room.

And rage, unlike anything I'd ever felt before, consumed me whole.

18

Faye

I couldn't look at him. If I did, I knew the Drude would know the part I had to play. The part that I was born to play.

Not his witch.

Not his weapon. Not today. Never again. I felt it as sure as the magic that hummed—no, not hummed… It roared in my veins, waiting for the moment to be unleashed. Not because of fear, but because for the first time in my existence, I understood why I was given these abilities. Why I'd been different. Why I'd been trapped here for so long.

Because I had spent most of my life trying to be something that I could never be.

I was a healer and a wielder.

Reapers and the damned bowed before me.

I was a soul mate to a demon prince.

I knew how to swim.

I knew that you had to heal before you found your place.

And I knew that I would fight every day for the rest of my existence to allow souls that dignity. The same privilege that Kharon had given to me.

And I loved him for it.

I loved him.

My power coiled like a waiting snake. I loved him, and this creature threatened us both. I would not stand for it. Never again.

I swallowed, forcing my eyes to the Drude as he stood, leaning over his big desk, watching me with those odd black eyes.

"Welcome home, witch."

Never again.

My throat tightened as I fought a gag. Instead, I pushed a smile to my face. I had to play this part, the same one I'd been in for such a long time. It would be nothing to play it for a few moments longer.

"Master." I nodded, moving to stand in front of him, between him and Kharon. It made it easier to avoid looking at my mate. Surely the Drude will see the love if I were to look at him. I keep my eyes cast away.

"Where have you been?" The Drude was rattled. I could feel it in the marrow of my bones.

Never again.

"He threw me back into the Underworld. It took time to find my way out again," I said casually. "My apologies for being late."

The Drude eyed me. I could still see the suspicion in his eyes.

"You can ask any of your people. I had to walk in the front door."

"You made it out of the Underworld," the Drude scoffed. "How?"

I ran my fingertips over the edge of the desk, the smooth wood cold against my skin. "Isn't that what you wanted me to find out?"

The Drude lowered himself into a chair, casting a hand towards the other one behind me. "Sit, tell me everything." He looked to the male behind me, *my* male. "You can go." His gaze jumped back to me, his need for the information I had making him sloppy. He was so sure of himself. It would make this all the more important.

But then the Drude's dark eyes narrowed. I could feel his own magic, always throbbing in his chest, sweep over the room. The lights around us dimmed. "Unless there's more. Maybe you came for him…"

I wasn't going to lie. The words flowed from my mouth, the truth the sweetest flavor. "I came for what is mine."

Master's head slowly turned, cocking as he observed me. I knew his magic was working around me, feeling at the edges of my being. He wouldn't find anything. My magic lay just above my skin, a proverbial layer of protection from his inquiry.

After a moment, it intensified, and I heard Kharon grunt behind me, as he no doubt underwent the same treatment. The

Drude's skeletal, deathly face was so intent upon me that I could almost feel the desire to shift under his gaze.

But I didn't.

Because I no longer cared what he thought of me. In fact, I wanted him to see. To see what I'd become. What I'd always been. What he had tried to undo.

I could see the moment he realized he could no longer get under my wards. When he recognized for the first time that he was out of his depth. "Witch…" He meant to warn me, but I liked it, the name he'd never used on me before. I'd always been Faye. His sweet little Faye.

Not anymore.

My eyes found his, holding them boldly. "I came for my mate. I came for my freedom. I came for everything in my life you stole from me."

The Drude sighed dramatically, but there, right where his hood met his forehead, I could see the sheen of sweat. "I gave you power."

"You gave me pain."

His sneer was cold. "Same thing."

"Not for me." I realized I was shouting, and I lowered my voice. "Teacher would never have let this continue on. You and I both know that."

The Drude glowered. "You know nothing of your precious teacher."

"I know enough." I pointed at Kharon, my hand steady, magic making my skin glow soft in the office light. "Release him."

"Or what?" The Drude raised his hands. "You are surrounded by an army you helped me build. Think of the blood that will be spilled."

My heart pounded. I hoped to God this worked.

"I thought of that too." I stepped towards him. "I knew you wouldn't want to face me one on one. Not without *her*. So, I brought a little help."

I did not look away.

I wanted the Drude to know. To understand what this meant.

He didn't.

Not yet.

"To me!" he cried out.

The door behind me burst open, men filtering in, carrying a variety of weapons. I stood silently, feeling Kharon move closer as the room began to feel entirely too small.

And yet, some small part of me rejoiced when Kharon's hand brushed my hip. "Hello, witchling. I suppose you have some kind of plan?"

I smiled but didn't take my eyes off the Drude, not that I had to.

Kharon moved boldly as he always did, pressing close until his front was warming my back. I could hear the soft huff he gave just as he leaned in and pressed his lips against the side of my neck. "Yours, eh?"

"Only if you want."

His mouth curved against my skin. "Oh, I want." I could almost feel him look around the room. "Shall we dispatch with these creatures so we can go home and discuss more about this whole 'mine' situation?"

My skin heated, but I didn't break my stare with the Drude. I couldn't let him out of my sight. If he ran or hid, I didn't know if I'd be able to find him again. This had to end now. The dead were not tools for his power-hungry campaign to steal the Underworld. I would not allow it anymore.

"Absolutely," I whispered to him. "But just one more thing." I shifted, raising my voice. "No one needs to get hurt today."

The Drude laughed and then held his arms out to the corrupted soldiers around us. "Do they look concerned with injury?"

"They should be. All of you who are Corrupted, this is your chance. Your last chance. If you surrender now, I will work with you to find a new purpose for this life you were given. However you came into this world does not dictate how you exist within it."

The Drude crossed his arms, crooked smile on his face as he watched. I pushed on, feeling Kharon's warmth at my back. "But if you take up arms against me or mine, then you should know that we will send you straight back to the Underworld. And it will not be peaceful." As a show of power, I released some of the hold on my magic, letting it bloom along my skin, glowing bright. One soldier shifted, his weight moving ever so slightly.

He didn't want to die again.

But still, they held their spots.

The Drude slowly came out from behind his desk, his hands spread wide. "It was a good try, Faye. I know this must've been hard for you. But why don't you let my souls take Kharon now, and we can talk again? Face-to-face. Master to—"

"I serve myself now." I reached back, pressing my hand against Kharon's cheek as his face hovered over my shoulder. "Please remember that I tried to reason with you."

The Drude snarled, but he didn't have time to do anything else. Because the moment my hand brushed Kharon's cheeks, I pushed my thoughts to him.

"Don't move."

He stilled, not even breathing as I reached deep into myself, where the roiling black smoke lived. I pressed into it, freeing it from its hold. And a moment later, they arrived. Coming from every corner, bleeding from the floors and shadows underneath us.

The reapers.

I called them, guiding them. Reminding them of the souls who had evaded their capture. Sending picture after picture of the corruption we faced. And they launched themselves, the swirling black shapes too fast for even the Drude to move against. They carved out the stolen souls, the Corrupted who had once escaped hell. Now they were held—captured—

glowing against Kharon's creatures. After each soul was collected, they dove back into the shadows, taking the soul back to the river for processing. And then they would come back, streaks of black ink in the flurry of colors and fury all around us.

Kharon's body hummed in surprise, but all I heard from him was a deep laugh. "Clever mate," he said into my hair.

And when the Drude struck, I was ready, my magic deflecting his blast of pure energy into the wall behind me. Kharon spun away, cackling and joining in with his reapers as the Drude stepped closer to me.

"This ends now," I said to my former master. "You need to leave the Underworld and its people alone."

The Drude snarled, his palms burning with glowing black magic. "Never."

"I wasn't done," I interrupted. "And I want my freedom."

"You have always been free."

"I have never been free. No more threats to my family; no more looking for me. It ends now."

"You think I would put twenty years into training you, guiding you, only to let you go like this?" The Drude cursed. "I raised you. You are mine."

"Yours?" I laughed at him, this desperate, frothing male. "You made me afraid."

"I made you strong. You must be to survive in their world. trust me, Faye, I—"

"Agreed to disagree, I guess. I need your word, in blood, sworn in the old ways, that you will leave my family alone."

The Drude spat at me, "They didn't want you, you know. They were terrified of you. It was so simple to find them, to convince them to let us take you. We visited a dozen witch families, none of which wanted to give up their children. But you, your parents practically threw you at me."

The lump in my throat ached, but I ignored it. "Your word."

"You can't have it. You don't deserve it. We are alike, you and I, Faye. Our families threw us away. Our power was all we had. And we can bend this world, push it to its knees, so that nothing can stop us or tell us we are not worthy of a place in it ever again."

"I know my place, Drude. I am happy." I whispered the last part. "Let me go."

"No!" the Drude roared.

I was done waiting. I released my magic, citing spell after spell that my teacher had taught me. I did not know what spells would work best for him, because after all these years, he thought he knew me, but I knew that I had no idea who or what he was.

It was time to find out.

The first spell hit him and spread over his form. Like water, it dripped over him, sinking in as the magic spun back to me, sending me information.

He was…

He was pissed. That was all I got before, with a roar, the Drude retaliated against my investigative magic. His magic was dark, sweeping over the room, crisscrossing over the forms of the Corrupted who had sunk to the floor. They rose again, no longer filled by souls, but by some strange, ugly version of his magic. They moved awkwardly, lurching towards us as if they were still alive.

"What is this?" Kharon's voice was filled with disbelief. "You're a necromancer?"

The Drude's face was pinched, angry. "I'm everything you are too afraid to do. You and your family, you believe you deserve the Underworld simply because you created it. But all of the abilities you left on the table, the things you refused to use because of your family's misplaced sense of pride." Drude dragged air through his nose. "Such a waste. And now you're going to see all of the things that you wish you could do."

19

Kharon

There were only a few things that my father claimed we would never stoop so low as to do.

And what this creature had just done, with a sweep of his hands, was the first of them. The Drude was moving these bodies, possessing their dead forms, using them as weapons. Watching the dead stagger towards us, I was disgusted. I should've known—we should've guessed after the implantation of the Corrupted souls that his powers aligned somewhere in this area.

A necromancer.

I could never have guessed. I had always assumed, like my brothers, that the Drude was a demon with more than usual power. Or perhaps a creature the Seraphim had accidentally dropped into our midst.

He moved through the living world like he belonged there.

He knew the Underworld and my family like no other.

And now, this. He was a necromancer, a rarity in every world and realm. He might be the only one left. My mother had made it her personal mission to track down and remove that ability from every creature she had found. It had taken hundreds of years. But she thought she had done that.

Then again, she also never would've left us willingly. Things didn't turn out like they should've.

"You should not play with magics that you cannot control," I told him, watching as Faye observed both of us closely. Her spell seemed to have disappeared, but I knew it hadn't. I knew that it was still sinking into him. Searching for a weakness or some kind of way in.

Because this ended today. Just as she said.

I stepped up, drawing his attention. "The dead deserve to sleep, just as the living deserve to live. You do not belong here, Drude."

The Drude coughed out a short laugh. The bodies around us still struggled to stand and move around the room. They looked like puppets with half their strings cut, limping around wildly. "I belong nowhere."

"Welcome to the party." I spread my hands wide. "Let Faye cuff you, and let us speak with my father. Let's end this war before any more lives are ruined."

The bodies all paused, and then the Drude burst into laughter. A moment later, dark shadows leaped towards us. Faye threw up her hands, a magical shield blocking the Drude's magic. We moved, shifting as the bodies attacked, throwing fists and legs wildly as the Drude directed them. Faye's face was pale, her eyes wide as she clearly debated about attacking the dead he controlled. They were already gone, but this kind of evil went so far beyond what was normal. I could see the way it solidified in her gaze.

She was done playing nice. But I didn't want her to be alone in this. I let my hands brush over the sleeves of the flailing bodies, my healing pulling from me as I sent those bodies back to the floor. For a permanent rest now. I could see the darkness leave them, sinking into the ground as I battled them back from Faye's form.

She was hurling magic at the Drude now, slices of water, curling darts made of ice and air. He was blocking them, but I could see the way that the magic he'd used to animate the bodies did not return to him. He was weakening. Faster and faster as her magic soared between them. They may have once been master and student, but now, the tables had turned.

I jerked my head up, looking at my soul mate as she threw a bright white ball of magic at the Drude, making him duck and shift. His face now betrayed him, the dark hollows of his skeletal face showcasing his fear.

Because Faye stood confidentially, her back straight, the dress she'd worn blowing lightly around her. She was a goddess, the light and love shining from her, taking the form of what we needed most.

I knew what had to happen. She would kill him, which he deserved. But just like the souls that sought me out every time, I needed to do something else too. Not just for me.

But for him.

The Drude was throwing black fire towards us now, Faye's palms pushing it away from us and into the walls as he dueled forward. Her curls swung around her face and her eyes blazed with power as she nearly fed off his distress.

I moved forward, the last of the bodies finally on the floor, and stood behind her. I leaned in, a moment within the chaos, and whispered in her ear, "I need to do this."

Her magic blazed across my heart, her answer flickering across my mind. *I know.*

The next moment, her eyes blinked, closing hard and opening, another more powerful wave of power curling around both of us before she turned, eyes focused on the Drude.

"Last chance," she told her former master.

He was breathing hard, his thin chest rising and falling under his cloak. The rattling sound of his breathing was enough to let us both know that there was only one way this would go.

"Fuck you," the Drude cursed, sounding more human than I expected. "You have no chance. I will win this war."

I approached him, my hands out, my magic already curling towards him, drawn to his pain, to his distress. "This doesn't have to end like this. There are other ways."

"There is no other way." The Drude spat blood out onto the floor. "You have already played all your cards, River Lord, and I have yet to even show mine."

My stomach twisted as I saw his eyes dart around, an eerie glow settling in the center of them. He appeared demonic now, but not a creature, not one of my father's. His eyes glowed like my brothers' and mine did.

The Drude coughed, a rasping noise.

"Let me heal you," I said, moving forward. "Then we can talk."

The Drude's head dropped to his chest, his shoulders still moving up and down too quickly. My body moved involuntarily, stepping to his side, my hands nearly on their own, settling on his side for a long moment before either of us took a moment to breathe it in.

I gasped as the power was dragged from me. The pain this creature contained was sucking my magic from me like a siphon. My mind, my lessons, everything my mother had taught me dimmed in the darkness that was him. Attached through physical touch and magic, I felt everything, saw all of him. The Drude was empty—a body, a living body scraped clean. He was…damaged. Deep and harsh lines strung across his body and soul.

I wasn't sure I would be able to heal this. Not below the skin. This was something else entirely.

Suddenly, strong, heavy hands gripped my wrists, wrenching them off him. Our connection was severed in an instant. Relief flooded my body as I staggered back a step, exhausted. "I don't need your pitiful excuse for magic, nor do I want it." But when I looked up, I wasn't looking into the skeletal, corpselike face of the Drude any longer.

He had changed, my healing dragging something out of him that had turned him from the dark creature that he had been to a broadly featured man whose ear-length curls were dark brown, nearly the same shade as the eyes that found mine.

For just a moment, there was shock and awe, and then it was gone in another instant. The hands, which had filled in, briefly felt over his clean-shaven jawline before curling into fists at his side. "What did you do?"

"I healed you, on the outside," I snarled as his magic immediately bloomed around his closed fists. "No one in this world has the power to heal what you have going on inside."

Faye's magic gathered, an incoming storm at my back. And I nearly smiled at how easy this was for her. My witchling had turned into quite the dueler, just like he'd always wished she would. The only problem was who and what she was fighting against.

"Move, baby."

I stepped aside, my healing snapping back into my chest as I released the Drude. Faye's beautiful eyes burned wildly as the magic began to pour down her arms, creating a maelstrom of vivid blue fire at her fingertips.

The destruction there. The power. It was beautiful. And I could see in her expression that she was ready to do this.

"Wait!"

For a long moment, the light between us seemed to pulse, making everything bright and wild between us. We were still, staring at the sparking of light just between the Drude and Faye and myself. A figure was there, appearing slowly, materializing out of thin air.

Blinking, I stepped back, my forearm coming up to shield my gaze from the light.

"Faye, wait. You cannot."

I blinked again, the light dimming as I stared at the woman in front of me. Because I know her. I'd seen her every day for hundreds of years. I'd felt her love, learned from her teaching, and battled the grief when she had disappeared.

Nicola, the first witch—my mother—stood in the middle of the room, an arm outstretched either way between Faye and the Drude. Dressed in jeans and a black sweater, she looked like she was just stepping from the living world.

Father had protested for so long, trying to explain how she was not dead. How she could not be dead. But seeing her here, alive, was something I could never have prepared myself for.

"Mother," I whispered, shock making my voice shake.

Nicola's eyes slipped over me, a half-smile on her face before she jerked her head back to Faye. "Faye, you can't. This isn't the way."

"Mother, what is going on?"

The Drude stepped up, shocking me again with his still human-looking face. Faye spoke, her magic quivering as she struggled to contain the magic she had gained. "Teacher…"

"Teacher?" I craned my head, staring at her. "What?"

Faye's face broke, a tear slipping down her face, "I'm so sorry, Kharon. I can't. Teacher…she told me…"

I stared at them, despair filling me to my very core. Even in the space that my soul had once rested. It ached with the betrayal and confusion of the moment. My mother… That was who had taught Faye.

These years that she'd been missing, at least part of these had been here, with her. I swallowed, staring at my mother once again. Her expression was tortured now, her eyes wide and fearful as she stared at Faye and me. I understood in a moment. She was… She was afraid of us.

For good reason, yes, but I still hated it. My guard lowered, and behind me, Faye took a short breath, releasing part of the magic she'd been gathering. We could not kill my mother, that much was certain.

I spoke loudly, over the rasping pants of the Drude. "Why are you here? What's going on?"

"I wanted to come to you so many times, Kharon. I thought about it, dreamed about it. Especially after Arafel found his soul mate. But I was…detained." Nicola looked back at the Drude. "Please." Her voice was low. "Please don't let this happen. You two cannot face each other. It will only end in pain—so, so much pain."

"She came here," the Drude hissed. Behind the shadow of my mother, I saw he was still leaning on the edge of a chair. "She knew what she began when she chose the Ferryman."

Nicola swiveled back and looked at me, her mouth curling in the smallest smile. "She chose you."

"Kharon is mine," Faye said softly from behind us. "But I cannot let the Drude continue to torture these people, these souls. Stand aside, Teacher. The time has come to end this. I cannot let him do any more damage to my home. To *our* home."

The last words were thick, my soul mate's voice choking on the words.

Nicola's eyes watered, her teeth biting into her bottom lip. "You are so much more than I dreamed you would be." She looked at me. "Both of you."

I knew the moment that she opened a portal. It was her bread and butter. She had been the foundation of the Underworld, after all. They always had this particular feel, the way the air in the room all seemed to be pulled in one direction. "Mother, please don't—"

But she was already moving towards it, the blinding light making me blink as another portal appeared to the side. "Don't!" I shouted, stepping towards her, between her and Faye, as she reached back to grab for the Drude. A million thoughts raced through my mind. I should've called my father. I should've called my brothers. I should've done *something*.

But there was nothing but an overwhelming need to step between my mate and my mother…and the creature she now protected. Call it intuition. Call it instinct, but I knew this would not go the way I believed it would.

And I was right.

Nicola disappeared into the portal, her grip on the Drude's arms yanking him in after her. But not before he looked right at me. And with a snarl, his magic exploded from him. A dagger of pure power and hate exploded out of him, spearing across the room within a breath, and pierced me straight in my chest.

The portal glowed as the Drude toppled through after my mother. And I stumbled back, feeling slender, tight arms gripping me around my middle as my vision became strained then blurred.

I reached back, finding Faye's curls with one hand. The other habitually went to the now gushing wound on my chest. My power flickered to life but then dulled.

"This is a bad one," I whispered to her, the sound gurgling as I tried to see her.

She was talking, her mouth moving fast as her hands fluttered over the top of me. What was she doing? Why was she acting like this?

Something dripped onto my cheeks, and I moved to brush my hands over the moisture. Tears. She was crying. Something clicked deep in my chest. I wasn't killable. But this, this felt different. Different than any other time that my brothers or I had been injured. I was soul-less. And fates, I was so tired.

And most of all, I was scared.

I closed my hands around her and let my eyes close.

20

Faye

My hands shook—my entire being shook as I crouched over Kharon's body. I needed to get him out of here. He was a Prince of Hell. We couldn't lie here in this place where more of the Drude's Corrupted might show up. Kharon had told me once that he was very hard to kill.

But something about this wound, which was sluggishly oozing dark-red blood, made me anxious. I hadn't really learned healing, not like this at least. But I knew one thing.

I had to get him home. I had to get him back to the Underworld—back to where he would be safe.

Leaning in, I pressed my lips against his forehead. I was not as good at portals as he was, or even his mother. She was, as she'd just demonstrated, extremely talented at the skill. I wasn't even sure if I could get one open right now, least of all to a forbidden place.

And so I strained, my magic an angry swirl at my center as I attempted to break back into the river. I strained, I begged, I pleaded, but there was nothing.

Sobbing, I leaned over Kharon's still body, holding my head against his chest as I listened to the soft but steady beat of his heart. "I have to get us home. I have to."

To my surprise, something brushed over my hair, pushing my curls out of my face. I gasped, unleashing the rest of my abilities as I stared up at the stranger. But it wasn't a Corrupted. Or anyone I would've expected.

"Daughter." Lucifer stared down at me, his face more serious than I'd ever seen him. There was no smirking male, there was no sparkling eyes. His expression was dull. Sad.

"Lucifer," I whispered, "I tried to get us home, but I couldn't. My power—they never wanted to show me how to do portals since that meant that I'd be able to—"

"To escape," Lucifer finished, nodding a little. His dark hair was cropped short, curling lightly around the swirl of horns that arched up above his scalp. "That's alright. Everything will be alright now."

I gulped, watching as Lucifer briefly looked over Kharon's body. "He needs to get back to the river. The souls there, they will know what to do. And his soul, it's there, waiting for him."

Lucifer's cheek twitched as if he wanted to smile but couldn't muster the effort. "I felt it, that day he gave it to you. He trusted you, completely. Something that speaks volume of the relationship you must share. Bond or no bond." His eyes flickered over me. "You are injured as well."

"I will figure it out once we get Kharon settled," I said steadily, ignoring the concern in his voice.

Lucifer nodded, helping me to my feet then moving to stand between Kharon's prone form and me. He reached a hand out for me. I took it, worried for some reason that my bloody, dirty hand might stain this king's. But he didn't even look at me, just continued to stare down at Kharon.

I shook my head. "I failed him. I failed all of you."

Lucifer's head jerked, black eyes meeting mine and making my tongue thick. "You believe you failed? You rescued my son, you channeled power into the Underworld, and still managed to take on the most powerful enemy I have had in a very long time." His grip on my hand tightened. "You did not fail." His chest rose and fell. "I did. But I will not fail again. Not you. Not…any of them."

He looked in the direction of the portal, to where his mate had disappeared with his greatest enemy. "I had hoped she was dead," Lucifer said softly, "rather than the alternative."

I nodded, feeling defeated and tired as I watched Kharon's chest rise and fall. "She never did anything without reason."

Lucifer gave me a short nod, and then I felt the heat pulse in my hand as his magic zipped through me. Right as the world around me dissolved, I heard him say one final thing. "That's what I fear the most."

And then I was crashing into the sandy banks, the docks of the Pier and Kharon's cabin just behind. Kharon was laid out beside me, his head tilted towards me as whatever magic Lucifer used to send us here dissipated.

Kharon groaned, and I moved over to him. "Hi there, can you hear me? I'm going to get you into the water, okay?"

The muscles on his face danced, his lashes fluttering as if he fought against the sleep that held him. But I knew that the river held the key. Mustering all the muscle I had in my body, I grabbed ahold of his arms. Pulling with all my might, I was finally able to get Kharon sliding through the sand until my ankles, then my calves, and then my knees were in the river. The water lapped at my skin, and subconsciously I could feel the eyes of the souls passing by on me. I heaved Kharon's weight until I had his entire body in the water. Bending down, I wrapped my arms under his chest, and making sure to keep his face from the water, I backpaddled and pulled us deeper into the river.

"Do you feel that, Kharon? Do you feel all that water?" Glancing down, I could see the way the river water brushed over his gills, and I hoped to God it felt good to him. I stopped there in the shallows because I didn't trust myself to go any deeper. Not without him there to hold me up.

I sniffled, surprised to find more tears slipping down my face as I stared down at Kharon's form, the soft blue skin so at peace with the water that surrounded it.

I pressed my face to the side of his, the water making my hair stick to my cheeks as I held on tight and tried to breathe him in. "I'm so sorry I didn't tell you about your mother. I wanted to, but I wasn't sure what it meant. It thought maybe if you knew she had taught me that you would think this was all some game. But it wasn't a game. It was never a game. You gave me a purpose. You believed in me when we were still enemies. But at the end of the day, nothing could keep me from you. I'm not sure how I can live here, or if I even *can* live here, but I will make this work. I will find you. I will make sure you forgive me, because nothing else is acceptable."

I pressed a kiss to his temple. "Nothing."

A soft sigh escaped Kharon. "Witchling, I had no idea you were so poetic."

I laughed, the sound wet and choked as I clutched him tighter. "You jerk. How long have you been awake?"

Kharon shifted but didn't regain his footing yet. "Not long. I was having the strangest dream." He moved his head. "Did my father show up in the living world?"

I laughed, running my fingers over the slope of his ear. "He did. He's the one who sent us home."

Kharon's mouth curled. "My mate nearly conquered the devil's number-one enemy. That's the least he could do."

"I don't even care, as long as we are all safe now." I watched as Kharon's body flexed, and I could see him moving until he was sitting up in the water, his feet brushing the sandy bottom.

Kharon wordlessly reached out, his eyes widening as a soft glow of green entered them. The hole in his chest was closed, the ripped shirt drifting lightly in the current as he stared down at the water.

I gasped, nearly jumping backwards as tendrils of bright blue threaded up from the water, skipping over me and wrapping themselves around Kharon's skin. Afraid to take a breath, I covered my mouth. "What's happening?" I asked in a barely there voice.

Kharon's gaze found mine, and then he looked out at the river, where dozens—no, hundreds—of souls seemed to have held their place in the current, filling the river with an opalesque appearance. They were…giving him something.

"Kharon?"

His face was filled with awe. "They are giving me power. They are helping me heal."

We both paused, watching wide-eyed as a soul rose from the pack, moving by us with her ghostlike form, her hand extended, a blue tendril leaving her hand and tangling itself around Kharon. He straightened, looking down at where the power had entered his skin.

"For the Ferryman," the soul said, her smile sad and dark as she drifted back to the current.

Another moved forward, the shape long in the water as they wrapped themselves around Kharon. Another tendril, another startled look from Kharon. "For the Ferryman."

And then another.

And another.

They came in groups then, brushing past us as they tilted those dark eyes and nodded to the Lord of the River. Each tendril only made Kharon's eyes glow brighter, more power suffusing his body as he accepted their gifts. And I stood at his side, watching as the souls he fought so hard to heal in turn healed him.

"Has this ever happened before?"

Kharon shook his head. "Never."

I stepped closer, and immediately Kharon reached for my hand. His fingers tangled with mine, and I leaned my head against his shoulder. "I'm so sorry I didn't tell you."

"I know," Kharon said, his voice sad. He turned to me, looking at me so long that a blush rose to the surface. But then he leaned over, pressing his lips to my forehead, then my nose, and then my lips. "Good thing we have a few hundred lifetimes to work on that."

I nodded. "Good thing."

Kharon sighed, turning his head to look out over the River Styx as we took in the enormity of what had just happened.

"What happens now?"

His grip tightened, and I could feel the fear in his body once more. "Three of the lords souls have been returned to the Underworld. We can begin to rebuild this realm as well as the others."

"I meant with…"

Kharon was still for a long moment, and then he slowly tugged me out of the water. "Then we begin again. It is more important than ever that we protect these souls. Especially now that we know what…or rather who we are up against."

His mother. My teacher.

She served the Drude. And not just the Drude that I had known, but something had happened when Kharon had touched him, some kind of healing.

"Would you have really healed him? Tried to talk to him?"

Kharon looked at me sharply, and then a wide smile curled his lips. "Of course. This life is built on second chances."

And he curled me forward, pressing his lips against my hairline.

I sighed, letting him enclose me tight in his warmth, in the glow of his power, the same power that once overflowed his abilities and now trickled into my own.

Bonded.

Mated.

I'd gone from being an abandoned girl no would get close to, to a witch princess.

"What are you smiling about?" Kharon asked as he guided us out of the water and up onto the banks.

"I just did not see this coming."

"Of course not. You were too busy hating me to realize that you were falling in love with me."

I snorted, pressing close as he moved up to the front door. "You think so?"

"Oh, I know so, witchling. You wanted me from the moment I fished you out of the ocean." That familiar, beautiful face of his curled into a smirk. But this time, I loved it.

"Is that so?" I leaned in, rising up on my toes so that my lips were closer to his. "And what about you?"

Kharon pressed a soft kiss against my lips, his hands on my hips, simply breathing me in. My fingers dug into his shoulders, my body pressing against his, soaking him in until his breath coasted over my ear.

A secret—no, a confession.

"I've been waiting for you my entire life."

21

Kharon

"Are you sure you want to do this?"

Faye leaned into me, a smile on her perfect lips, but the grip on my fingers told me something else. She was nervous. Not just nervous. Terrified.

"Not really," she said finally, looking up at me.

Just because I could, I leaned in and dropped a soft kiss on her mouth. "I can call him off. We can do this anytime, Faye."

"I want them to know, to understand. No more lying and hiding. This will be easier." Faye huffed out a short breath. "I wish you were more…*you*. I still can't get used to seeing you like this."

I reared back, mock offended at her critique. "Do you not like this look? I kind of thought it worked for me."

Faye's eyes swept over my human glamor, the very same one that I'd worn the day I'd rescued her from the boat. It seemed like a lifetime ago, when really it was only weeks. Fates below, the fight with the Drude just days before already felt like a decade ago. Sighing, I leaned in close to my mate.

I didn't love wearing the glamor, but there was no way in Heaven I was letting my Faye out of my sight anytime soon.

Faye giggled then pressed back into me. "I like you much better in blue," she said, straightening the lapel of my white shirt. Her eyes danced in the way that I loved so much, and the bond in my chest nearly bounced with joy. Our bond.

It felt like nothing else ever had, healing sharp edges that a lifetime of stress and trauma had created. Better than that, it was healing her. But in some aspects, Faye was going to have to take the lead on healing.

Beginning with this one.

We paused on the sidewalk, looking up at the beige split-level house. Its sidewalk was lined with carefully trimmed bushes leading to a dark-brown front door. The handle there gleamed, as if beckoning us closer.

"This is it?" I asked, taking a deep breath. It smelled like oak and dirt and was uniquely living world scents to my senses. No traces of a Corrupted here. Perhaps the Drude had been bluffing.

"It is." Faye fiddled with the piece of paper in her fist. "Or at least, that's where I sent Kadmiel, so I sure hope it is."

I curled an arm around her shoulders and began walking forward. "He's here too, so don't worry. Just keep walking, one foot after the other."

"Oh, gosh, you know what, I'm not sure…" Faye nearly tripped as she halted on the walkway, her eyes frantically sweeping over the house.

"Yes, you are. This is what you were waiting for. This is the stand you made, witchling."

Fayed turned to me, her face drawn and tight. "What if they hate me?"

I leaned in, brushing my nose down hers. "What if they don't?"

Faye blinked and then, without another word, turned and marched the remaining steps up to the front door and then pushed the doorbell.

The bell tolled, and we both waited, me a step or two back from her. There were footsteps on the other side, a variety of voices, and then the heavy door swung open. A woman, so similar to Faye that I had to blink for a moment, answered. No, not just like Faye. Her eyes were a little different, lighter. And the soft gray swirls hidden in her curls, I saw them now too.

But mostly, I saw the look of utter shock that swept over her face, replaced instantly by joy. Overwhelming, wild, profound joy.

"Faye?"

Faye flinched, her hands curling and uncurling at her sides as she stared at the woman who had to be her mother. "I'm sorry to bother you. I—"

But she couldn't finish her sentence because the older woman was on her, wrapping her arms tight around Faye's body. She was muttering her name, over and over, the door swinging wide as they stumbled a little on the narrow stoop.

I pressed my hand to Faye's back, our gazes briefly meeting before she was turned away again. The other woman pressed her hands to Faye's cheeks. "Honey, I'm sorry, are you alright? I thought I was dreaming. I thought I had made it all up. That I would never see you again."

"Hi, Momma," Faye said softly, tears slipping down her face as she looked at her mother.

"Greg!" the woman shouted. "She's home, Greg. She's here!'

A bespeckled man, a few inches taller than Faye's mother, appeared in the doorway. He quickly took me in before seeing his daughter. And then he didn't have the least bit of interest in me. He was wrapping his arms around the two of them.

I stepped back, content and warm with her joy as the family stumbled about, talking over each other, hands and hugs flying as they all stared at one another. And then there was her brother, showing up bleary eyed and a little confused at the door. Only to be dragged into the hug circle for more.

And when Faye finally emerged again, I could pick out more of the conversation. "I knew it as soon as he showed up. Said he was from Witness Protection, but I knew better. I knew you would always find your way back."

Faye was shaking her head. "What? What are you talking about?"

Faye's mother sighed. "The demon you sent, I knew he had to be from you. He's been out there for days. I so hoped that you would follow. I wasn't sure, but I just had this feeling."

I glanced over my shoulder at the direction that her mother pointed and immediately grinned at Kadmiel, who was sitting on a bench across the street, looking very much out of place in the rest of the neighborhood.

"Who is he?" her father asked. "Someone important?"

Faye laughed. "He's a sort of brother-in-law."

Faye's father and mother both went still then slowly turned to me. Her father swallowed. "So you're the one, then, the son of Lucifer."

My brows rose, and I tilted my head. "The one?"

"He told us that if we did not give her to him that a son of the devil would come for her. It took us years to find out more. To track down the other original families." Her father turned to Faye. "If we had known, if we had educated ourselves, then we would've known that being a soul bond to the demon lords was a far better cry than to serve that monster. But we didn't know. I'm so sorry."

Faye's face was shocked. "You knew?"

Faye's mother took her hand. "Not until after. He came here, claiming he could protect you, that he could teach you to protect yourself from the demons."

"When all along, he was the enemy," Greg finished, his face grim. "We are so sorry, honey."

Her brother was nodding along, swiping at tears. "We looked for you, sis. But no one could find you. They all said you were a runaway and that you would come home when you were ready."

Faye shrugged. "I had to stay away, but that's a long story. I'm just glad that I can come home now."

Greg held out his arms, ushering the family back towards the door. "Yes, yes, a hundred times yes. Please, come in. Let's get you some tea, and you can tell us everything. Bring in your demon. I'm sure that he is getting itchy in that glamor."

I tilted my head, surprised at the vernacular, and followed Faye's family into the house. There were a few words of basic conversation, and then Faye sat down, questions falling from her lips like the rain as she stared into her mother's face. On her lap, their hands were intertwined.

Greg approached me. "It's Kharon, isn't it?"

I turned, nodding. "How did you guess?"

Faye's father gestured. "Come down here. You should see something."

Fighting down the wave of unease, I followed Greg down the stairs and found the basement cloaked in darkness. Greg hit a switch, and a moment later, the room was illuminated. I snorted out a surprised breath, looking around.

"We never stopped looking. Our ignorance cost us our daughter." Greg stepped back, his hands gesturing around the room. "I'll never let that happen again. And if you let us, we'd like to make it up to you."

"What is all of this?" There were papers everywhere, strewn across every wall with yarn and dots connecting various pieces.

"This," Greg said, his voice serious, "is the original five families and their heritage."

"The original five?"

"The original five witch families who volunteered their powers to bind the Princes of Hell to humanity."

I moved over to a snapshot of a painting, my mother the centerpiece in a group of women and men. The smile on her lips was honest and true, and on her shoulder perched a perfect black crow. My father, in his favorite form.

Greg stepped forward. "We descend from the Suileabhains." He pointed at the tall, fair-haired male standing in the corner, a coy smile on his lips, a patch over one eye. "We believe that the Drude wants each of these family's descendants. And we were too stupid to understand at the time."

"You did all of this?"

"I wish I had done more, but I knew someday, we would find her. And I would be able to share this with her, to try to help her understand why she was made this way." Greg fiddled with the pen in his hand. "She seems so happy."

I cast a wary glance over the man before me. "She is." I moved to the window, leaning over to look at more of the papers, these a long, elaborately colored family tree. "But I think that she could be happier."

"We want to help."

I nodded. "Then talk to her. Answer her questions. And when the time comes, tell her what you've done here."

Greg nodded and began to walk back up the stairs. He paused at the base. "You might have rules, but just in case you were wanting to, feel free to drop the glamor around us. That's the least we can do for making our daughter happy when we could not."

I rubbed a hand over my head, smoothing the glamor from my skin with a sigh. To his credit, neither he nor his family had more than a quick double-take as I walked back up the stairs. But my mate, she grinned at me widely, surrounded by the family she thought she'd never see again.

Peace and joy, both mine and hers, filled the bond in my chest.

For now, all was right in the world.

Epilogue

Kharon

"What happens now?"

"Now?" Kharon's voice was nearly a rumble as he pressed his mouth against my shoulder blade. "Now I keep you here, ravish you until you don't know your own name, and then insist you take mine."

I sat up, turning to look at Kharon where he lounged on the bed beside me. "You have a last name?"

Kharon made a face. "Unfortunately no, but we also typically don't have weddings."

Faye raised her brows. "Really?"

"Really. Horribly outdated concept that the living have ruined with a variety of methods of cheating and incorrect obsession."

"So…" I stretched against him. "What do you suggest?"

Kharon's hands slid up the back of my thighs, over my ass, and up to my side, where he gripped me, curling me to my side so that he could form his body against my back. He ducked his chin, tucking it close to my ear. "A lifetime of devotion, my soul in return for your love. Whatever you want."

I turned so that I could see a little more of him. Since we'd arrived back from the living world, we hadn't done much except hold each other in this bed.

Now, I wanted more. And I had a very real idea on how to make that happen.

"A lifetime of devotion."

Kharon's eyes were heavy-lidded as I arched into his body, my hand skimming down his chest. "Without question."

I threaded my fingers through his then used that vantage point to push him off of me. With a squeal, I raced to the door in just my underwear, turning back to him. "Come and get me."

Kharon rose to his elbow, one brow lifted. "Witchling, this a very, very bad idea."

My lips curled. "Only if you catch me."

And then I took off, racing across the house, throwing the door open wide, and cutting off back to the property behind, the soft grass cool under my bare feet as I heard Kharon's roar of laughter. And a moment later, there were footsteps behind me, falling heavy and fast as I sped through the grassy field leading to the edge of the wooded area.

"Faye," a deep rumble sounded, "you should not have run from me."

My chest was heaving as I pushed harder, the delightful pull of my muscles making my breathing ragged. But none of that mattered because here, under my powers, under this world, I was prey. Only prey.

And he was the predator.

Just as I reached the soft shade of the woods, I felt him. A breath later, he was tackling me, twisting and turning until he was on his back, my body saved from the fall by his arms.

I didn't have time to cry out before his mouth was on mine, his leg pressing between my thighs as we rolled against the ground. When we stopped, my body eagerly arched into his weight. "Kharon…" I couldn't stop the way my hands clutched at his sides, trying to get even closer.

But he resisted, pushing away until his knees straddled my belly. I looked up into glowing green eyes, my core clenching as he held up one hand, black claws gleaming. "Hold still, mate."

I gasped, holding my breath as those deadly claws sliced down the front of my clothing, straight down to my bra. In the next moment, his hands were spreading it open, exposing my body to his hungry eyes.

My hands twitched, old habits telling me to cover up. But only for a second. Because Kharon's head fell back, a deep roar echoing the surroundings. When he finally quieted again, his chest heaving, he walked back on his knees until he was only over my thighs.

"Roll over, witchling, and let me claim you."

I began to move, and instantly his hands were there, his body curving over mine as my knees pressed into the soft earth. The moment my ass touched his pants, he was up and cursing, throwing and tearing fabric until he returned to me with a grumpy-sounding huff.

I almost smiled at the usually unfazed male but ended up moaning instead. His hands moved my hips high, the throb of his length pulsing against me. But he didn't fuck me yet. No, his hand wrapped under me, between my thighs, where his fingers circled my clit slowly. "Are you ready for me to take you, witchling? The way that a demon takes his female."

I moaned, hips pushing up into his grip as he drew it out, making my core burn with the need for more. Kharon's other hand moved around to my chest, pushing me up until my back rested against his belly.

"You are mine, Faye Sullivan. Say it back."

"I am yours," I said in an instant, the truth of it settling into my skin as the delicious pressure from his fingers grew heavy.

"Always."

I smiled into the Underworld. "Forever."

Kharon pressed a kiss against my shoulder, and then his hands were on my back, pushing me down until my back arched, my thighs shook. His cock pressed against me, the core of me already clenching against him.

Desperate for whatever my mate would give me.

And then he was deep inside, shouting his victory as he pulled back, only to thrust himself back in even harder, in and out. My body shook in his hold as my demon laid his claim to me. And I loved it. I loved the way he groaned my name, his hands tight on my hips. There was a reverence in his movements, as if he might die if he could not continue.

And I understood, because even as my release built up, I was already mourning the end of this moment with him.

"Faye," Kharon whispered. "Mate. I love you." His hips were stuttering, the release we were both so close to beginning to overwhelm us.

"I love you too," I whispered back.

Kharon thrust forward, his hips flush to my ass as he curled a hand low, one finger pressing on my clit. My orgasm washed over me, making my body jerk against him as Kharon joined me in bliss. His entire body was throbbing against me, his hips giving little jerks as he released deep inside me.

Finally, my body relaxed, sagging in his arms as soft, warm lips traced over my shoulders.

"What happens now?" Kharon asked finally, his hands smoothing over my skin as he held me.

I looked over my shoulder at the male I loved so much.

"Let's go for a swim."

The End

The Lords of the Underworld series continues on in book four which will be Kadmiel's story, coming early 2025.

Preorder Shield of Fire and Fate now!
Signed Hardcopies Linked Here.
Ebook via Maggiewhitebooks.com
Ebook via Amazon.

There's a small snippet from the story to follow.
Want to be first to learn about details for upcoming releases, fun behind the scenes tales from the underworld and character art? Find me online here. Or check out my patreon.

There are thousands of books published every day, I'm so honored you chose one of mine to share your time with. I have loved sharing my stories with every single one of you.

To my husband who doesn't have wings, or horns, but continues to remind me every day of how powerful love can be –I couldn't do this without you.

And to my parents, who never stopped believing in me. I love you…please don't read this.

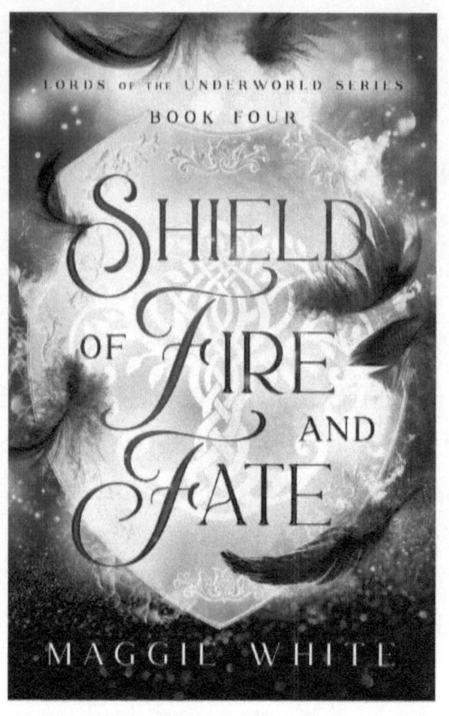

And now, a little scene from Tabby and Kadmiel's story:

"My name is Kadmiel."

"Kadmiel?"

"My parents are old fashioned," he said with a one-shoulder shrug. The elbow that still clasped my hand between massive bicep and curling forearm didn't move.

I stared up at him, wondering why I was even letting this conversation continue. "Why are you here?"

"Because you need me."

I laughed, but it only lasted a moment, the surprised sound a sharp noise in the relative quiet of the park. "I need you?"

"You do," Kadmiel said, eyes shimmering as he swept his gaze up and down my form. "You may be the most powerful witch I've met in a long time, but you can't save your friend." My heart was pounding in my chest so loud I could barely hear the words that fell from his mouth. "For that, I think, you will need my help."

Taylor Fucking Swift, I was screwed.

"A witch? Are you crazy?"

His dark brows rose with a smirk. "I've been called worse."

I huffed, moving off, nearly dragging my hand free before Kadmiel gave up and walked with me. I was scanning the landscape now, looking for a way out. But at the same time, I couldn't make myself yank away. Every instinct was screaming to stay put, to stay close.

"The fates controlled his death, *lioness*, and to get to them, you must go through me."

Preorder Shield of Fire and Fate now!

<u>Signed Hardcopies Linked Here.</u>

<u>Ebook via Maggiewhitebooks.com</u>

<u>Ebook via Amazon.</u>

9 7 9 8 9 8 7 6 0 9 3 9 2